LAST NIGHT

LAST NIGHT

By Brendan Lemon

alyson books
los angeles | new york

© 2002 BY BRENDAN LEMON. ALL RIGHTS RESERVED.

MANUFACTURED IN THE UNITED STATES OF AMERICA.
PRINTED ON ACID-FREE PAPER.

THIS HARDCOVER ORIGINAL IS PUBLISHED BY ALYSON PUBLICATIONS,
P.O. BOX 4371, LOS ANGELES, CALIFORNIA 90078-4371.
DISTRIBUTION IN THE UNITED KINGDOM BY TURNAROUND PUBLISHER SERVICES LTD.,
UNIT 3, OLYMPIA TRADING ESTATE, COBURG ROAD, WOOD GREEN,
LONDON N22 6TZ ENGLAND.

FIRST EDITION: APRIL 2002

02 03 04 05 06 a 10 9 8 7 6 5 4 3 2 1

ISBN 1-55583-645-3

For Bill Schneider

They're coming for me in the morning. Whether the news will be death or deliverance I do not know. Though my execution was supposed to be a secret, word of it has seeped out of the prison walls, and there is now talk of intervention at the highest levels in Washington. According to Demosthenes, a guard here who is covertly my envoy to the outside world, in which capacity he acts as the bearer to you of this alarmingly long letter, the Cuban authorities have made noises about the "integrity of local law." I killed a young man, they say, in their country, and must be appropriately punished. The Americans, I am sure, object that the handling of my case flouted conventions of international jurisprudence. After our apprehension, I was never allowed to contact the diplomatic custodian of yanqui interests on the island. Moreover, my case has been conducted with utmost irregularity: no initial charges, an aborted trial. I can hear the Cold War behemoths bellowing in the press about my "outrageous" situation. They have an idea about the sham justice but not necessarily about the love denied. Perhaps it is just as well that the old Cold Warriors don't know everything. The irony—their taking up an action involving the kind of love they habitually condemn—would be lost on them. As would, perhaps, any irony, belonging as it does not to the powerful but to the put-upon.

Eduardo, I am sure you are wondering why I would spend what may be my last night on earth writing a letter, or should I say *assembling* a letter, since my task this evening is to fuse fragments I've composed along the way. My feet stretch out over the abyss: Shouldn't I be calling for a priest, even in Communist Cuba? The truth is, to distract myself from the anxiety, I would rather be watching reruns of *Rat Patrol,* the favorite show of my youth, or any recent movie with John Gielgud—*Arthur* perhaps, the scene where Dudley Moore is enjoying a luxurious warm bath and Gielgud, poised and supremely astringent, asks, "Would you like me to wash your dick?" I would like such company as my hand scribbled across these pages. But inside Havana's Morales prison in 1987, there are no televisions. You are your own *Late Show.* My mother, may she rest peacefully, would be happy about this. Throughout my childhood, she used to bewail the effects on me of "the idiot box." She wanted me to read instead; for her, to watch was to waste. Until the past nine months, when I have been intermittently allowed to immerse myself in reading, books took third or fourth place in my life. I never seemed to have enough time for them.

Just as there would never have been enough time to tell you everything yesterday, had I agreed to see you, Benitez, my detective, honored a promise to me by allowing you to visit here. I suppose I should feel grateful to him for proving true to his word. Instead, I hate him for having presented me with a dilemma, one whose consequences, much more than those of that boy's death in the park that night, are what drive me. Little did I expect that elaborating my strategy would require me to explain my life. But it does, a task in line with what has been happening to me behind bars. In jail I thought my task would be survival; instead it has been my Self.

Please believe me that not seeing you was really the only way, even if it now requires me to strip my character bare. (How appropriate that verb is to prison!) How else can I be sure that if you will not excuse me (or I, perhaps you), that at least you might understand me? I cannot do that without reference to the quite random series of events that make up my life and that you say you have never quite understood. I believe that is why you took the action you did: You did not understand me. So I have no choice but to tell you my story. To bequeath you a true version of our time together, in contrast to the forced falsities of our official confession.

If, after leaving the prison yesterday, after I refused to see you at all, you may have asked yourself why I could not at least have granted you the 10 minutes we had been allotted face-to-face, obviating the need for you to pore over this document. Of course I thought about that. I wondered if it might not have been more humane to say goodbye in person, to convey our farewells through touch rather than correspondence. But just imagine the scene. We would have been surrounded by guards. There would have been little chance for either intimacy or spontaneity, and how could our emotions have combusted without those sparks? I tell myself that I would have disregarded the onlookers and, despite all that has occurred, devoured you with kisses. I would not have given a straw about their undoubted distaste. Why? Because when it comes to disgust, it is only the disgusted people whom I find disgusting.

But what about you? Could you have braved those censorious gazes? I wonder. I would like to think that you would have sat patiently beside me, listening to my recital of all the sorrows I've accumulated during these months in prison. But the vestiges of your humanity would have made you want to halt my confession. And I might have been grateful to you later, back in my cell, when I suffered the embarrassment that last-minute explanations might have caused me. I might have also been secretly resentful of your interruptions, and it is not resentment that I want to engrave on my heart as the memorial to you. So I chose to spare myself all that. If you decide that I elected this course merely to manage the emotional flow of the situation, perhaps you would be right. Though our story strongly suggests to me the folly of assuming one is ever in control of anything, I can acknowledge in advance your annoyance that it is you, not I, who is left holding the bag. After all, you are a boxer, and you prefer to be the one throwing the punches. So here is a suggestion: Before you read the rest of this letter, take a moment to plant one right between my eyes. Stun me. You have so many times already.

✳

You do not understand how I could have landed in this mess. Nor do I. But before we get to the crime, a subject somewhat familiar to you anyway, we must take a little time to lay out my story. I promise it won't bore you.

I had such banal beginnings. First there is my name, John Webster, which you were always trying to jazz up. "Johnny Baby." "Webster febster." You had never heard that a long-ago English playwright with the grisliest, most gruesome tastes had also been called this. (Don't worry, I'm not about to tell you just how similar I am to *that* forebear.) To me, my name has more consistently suggested someone of New England stock and a plodding disposition. From all these qualities, I have always claimed exemption. My 19th-century ancestors had bypassed the high-toned American acculturation provided by the Northeast and migrated directly from England to Montana, where my great-grandfather taught music in a Christian Academy and lived to be 72, then a fine old age for the plains. His wife, a seriously devout Methodist, met an earlier end: She survived passage across the Atlantic and a cross-continental trek only to die of dysentery shortly after her arrival. During the past year I have flattered myself that I am her reincarnation, at least of the fervent side of her nature. Not, as you know, that I am religious, but that I am dogged and self-sacrificing in pursuit of a goal.

Emotion was certainly in the air last autumn, the fall of 1986, my 33rd year, when our story began. Within the previous 18 months I had lost my father (my mother, of whom you have rarely heard me speak, died when I was 19) and my lover, Josh. When the bank for which I had toiled 10 years as a financial analyst would not give me leave to care for him, I lost my job, too; or rather, I chucked it. I had built up some savings over the decade, but what with all the medical bills and Josh's lack of insurance, the money had run out ridiculously soon.

I have always brushed aside your questions about Josh, but now I guess I should share a few things. As you know, he died of leukemia, so I was spared the deepest hell endured by other men I have known. I was not, however, spared a kind of reverse, battle-induced snobbery at the memorial. "At least it wasn't AIDS," someone said to me on our way out of the temple. As if illnesses were an ouch contest and Josh had not been a big winner.

But if you think this account is going to be one more elegy for a dead friend, one more Lycidas loved and lost, you would be mistaken. I had promised Josh I would not take that path. Besides, it is too obvious. Though I know you have been spared exposure to them, trust me when I say that there are so many (too many?) stories of young men fallen prematurely that I could not bear to relate yet another, even though I know that the archaeology of AIDS in particular will for a future generation be a monumental undertaking. It was another sort of excavation that was the backdrop to my promise to Josh. It was our last trip together, to Egypt. Under the harsh light of midday, we climbed the Cheops pyramid and ran across an inscription that inspired our final contract. No grand apothegms carved by Napoleonic visitors, nor cheery slogans etched by victorious members of Rommel's army. No, it was a much more recent, Magic Markery scrawl that pointed the way. "Fuck nostalgia!" was what the visitor had been moved to say. Josh read the phrase first, pointed my eyes toward it, and murmured with a difficult, heaving breath, "Exactly."

I did my best to keep that promise last year. I was in a kind of free fall, I guess, a state of alarming descent that I had previously experienced only in my dreams. I had flirted with such a surrender to gravity only once before, during a college term when drugs had sent me on a first pleasant, then perilous spiral. I was trying to see if I could shed my good-school-citizen carapace.

I regained my general footing when I realized I could not face the shame of having died while either of my parents was still alive—as if emotion could follow me into the crypt. Now that they were both gone, I felt free to descend, without fear that the hot tears of heartbreak would be shed if I disappeared. Andrea Mills, my best friend, would see to that. "No dirges at your funeral, darling," she had said when the subject last came up. "Xavier Cugat at full concert pitch."

My resolutely aimless attitude of last year was, I realize now, in one sense colossally ironic, for I was about to be as doggedly in pursuit of a goal—you!—as I had ever been. The combination of passion and irony may still be new to you, but to me it was very familiar. I have always believed in the necessity of their coexistence, passion warming up irony, preventing it from hardening into brittle cynicism, irony making more endurable the suffering inevitably arriving in passion's wake. Although I had no trouble rustling up dates on Saturday nights, dates that generally extended smoothly into Sunday mornings, I had persistent difficulty meeting anyone who genuinely interested me. I was not alarmed by this, and sincerely told myself that I had been lucky enough to live with a great love and, if another never coalesced in that miraculous alchemy of timing and mutual interest, that I should not be disappointed. My coupled friends suggested that this was only a cover for my loneliness, my putting a brave face on loss. When such sentiments were voiced, I could have just as easily replied that marriage was the refuge of those afraid to live alone. Marriage can conceal loneliness just as surely as bachelorhood can mark connection.

Andrea disbelieved everything I said on the subject. "All I know, kiddo, is that you're a Cancer, and Cancers like the home, and sooner or later you're going to want someone to share yours."

That I might relish the breathing room I now had in my apartment did not occur to her. Even though your own apartment in Havana is a relatively spacious two-bedroom, you have had enough experience of cramped quarters to realize that even in my modest one-bedroom there could be solace in a few extra square feet. Josh and I had moved into the apartment, in that nondescript Manhattan neighborhood known as the East 20s, shortly after college and, despite a steady pile-up of possessions, we had managed to keep it orderly. After he died, however, whole sections of the home, in post-Tito domino fashion, collapsed. For months I neglected to put things away. Clothes did not hang crisply from hangers but now dripped from dressers. Wrinkled items consorted openly with clean. The place might have become utterly uninhabitable had I not, one weekend, abruptly cleared it out and given boatloads of belongings to charity. That same weekend I severely cropped my hair into the Marine look you so like.

Doing these things simultaneously made sense to me. I was merely illustrating one of my long-held dicta: It is not people and pets who grow to resemble each other, but people and apartments. The incorrigible pack rat who cannot stand to throw anything away is the same man who cannot bear to clip the hairs sprouting from his nose. The sight-impaired woman who should have had her eyes checked ages ago is the same woman who neglects to polish her windows.

In my own case there was a correspondence not only between house and haircut but between my apartment building and my body. Both were starting to feel the effects of age. Yet both repaid inspection. At first glance you didn't necessarily notice the ironwork cornices, or the trapezoids tightened just so. But by the third stare each was unmistakable—as Henry James once said, the production of interest takes time.

As for the rest of me, my features were decent enough—you would say much more than decent—but I have always been suspicious of compliments. I have always felt, in fact, that my coloring is all-American standard issue: fair hair, blue eyes, ruddy complexion. I have always been the type of guy that people pick out from class photos: well-groomed, chipper, eminently presentable. During the taking of one group picture at a fraternity gathering second year at Dartmouth (a glacially cold school I was able to attend only because of a full scholarship), I stared at the sexy guy to the left of me—a pretentious bastard named Dusty Lloyd-Jones—and went through sex, marriage, children, and decline with him before the photographer had finished the snap. Such fantasies might have gotten me in trouble, had I not dropped out of the chapter house the following semester. By the age of 19, perhaps because I had already endured a year at what was still a mostly male school, homosociability (except when it involved the tribal ritual of disco dancing) already struck me as tired. I have never been able to fathom why adult men of any age or persuasion would not want to enjoy the company of women.

In that company I counted not only Andrea, but Sarah. From meeting my sister at that baseball game, where she adored you almost as immediately as I did, you have a sense of her sophistication. You'd never know that this mid-echelon fashion editor had ever been barefoot and dungareed in Great Falls, Montana, or that her life can be riddled with inefficiency. She has the looks of a Marie Claire model: creamy pink-and-gold coloring and a height of 5 foot 11, only two inches shorter than me. Apart from her tendency to believe that the only real problems in the world concern children, I tend to like her. I like her husband, George Pavlos, a computer salesman, even more. He is a kind, rather diffident man who is often away on business. His love of Becky's profession and of bridge and baking used to make me wonder whether he might have been a better mate for me than for her, but any suspicions I had about the set of his sexuality were superceded by the affection I feel when I see him with his 6-year-old son, Jackson. No matter how tuckered out from a long trip or a difficult day, John always gives him his utmost attention. He and I have long vied to be the child's principal spoiler. I would like to think that what my avuncular efforts lack in frequency they make up for in volume.

I can hear you saying: He is providing me with so many details of his past to suggest how first idyllic and then full of feeling it has been, and what a contrast it offers to his present stressful state of suspense. You are wrong. I do not, even for the sake of sanity, romanticize the past.

Well, maybe a little; maybe the day I first saw you. It was a Monday: October 5, 1986. Jesus, do you remember? All too fittingly for my story, it was Indian summer; a golden, slightly muggy warmth enveloped Manhattan. Monday was one of my normal days off. (I told you I was out of work when we met, but strictly speaking that is untrue. What I was out of was meaningful work, having taken a part-time job proofreading documents at a second-tier law firm while I reassembled my life. Why did I never mention this? Because I did not want you to think that I was neglecting a "career" just for you.) I returned from a round of late-morning errands in my neighborhood to find that Sarah had canceled our appointment. I frittered away the afternoon, not even making it to the gym, and nodded off around 5. A half-hour later, the phone awakened me.

I heard Andrea's contralto booming at me: "John!"

"Where are you?"

"At the Angolan consulate. At a reception for the Cuban delegation. I think you should join me. Right away."

"Um, all right."

Andrea was in her element. To her, a party was a stage set. Andrea, as you know, was an actress, or should I say is an actress, because, though she no longer practices her profession diligently, she will never completely renounce it. From time to time she will have too much to drink and mutter, "It's over, it's over," but when I point this out to her the next day she claims she was referring to the ballet, the cinema, civility—anything but her career. She maintains her membership in the actors union by means of the occasional commercial; she maintains her craft by practicing roles on her friends. It is nothing for her to ring me in the middle of the night, insist that I switch on the television, and listen as she plays the part of Spring Byington or Mary Wickes in some sub-B trifle. She treats old movies as if they are "Music Minus One" records where a part has been left out. I put up with her habit of phoning me at odd hours and insisting that I drop everything because she embodies something altogether lacking in most Manhattan life: spontaneity. As long as I have An, I told myself in those New York days, days that seem three lifetimes ago, I haven't become one of them: the New Yorkers who ossify not because of age but because of lifelong dependence on the dictates of their datebook.

Though Andrea's urgent enthusiasm made it seem as if I must drop everything and race to the midtown consulate in a cab, I took my time putting on a jacket and tie, and took even longer reaching the destination: I walked, a zigzagging route up First and Second Avenues that I would use whenever I needed to get out of the house and clear my head after attending an ailing Josh. Ambling along that October evening, I again thought of how, when one is unhappy, there can be something soothing about the anonymity of city streets. So many times when despair overcame me during Josh's illness, I would step outside and feel immediately less significant and therefore calmer. At 6 o'clock in the evening I would emerge from the sickroom into an uneventful day, some clouds overhead or the sun still beating down, while on the thoroughfare all kinds of other people, seeming, in that mood of mine, nondescript, walked along at the same pace, as if ears were all cocked to the same invisibly ticking metronome, shuffling about with real purpose or with no aim whatsoever, shouting greetings or staying mum, lost in thought or emotionally alert, cruising passersby or steering clear, planning to shop or no longer able to, and out of this theater of real life I would draw tremendous consolation. Other lives were going on, even if Josh's soon would not be.

I reached the corner of 47th Street and First Avenue, idling on the curb as the light changed. And then you passed me, on the left, not even waiting for the traffic to clear. There you were, a boy in a blue blazer and blue jeans, artfully torn. I estimated your age about 18, exactly right as it turned out. Your looks seemed so at odds with your preppy garb: You had rich, dark skin that suggested a Spanish lineage into which a tincture of African blood had been spilled; eyes dark as Claudette Colbert's (how I laughed when I told you this later and you said, "Who the fuck is Claudette Colbert?"); and a slightly uneven mouth. Individually, your features were merely above average; cumulatively, they were riveting.

I slowed to stare discreetly at you as we passed, but the impression was quick, a little blurry; I have only sorted out your appearance in retrospect. Only in memory, too, do you remind me of Ezra Pound's line, which I ran across in one of my prison books and which I have slightly amended: "The apparition of this face in the crowd/a petal on a wet, black bough."

I reached the opposite side and looked back, hoping you would turn around too—as if I were an Old Testament city and you were Lot's wife. You did not. You disappeared up ahead into the crowd, and I stopped, stood against a building for a second, shrugging my shoulders and telling myself that, if I waited there long enough, another boy equally attractive would cross my path. But none did that day; none has in prison. I keep trying to recreate what exactly you gave to me, and I can come up with no better answer than this: your beauty. That quality revealed to me daily in memory, that one of my prison books defines eloquently as "the involuntary giving away of what is hidden even from oneself."

✳

One of the prison guards is about to pass my cell, so I must put out my penlight (a gift from Demosthenes) for a moment. I listen intently to the deep-night sounds of the prison: the guttural coughing (product of furtively smoked cigarettes), someone talking in his sleep, someone else whispering fiercely to the dreamy chatterer that he should shut up. The place's animal odors, which during the day are so repulsive, especially to a newcomer, at night are merely fetid.

The guard is gone now, so let me resume the narrative of our first day.

I chased you. I chased you through the rush-hour crowd up First Avenue, knocking into a couple of old ladies, upending groceries. I slowed down only as you turned left onto 48th Street and climbed the steps of the Angolan consulate. That you were attending the same function as I did not make me utter a "Yes, there is a God!" exultation. No, I stopped behind you on the sidewalk, watched you enter the town house, and plotted my next move.

Once I was inside, Andrea greeted me as if she herself were hosting the affair, which in a sense she was. Despite the setting, African nations maintained meager staffs in New York, which generally included few women. So these diplomats—a network Andrea knew through a fling she'd once had with a high-ranking U.N. diplomat from Gabon—often invited her to events to assist them informally. She liked the attention; she loved the mounds of often spicy food the Africans served. At the consulate, she Miss Kitty'd around the guests, encouraging them to drink and making introductions. I have always marveled at how many obscure African functionaries she knew ("Mr. Ahmad, I'd like you to meet Mr. Bah. Mr. Bah is the assistant to the Undersecretary for Angolan Corn Exports, you know"), even though I knew the primary motive for her keeping up this vast acquaintance: She likes sleeping with black men. Not for the most stereotypical reasons. She exhibits many of the traits the world associates with homosexuals—love of opera and old movies, for example—but an obsession with penis size is not one of them. Andrea likes black men because they like her. White men, American men, find her strange; African men find her exotic, exactly as exotic as she finds them. The fact that she was also available sexually (or had been: She claimed to have given up her love life, a renunciation I found as credible as her exit from the stage) was also thought appealing. Her full, heavy breasts exert an allure quite hidden from me. Early in our relationship, 10 years ago, we had stumbled drunkenly into the same bed, but nothing had happened. My experience with women had been—

surprise!—with boyish types, and nothing about Andrea was boyish. I would call her figure matronly, if matron did not imply a sadistic warden or Mayberry's Aunt Bee.

"If you think I'm making small talk about the price of maize in Madagascar, you're crazy," I whispered to Andrea as she took my coat. "I'm looking for someone."

"Let me guess. The luscious man-child who came in a minute ago."

Andrea laughed, implicitly approving of my urges, despite the age of their object. Given her own unconventional love life, she would never have disapproved of you in principle; in fact, she would have stoked any romantic interest on my part, so nudgingly did she want me to find a new boyfriend.

"Where'd he go?"

"Upstairs. As soon as he walked in, he met up with an older woman who looks like his mother."

"You mean you didn't introduce yourself?"

"I tried to when they arrived. But just as I was about to offer my hand Ishmael horned in. He's always spoiling everybody's fun."

I had no idea who Ishmael was. Andrea speaks of all her men friends as if they were characters on a television soap opera that everyone is assumed to be watching. It is easier to pretend acquaintance than to be brought, wearily, up to date. And even if I keep current, it makes no difference. For her own amusement, Andrea is always assigning nicknames to her friends. She has christened more creatures than Adam, and every time I memorize one of them I risk embarrassment. I once greeted a pal of hers as "Forrest," because she referred to him as "Forrest Gump," and the man looked at me as if I'd forgotten to take my Lithium.

I broke free of the downstairs crush and climbed the stairs. In a small former ballroom, waiters were circulating with tapas trays, though most of the guests were clustered in an adjacent ante-chamber. Near me was a regal-looking lady surrounded by men. The woman's affect was poised and warm; the discreet red cut of her dress conveyed a subdued boldness that I somehow associated with aristocracy, or at least a country's governing class. Every time she moved—to gesture, to laugh—you moved, too, Eduardo, as if you were not merely a satellite but one of those mini-moons of Saturn that are embedded in the rings and revolve in concert with them.

As I approached the room it became clear that the woman's consort was you. You were taller than I remembered. But how could I have assessed your stature accurately before, since you had whooshed past me on the street and I had seen you mostly from behind. In your coloring you suggested a Spanish conquistador without a beard and armor. You had on your jacket and jeans, but your mother had obviously insisted that you wear a tie.

I lay back for a moment, observing you. Had I been younger I would have used more extreme tactics: I would have dived into the crowd, counting on my own modest attractiveness to secure entrée. As I had aged, however, I had had to acquire other means of introduction. I searched your face for clues. Which remarks made you laugh? Which made you frown? Would you ever break free of your mother's orbit? (I am still asking the last question.)

Grabbing a drink so as not to seem a gawker, I stood unobtrusively in the corner and sipped champagne. I was sure you didn't notice me. I meditated on the many factors that had combined to make that moment occur: the happenstance of my strolling up First Avenue at rush hour; the fact that I was, unusually, home at 6 on a weeknight, rather than at the gym. And then there were the more cosmic, or should I say biological factors: not just the happy strands of DNA that had combined to form your face, form, figure, but the algorithmic accidents that had collided to form the eye, its evolution so inspiring to Darwin. Just as these impressions had removed me for a moment from my aching desire to possess you, a drink was spilled on my back.

The culprit was an errant waiter, who in an awkward effort to dry the mess spilled even more liquid on me. He was passing soda water, so the damage was minor.

That was when you—breaking free of your mother—ran over.

"So," you said, "do you think the stain will come out?" With your right hand, with its bitten nails and skin much rougher than I might have imagined, you touched the damp spot on my back.

"It doesn't have much of a smell," I said, not sure whether this was true or whether the drink's fragrance was smothered by the sweet boyish after-shave you were wearing. "It's probably just vodka."

"Yeah, yeah, you're probably right. Not that I'm, well, not that I'm an expert in vodka. Rum's what I'm used to." You smiled, exposing a front tooth whose chipped bottom third made it resemble a map of Mississippi. You also looked directly into my eyes, which I'm sure, like yours, were a little watery from the cigarette smoke clouding the room. I wished that someone would open a window so that an evening breeze might carry away the lingering smell of cigarettes and take us with it.

"Looks to me like you're drinking Coca-Cola."

"It may look that way"—you touched my left biceps, which I immediately flexed, trying to impress you—"but maybe there's a little, well, maybe there's some Bacardi or Captain Morgan's in it."

"If you say so, amigo."

"Did I hear you say 'amigo,' bro?"

"Did I hear you say 'bro,' amigo?"

"Well, surfer speak is my third language after Spanish and English."

"Sorry, but I only speak English and Spanish."

"My name's Eduardo," you said in Spanish, the language in which we conducted ourselves ever since. "Good to meet you, dude."

We laughed at the colloquialism, sealing our acquaintance. I felt as I do when any significant person enters my life: that we had known each other long ago. In that sense, our introduction was not really an introduction but a re-acquaintance. We made a little more chit-chat, and your mother—Victoria Maria Luisa Teresa Ortiz de Montellano Garcia—moved over.

"Would you like to accompany me and my son downstairs? A drumming exhibition is about to take place."

I looked at you to gauge what you were feeling just then, back in your mother's orbit, but your smile had vanished. Trying to be polite, I focused on your mother.

"Please," I said, "tell me about what brings you to New York."

She explained her post as a high trade official in the Castro government and her reasons for attending a conclave at the U.N., and I nodded my head.

"Mommy, tell John about your involvement in the effort to erase the international debt of poor countries."

Your mother began a quite detailed discussion of the matter. I was grateful for all the technicalities. Trying to follow the discussion allowed me to avoid showering too much attention on you, even though my inner race of feelings for you determined every move I made. My feelings dictated that as the three of us descended the staircase to attend the drumming I walk along the banister, separated from you by your mother. The presence of this barrier conferred a tense pleasure on the situation. Though my attentiveness toward her was mere politeness, I was beginning to like her. I felt cocky enough to compliment her: "That was a very instructive analysis."

She laughed. Your mother had charm, a humor I did not expect from a committed revolutionary, and the confidence in her continued allure to men that is more present in Latin than in North American women. I did not know if she noticed my attention to you; if she did, she concealed it gracefully, as gracefully as she pretended not to notice all the attention she was attracting as we finished going down the staircase. I caught men staring at her, clandestinely or with brazen intent, the women checking out her quite fashionable dress and undoubtedly asking themselves where in Castro's Cuba she could have found it.

The situation threatened to sour when the seating arrangements for the concert began shaping up. The ballroom had been filled with small rows of chairs in groupings of four, and as we were making our way toward the front Andrea suddenly appeared with the party's official host, the Angolan vice-consul, who spied Victoria and decided that, owing to protocol, he must join our party. This would have been acceptable, had not the lustful Andrea, clinging to his arm, made her way in front of us, presenting the possibility that the row would consist in classic girl-boy fashion of you, your mother, the consul, and An. I would be left behind, to study the backs of your heads. Had the party not been so crowded, I would have taken Andrea aside and insisted that she excuse herself, for what is the point of friendship if not candor without consequences? But so quickly did the horde move to seat itself that in a few seconds I was faced with what I had feared: you four were in the first row, and I was left behind, fuming. (Another aspect of friendship: that the annoyance of today will have to be forgiven tomorrow.)

As if in awareness of my displeasure, you turned around, as the drummers took their places, and gave me a smile, not a smile to indicate awareness of my interest, at least so I thought, so much as a sign that you understood my anger and that I shouldn't distress myself: We were two men, and womanly wiles were only a temporary irritation. That was the first example of the unspoken bond between us, the bond that I counted on for so long, and that made it unnecessary, fatally so, for us to convey things in words. Until now, when words are all I have.

"So maybe after all this drumming you'll tell me a little more about New York. I mean, I know it was visited by the Florentine navigator Giovanni da Verrazano in 1524 and that the Dutch grabbed it away from the natives, but it would be nice to hear about it from a more contemporary explorer."

"I'd be happy to tell you what I know."

The concert began, and many people in the room moved their bodies discreetly to the percussive rhythms, natural impulses warring against diplomatic decorum. When the music broke, I remained in my chair. I was hoping you would come talk to me, and I felt too vulnerable—a vulnerability that after Josh died I had begun to guard, lest someone detect it and fall in love with me—to make the first move. But you disappeared, and I was left to stew silently. I would have liked to be alone to nurse my feelings, but I was distracted by a conversation Andrea was having with the Angolan vice-consul and your mother. It was a typical Andrea performance: nodding assent at everything a man said in order to engage his interest. In this case it meant agreeing with the Angolan's polite tirade against the forces of American imperialism around the globe, symbolized by President Reagan and the CIA. In principle, I had no problem with these opinions; only when the Angolan droned on about palace coups and conspiracy theories and American-backed commandos did I realize how rabid his views really were. That Andrea kept agreeing with him amused me; she would put up with a lot more than insults to her intelligence to end up with a solid, steady romp. I was grateful to the Angolan in one sense: His remarks gave me a chance to observe my rival for your affection: your mother. She listened politely to the vice-consul's speech, so politely, in fact, that I began to wonder how she had ever negotiated the hard shoals of Cuban politics. Just when I had decided that she must have slept with men at the top, and that her sexual hold over them was sufficiently tight to allow her to enjoy the unusual privilege of traveling abroad with her son, she asserted herself. She teased apart the Angolan's logic, deflated his reasoning, and reminded him that the problems of African peoples had as much to do with internal mismanagement as with the threat of yanqui mercenaries. She did all this without raising her voice or surrendering her smile.

Just as I decided that that it would be impossible to evade her in order to pursue you, and that your playing with me was not flirtation but merely teenage high spirits, you returned. You had not abandoned me. You had fetched me a drink. "Hey," you said, "I took the liberty of figuring out what you wanted." As you offered the beverage to me, I wondered why simple, considerate acts can move us so much more than grand displays of devotion—why someone's barely detectable nod while exiting our hospital room can affect us so much more than a blubbering bedside farewell. It has to do partly, I suspect, with the surprise of small gestures.

At first I had mixed feelings about your slang, only later finding it charming. Still, I was glad we were spared having to converse in the world's lingua franca, which is not English but, rather, bad English.

We sat silently for a moment, looking around the room.

"How old do you think this building is?"

"Dunno."

I found your questions sexy. Immediately, they reminded me why so many people, as they age, reject their peers and scour the schoolyard. Proximity to youthful beauty only partially explains the tactic. The desire to feel curiosity—to shed history!—is crucial when some of one's contemporaries have settled into a state of sclerosis. And if that youthful new pal can be as irritating in his demands for information as a professional copy editor (tell me again, John, who exactly was Farrah Fawcett?), well, all I can say is that ardor, love's breath, involves exhalation of knowledge as well as its absorption.

After a bout of speculative architectural history, we lapsed back into silence. I chose to interpret this hopefully. You weren't a chatterer, stuffing the conversation with details of your daily life in Cuba. No girlfriend was mentioned. Even if you had dropped the name of a girlfriend into the discussion, it was unlikely I would have aborted my pursuit of you. Eduardo, you came along at a time in my life when I needed to feel very deeply. More: I needed to know emotion openly. When my mother had died, I had cried only as an animal does: in the night. With Josh, I had been so busy consoling others—his family, mostly—that I myself had forgotten to feel strongly. And my father? I had gone on a crying jag with one of my aunts, but the wailing had lasted only for a few minutes. That was progress, though.

While listening to your questions I'd been tracking the exchange between your mother and the Angolan. It was breaking off ominously. You and your mother were about to depart, and I had arranged no other time to see you. Panicky, I lied: I said I had tickets to the Mets playoff game the next night and asked if you were interested in going. Did you detect my falsehood? It was part of a pattern that at that moment insinuated itself into our relation, though of course, I only noticed this ex post facto, just as it is only in prison that I have realized that in your deceit you were, in part, picking up on cues from me. At the prospect of tickets, your face lit up, and just as quickly collapsed. There was no way you could go without one of those bodyguard types who routinely accompanied Cubans abroad. Yours was named Zeus. Could I find a third pass for the policeman? No problem, I lied, giving you my phone number. Before your mother could sweep you out the door, Andrea slid over to talk to us.

"Were you trying to leave without saying goodbye, Theodore? And without introducing me to your friend?"

"Hi, I'm Eduardo Garcia."

"Andrea Mills."

"Why do you call John 'Theodore'?"

"Andrea telephoned me one day as I was watching a program on Teddy Roosevelt. She thought it so atypical—her words were: 'Why are you interested in that four-eyed imperialist bully?'—that she could not resist."

"You know who Teddy Roosevelt is, don't you, Eduardo?" asked Andrea, slipping her hand conspiratorially under your left arm, and emphasizing a little maliciously how easily she, as a woman, could insinuate herself into a man's company.

"Yeah, I seem to remember something called San Juan Hill," you replied, tilting your head so that only I could see how far your eyes had rolled upwards, and causing me to notice the dark curving length of your eyelashes.

"Of course you do, Eduardo. I'm sure your schools in Havana are much better than the baby-sitting services we call schools here." Andrea affixed herself more firmly to your arm. "Theodore, do you think the Angolan vice-consul liked me?"

This routine was a sort of joke between us, though behind it lay all Andrea's unanalyzed insecurities. Those insecurities had been a help to her early career, propelling her past rejection and often into a part: She would not rest until the director—the head producer or the studio chairman, if necessary—had told her what they didn't like about her. Casting agents loathed her, because she treated them disposably. But with interested men there was no appeal.

"I'm sure he liked you." I caught your eye, hoping you would excuse the digression. "He told me so himself. He said, 'That Miss Mills is the most delectable woman I've ever met.'"

"He did not. By the way, I think his dick is crooked."

I held my breath as she said this, sure that you would be offended. Yeah, right: a teenager would find dick jokes offensive. Sure enough, you laughed loudly. Here's what I secretly wanted to tell you, as you and An got chummy. I wanted to say that the leap from girlish denial to all-too-adult speculation is characteristic of her. Andrea treats penile estimation as a more or less exact science—somewhere between mesmerism and microbiology. I found it comforting that in our relation the stereotypical roles seem reversed: The woman is interested in sex, the man in love. Andrea was a relief from even the most sophisticated New York women I knew, who thought they could handle sexy talk or sexy literature but, when the narrative detoured from the roguish-man/reluctant-woman formula, were always somehow put off.

"Andrea," I said, trying to embarrass her and yank your attention back to me, "I thought you preferred *West* Africans to Central Africans."

"Not necessarily. They're usually Muslims, you know, and full of double and triple standards—to say nothing of double and triple wives."

"I'm not so sure Angolan Man is an enviable alternative. Can you trust him?"

"What are you saying? That because he's a Marxist and in cahoots with the Cubans that he'd have me under house arrest at the slightest sign of infidelity?"

I held my breath again. It was one thing for Andrea to flirt, another for her to speak of "Cubans" in the third person while you were present.

"Andrea, how could anyone," you joked expertly, "even think of putting you under house arrest? You're much too alluring."

This heterosexual flirtation must have sent up a scent toward your mother, because, all of a sudden, Zeus appeared to whisk you away. Angolan Man appeared just then, too. I was grateful, because it allowed us a moment away from Andrea's gaze.

"John, you won't forget about the tickets, will you?"

Of course I wouldn't forget, even though I'd had to sell my first-born to get them. "No, I won't. Call me in the morning."

"Don't worry. I'll call you."

"Angolan Man tells me that she's very well-connected," Andrea said as I watched your group leave. "Supposedly, the mother used to be Castro's girlfriend."

"Something tells me there's no 'used-to-be' before the phrase 'Castro's girlfriend.' You're either dead or living in Florida."

"Well, darlin', that's what he told me. I heard Mamacita talking about a baseball game. Are you behind that?"

"Yes. What did they say?"

"It was in Spanish, so I'm not entirely sure. You know me. My Spanish consists of exactly one phrase: *Mi gato es muy grande.*"

"But what was the general tone?"

"Seemed friendly. Until she drew one of her minions into the conversation. Then it got official."

"I knew it."

"Knew what?"

"Eduardo said she'd only let him go if he had Zeus in tow."

"A duenna."

"A fucking nuisance. But I'll have to endure it."

✳

(There is water dripping from my ceiling: just the thing to ruin my letter-compiling concentration. The conditions here: the leaks, the crowds, the noise! The dankness of this place engulfs me. I feel as if

22

I'm living—or rather, have been living—inside a septic tank. The distant slap of the surf, the constant humidity, combined with the drips: Water, water, everywhere, a frequent reminder that I am almost entirely surrounded by and composed of H_2O.)

I have always wondered why you Latinos love mythological names. I made it through an entire Montana childhood without meeting a single Hector, for example. In New York, however (to say nothing of in prison!), Hector and Achilles and Agamemnon surrounded me. I wasn't sure of the explanation—of the naming, that is. Was it the movies? I had a cousin named Sabrina, after "Sabrina Fair," and a friend named Atticus, after Gregory Peck. Had there been a famous ballplayer named Xerxes when your generation was growing up? I doubt that most of your parents were listening to Handel instead of salsa during pregnancy. Anyway, none of the classically named boys here in prison come from families of pre-Castro aristocrats or former tobacco tycoons. (Those boys have names like Arthur, Charles, and Victor; Osborne, Nigel, and Earl.) Not only has the derivation of these names been puzzling; their ineptness is also odd. The Hectors are anything but heroic, the Agamemnons are invariably unkingly, and no Achilles I have ever met would lift a hand to help a friend.

Zeus, our baseball chaperone, was in line with the lack of logic: Six foot four, stout, and mentally slow, he was born to serve. I noticed this predisposition right away. The fact that there were five of us that evening seemed to jazz him: He would have something to do. For Sarah and Jackson, and for you and me as well, he fetched Cokes, hot dogs, and ice cream; he would have shagged foul balls if you'd asked him.

You and Zeus and I were right to take the train to Shea Stadium. I'd been so anxious in the two days since we'd met about seeing you again that to encounter you amidst the camaraderie of a subway car, in a sea of Mets fans, rather than awkwardly across a restaurant table, was a blessing. The atmosphere allowed us small talk about your day (Ellis Island, Empire State Building); the massive, mustachioed Zeus leered at a high-haired, tight-waisted lady nearby.

"Hey, Johnny, what do you think of my new Levi's?" you asked proudly as we entered the stadium in a stream of shouting, screaming, whistling people.

Of course, I'd been noticing the jeans on the train, the way that they tugged at your crotch and the way that you kept shifting on your seat, as if their newness were slightly irritating. That the jeans did not show off your small, round ass made me wonder whether you were definitely homosexual. No gay—or confident Latin—man I knew would have bought Levi's that hung so loosely.

"I think that by wearing them you'll be the pride of Havana."

"Yeah, yeah, it took me a while to find the ones I wanted. There is so much to choose from here." You made the observation with such glee that I was surprised, a few minutes later, after we had taken our seats and you had taken in the bright bazaar on offer—the merciless hawking of souvenirs—to hear you issue a mild complaint.

"Man, there's so much shit being sold here, how can anyone keep his mind on the game?"

"You mean that there are no concessions in Cuba?"

"Yeah, there are, but not so many as before. At least that's why my mother says." I was surprised you didn't say "what my father says." Dad was still a mystery I didn't want to broach. "She says that at the Gran Stadium in Havana there used to be all kinds of stuff—flags and pennants and scarves. There was pork roasting on open fires just outside. But there's not so much of that now. A child has dinner before the game."

The hot dog I was shoveling into my mouth just then seemed suddenly gluttonous. "Did you go to games much as a child?"

"Of course, John. And of course I played. Everyone does. Even—what's the word you use?—sissies." There was no contempt in your voice as you said this, only equanimity. "The sissies got their chance to shine at the stadium. I mean, man, they would dress up, look sharp. Everyone dresses better than they do here." A note of condescension had crept into your voice, an attitude in contrast, Eduardo, with your attire: not just the jeans but the I♥NY T-shirt.

At the mention of clothing, as if on cue, my sister and her son arrived.

"The traffic on the way was horrible," she said. "Ninety minutes to get here from southern Westchester."

Number Seven Primrose Place, in Pelham, the house Sarah had come from, is on a studiously attractive street of contemporary homes, and the neighborhood resembles Sarah in a way: No weed would dare to push its unsanctified tendrils through one of its lawns. Just as Sarah would have died rather than leave home with a wayward thread showing, a trait at odds with her disorganization otherwise. Both her jeans and her red cotton sweater looked new.

Her son, with a mitt in one hand and a giant soda in the other, could not easily have given me a hug, so he instead gave me a kiss, an act unthinkable were he a year or two older—or with friends.

Introductions were made (Sarah smiled; Zeus grunted). Instinctively, Jackson sat next to you, and though the game, and its demand for attentiveness, was about to begin, you made a point of answering the child's questions, and I made a point of savoring the two of you. With his straight blond hair and smooth features, Jackson looked like he had cantered forth from an ad for Ralph Lauren's bambino line, and for a moment your thick, dark, slick-backed hair made you look like a '50s teen idol—Fabian, perhaps.

"Hey, boy, is that a new glove?"

"Yes. Uncle John gave it to me for my birthday. Mommy says that Uncle John was a really good pitcher when he was a kid."

"Yes," you said without looking at me but loud enough so that I, talking to Sarah, would hear. "I am not surprised to hear that your uncle is a good athlete."

"Would you like to try my glove on?"

"Sure."

You slid your rough hand into the glove's slick, hard contours, caressed the leather, and pounded your fist rapidly into its center. It would be poetic to say that the glove became a part of you, and to imagine your hand's shape and its sweat, to say nothing of line drives, leaving their imprint there, but of course a glove remains only an extension of the body.

You'd better watch out, John," Sarah said as you and Jackson talked shop, "or my son will steal your new heartthrob right out from under you."

"Is my interest so obvious?"

"My God, you're practically panting."

I felt a pang of resentment toward her; I thought of her insensitivity toward Josh—especially during his illness, especially about money. There had been many times during his last months when we had run out of funds, and had been forced to borrow from Josh's family. It would hardly have occurred to Sarah to have offered a loan. Not that she and George were rich. And in her defense, at the time she had been preoccupied with the decline of our father. She shuttled between needy child and needy parent, and I between needy parent and needy lover, and, though I hoped our terrible to-ing and fro-ing would bring us closer, more often it turned our encounters into competitions. Who had had the most crises that day? I ascribed this rivalry to a necessary survivor-like toughening on her part and did not want to challenge it. Perhaps on some parched dark parcel of the mind, I thought, Sarah and I might find a dry meeting place. Perhaps there could be a liking as well as an obstinate, often unvoiced love.

Her next remark shepherded us in that direction.

"I don't know why I'm saying this, John. Maybe it's just because he's getting along so well with Jackson, or maybe because I'd like you to settle down with someone again, or maybe because he's just so gorgeous. But I have an intuition about Eduardo and you."

"I'm still figuring out whether he likes me or not. And there's this other barrier: He lives in Cuba."

"A mere detail, sweetie. By the way, where'd you get such great seats?"

"It wasn't easy. As Dad might have said, 'I had to work as hard as a miner during a landslide.'"

"I'd forgotten that one." Sarah paused, as if searching for a memory of our father to offer in exchange, but, finding nothing, said, "George will be sorry he had to be away on business this week."

An ex-member of Menudo sang the national anthem, and the game, after an electric start, settled into mid-innings torpor: a long, loping sentence punctuated only by a couple of singles in the fourth. You were shocked at how many pitchers were used.

"In my country, if a pitcher cannot finish a game, he is considered a failure."

Although you chatted a little with Sarah, and quite a bit with Jackson, your comment about enfeebled American pitching was one of the few remarks you made specifically to me all during the game. I wish I could relate in detail the sensations I experienced then; I remember only that they were peculiar and, by the ninth, a little unpleasant. There was a drumming in my veins, a drumming as loud and unsettling as that at the Angolan consulate. Maybe you weren't so interested in me after all, and were only being polite.

By the eighth inning, however, as Sarah was busy telling Jackson why he could not have a third hot dog, and Zeus continued scanning the stands for floozies, you zeroed in.

"Johnny, do you ever come to games with your friends?"

"I used to. Now I come with my family."

"Do you worry that something will happen to Sarah, or to Sarah and her husband?"

"All the time."

"You'd end up with Jackson."

"I know. That worries me, too."

"Afraid you wouldn't make a good parent?"

"Yeah."

"But why? I'm sure you'd be great." You paused to let the remark sink in. *So you weren't merely interested in using me as your concierge,* I thought. *There was something more.* "But not as great as me," you continued. "I'd be the best fucking dad there ever was."

If your sensitivity struck me as preternatural, your confidence was still a little adolescent, uninflected with experience of the daily traumas—the toddler who slips down some stairs when you look away for a second, the child whose dry cough at bedtime will certainly turn into pneumonia by morning, the teenager who returns from a first date reeking of dope—of which parenthood is composed. But your ability to detect my unvoiced fears and calm them was virtuosic.

The game ended, and in the crowd's euphoria at the home team's win, you stood and said with thrilling matter-of-factness, "Let's say goodbye to your family, ditch Zeus, and go have a beer."

✳

My plan for shedding Zeus was simple. I would introduce him to a strip bar in my neighborhood, point out that you were too young to go in, and insist that you and I wait at a nearby diner while Zeus ogled silicon-assisted women. Then I would drag you off to a gay club down the block and hope for the best. Did you notice? In that event, I would have been more worried about you than about Zeus.

How easily Zeus acquiesced to the plan! After we dropped him at the strip show, and were walking down 24th Street toward the gay place, I took smug satisfaction in how easily I had succeeded. (If only I had triumphed so readily over other Cuban authorities!) I forgot my worry about whether you would walk into the club, do a quick 360, and run screaming into the night. As the club's Rick Astley beat throbbed at our approach, this fear resurfaced powerfully. Two boys were standing outside the place with their arms around each other. (I felt certain that your sports background had exposed you frequently to the sight of guys with friendly arms thrown over the shoulders of their teammates, but I wasn't sure how you'd react to arms thrown round waists.)

"Eduardo, there's something I should tell you about this place. It's a little, uh, loose. A little…freewheeling."

"You think Havana doesn't have a few places that can get a little wild?"

"It's not just the spirit of the place I'm talking about."

"Quit worrying, man. You're starting to sound like my mom."

"I just want to make sure you feel comfortable at—"

"A gay bar?"

"Yes."

You grabbed the back of my neck, pulled my face toward you, and gave me a full-on-the-lips kiss. Your mouth was still beery from the game. The kiss lasted so long that when we finished, the couple outside the club burst into applause.

"Are you satisfied?"

Immobilized by the current running through me, I couldn't speak.

"I've known all along, bro. The eyes don't lie, and your eyes have been all over me since the first. And my eyes have been doing a little work, too."

"But," I said, stammering for words and not quite inhabiting the emotion—elation!—that flowed through me, at least not inhabiting it fully, "why didn't you give me a few more clues?"

"We haven't exactly had a lot of time together, just the two of us."

"No. And now we're going into a club with dozens of guys and music so loud we'll barely be able to talk."

"Don't worry," you said, kissing me again. "We'll make up for it later."

We walked through the front door into the roar of music and shouted conversation. You surveyed the quality of the men and ran your hand vainly through your hair. You were not a novice.

I had been to that bar, the Quarry, several times with Josh, but since my last visit it had gone through some renovation. It was a little sleazier than I remembered. The decor, however, was unremarkable. There were mostly black walls and a couple of white TV monitors playing MTV videos. Metal gates and barbed wire hung from the ceiling. On one side was a mural of feather boa–sporting drag queens with fierce expressions, as if a German Expressionist were taking a stab at a Mardi Gras scene. Despite the offbeat visual effects, the place's smell of Budweiser and stale sweat reminded me a little of the sort of cavernous corner bar where husbands go to escape their wives, to spend a few rowdy hours with the eyes glued to a sporting event and their hands cupping a mug. Contrary to beer-commercial belief, it takes all kinds to make up such a place.

There were all kinds at the Quarry that night. There were loud guys and quiet guys, guys who wore underwear and guys who did not, guys with sideburns and guys with beards, guys with trust funds and guys in arrears, guys with variable-rate mortgages and guys whose mortgage rates were fixed, guys from the neighborhood and guys who wished they were from the neighborhood, guys with big dicks and guys with stubs, guys who were size queens and guys who said they weren't but were, black guys and brown guys and Chinese and Thais (but mostly white guys), guys sipping whiskey and guys guzzling gin, guys wearing loafers with socks and guys wearing loafers without socks, guys who slurred their exes and guys who slurred their guys, guys who had friends with AIDS and guys with AIDS themselves, guys who dated bankers and guys (a few) who did not, guys who got down to Janet and Whitney and guys who still grooved to Chaka and Teena Marie, guys who looked like Thurston Howell and guys who looked like Lovey and guys (too bad for them!) who looked like Gilligan himself, guys gathered around the cool hearth of video screens, guys gathered around guys—a succession of massed maleness: regular guys?

You pushed right through to the bar and ordered us beers, immediately attracting attention. As you waited at the bar for service, I heard someone say, "That kid is seriously cute." Pride rushed through me. Yet I did not want to share you. I prayed no one I knew would be there that night. I looked around. I was grateful not to recognize any of the bar's faces. There had been a time when I had many barfly friends, but in my memory now they seem less a clutch of flowers that has faded and shrunk from inattention than an array of balloons that has broken off and floated away, twiney tails squiggling haphazardly, like unsuccessful sperm.

My hopes proved hollow. Someone tapped me on the shoulder and said, "How are you, darling?"

I shrank from the endearment. You may have been ready for American gays but I wasn't sure you were ready for American queens, especially queens as East Side as that one, Allan St. Ives.

Allan, whose clothes were beautifully made but so timeless that they were never actually in fashion, inserted himself between us. Until I met Allan, a professor at NYU, I thought that intellectuals breathed air too rarefied to be much interested in the flesh.

"And who are you, dear?" He didn't so much extend his hand in your direction as grant you its touch.

"I'm a friend of John's."

"From your charming accent, I assume that you're not from Puerto Rico or the Dominican Republic—the homelands of so many Spanish speakers on Manhattan island."

"No, sir. I'm from Cuba. Havana."

"And what brings you to New York?"

"My mother is here on business."

"You're not here to work yourself? I can think of at least one business in which you could be very successful." Allan snorted, and sloshed his way to the bottom of a martini.

"So, Allan," you parried, making it clear that you would not be embarrassed, "what is your line of work?"

"Professor of film studies. But I'm tired of Truffaut and Godard. I'd rather study you."

He made a move to touch you, but you deflected it, took a step to the side, and put your left arm around me. You pinched me around the waist, a playful gesture with at least two serious subtexts: You acknowledged that you, too, thought Allan St. Ives ridiculous but that I should relax and enjoy his absurdity.

The more leering Allan's questions became, the tighter you gripped my waist. Persuaded that you were mine, however, at least for the evening, I disengaged, just as you were asking the professor about his childhood in Cornwall. Finally we were served. Clutching my beer bottle to my chest, I shouted that I had to use the bathroom and edged myself through the deepening throng. I was reminded why, since Josh died, I was so unhappy at a bar: At a social gathering, all I've ever wanted is to enjoy the primary attention of one person. Without that, I feel too often intimidated by the noise, the underlying ruthlessness, and the tired convention of tribal matings. But at the Quarry, for the first time in months, I felt giddy in public. By the time I returned, you were well into a second beer and exchanging the kind of jokes with Allan and a couple of his acquaintances that suggested you'd all known each other since the Last Supper. I plunged in, too. It was as if we'd all been inhaling helium, and while I can't pretend to remember the ensuing verbal fusillade exactly, or always recall who said what, as yet another Allan crony joined us it went something like this:

"Whassup, guys?"

"Not much. Unless you count the fact that God's gift to Western maledom just walked in and headed to the back."

"Make me a woman tonight," I said, winking at you.

"Where'd you get that shirt, Eduardo? I♥NY is so-o-o original."

"What's wrong with it, man? The bartender's wearing one, too, I notice."

"Which bartender? The one with the attitude problem?"

"No, the one wearing the Mets cap. You know, John and I went to the game tonight."

"Which game?"

"*Which* game? Where've you been living? The moon?"

"Hey, Allan, John, Eduardo. I want you guys to meet my friend Steve. Steve's from Boston."

"Yeah? How are things on the Cape, Steve?"

"I wouldn't know. I usually spend my weekends in Maine."

"Ogunquit?" I asked.

"Bar Harbor."

"Bar Harbor?" you queried, but the conversation moved along so furiously that I couldn't possibly have footnoted it for you.

"You must be from a very old gay family," Allan said.

"Where do you live in Boston, Steve? Beacon Hill? Back Bay?"

"No gay person's lived in those places since they rid the harbor of tea."

"The Boston Tea Party," you announced proudly. "1773. A revolutionary incident in protest against the tea tax and British import restrictions."

"He's a fucking historian," Allan cooed. "Brains, brawn, and beauty: the trifecta!"

"I live in the South End," Steve said. "Appleton Street."

"The South End? How original! Where are you staying while you're here? Chelsea?"

"Where's Bobby tonight?"

"Bobby?" you said.

"He's here. In the back. On maneuvers."

"Bobby's the only man in New York who can give Linda Blair a run for her money."

"Linda Blair?"

"Eduardo, don't tell me you've never seen *The Exorcist*?" Don't tell me that's banned in Cuba?"

"That means," said the film professor didactically, "he can turn his head around a full 180 degrees. To track prey."

"Hey, guys. Check out this video. Can you believe the bulge on that wrestler?"

"About as authentic as his hammerlock," you scoffed.

"You mean those guys aren't for real," I mocked, kissing you so you wouldn't think I was patronizing.

"John, you need a better bullshit detector."

"*Mi amor*," Allan purred, "where the hell did you learn a phrase like that?"

"*Top Gun*."

"Speaking of *Top Gun*, is that what I think it is on the screen?"

"Tom Cruise's next picture. A trailer. Not much in the bulge department there."

"There's a rumor going around that he's giving up acting. Can you believe it?"

"What?" you shouted, genuinely concerned. "Tom Cruise is giving up acting?"

"To turn your back on your art form before you're 30," Allan asked. "It's unheard-of."

"No, it's not," I said, poised to exercise pedantry, before others in the group beat me to it.

"Look at Rimbaud."

"And Congreve."

"And Deanna Durbin."

"God, she was great," Allan aah-ed.

"Speaking of greats, here comes God's gift. Be still, my heart."

"You mean the six-footer with executive skin?"

"Yeah. Amazing, huh?"

"Definitely a 10."

"Ten out of 10."

"I thought he was a 10 once, too."

"What happened?"

"We met."

On and on it went, an explosion of small talk. It was exhilarating that night, although something about it now strikes me as a forgotten language, one that I understood perfectly well then but can no longer speak. Gay-bar camp is not a patois one hears every day in prison. (Prison: It has been eerily quiet for several minutes now; the guard must be on bathroom break.)

"Eduardo," I said after we had had another beer, "shouldn't we get back to Zeus?"

"No, let's go to the back, to the dance floor."

In a crowded nightclub, that would normally be the last place to which I would flee—too many flailing arms and whiplash hips.

"I don't know, Eduardo. No one really dances here."

The look in your eyes, vulnerable yet firm, made me relent.

Squirming through the crowd, we greeted a few more of my acquaintances. I realized again how severely I'd let my social life slip away since Josh died. I followed you dutifully, still nervous after being absent for so long from the dance floor. To twist and turn with you on an empty dance floor was to announce a selection: Was I ready? Were you? My doubts began to dissolve when we walked onto the polished-wood floor. A song by Depeche Mode, one of my favorite groups, was overtaking the sound system's mix. You liked the tune, too, and as the song's slick and jittery rhythms wound their way around us, we progressed from free-form gyrations with no contact to a series of coordinated steps in which we each felt free to touch the other occasionally. We sank into a kind of provisional emotional state: no longer strangers, not quite in love. I was elated, but I dared not think either *happy* or *unhappy*, lest one of those words strike me on the spot, like a strobe.

I was struck by what a good dancer you were. Most white-boy American teenagers are embarrassed to enjoy dancing, believing such pleasure indicates a lack of manliness rather than its full, joyous expression. Your hips moved at half-time to the caffeinated disco beat, as you were determined to show off slithery, rumba-like pelvic movements regardless of the musical accompaniment. But what impressed me most was your agile footwork with its effortless display of difficult combinations. This was a skill that made perfect sense, once I came to Cuba and learned one of your mischievously withheld secrets, but it was somewhat baffling at the Quarry.

Two couples joined us on the dance floor, and the presence of others released a few of my inhibitions. I placed my left hand on your ass. It tightened for moment, then went slack. Picking up the cue, you put your hand on my crotch and met the reverse sensation. Half-hard. Getting harder.

"John?" you said.

"Yeah?"

"Let's go back to your place."

✳

Thank God for strippers. If Zeus had not fallen for one that night I don't know how we would have stolen any more time alone. You would have left New York, and I would never have had those three perfect days with you. I would have spent the following year recuperating from my impossible infatuation with you, instead of languishing in jail. Maybe more than a year, since there is no strict correlation between length of affair and length of recovery. I've known people who take up with a new, genuinely compatible partner just weeks after their previous one dies, and though this tends to shock some, it never surprises me. You don't always have to wait an hour after lunch before going back into the ocean.

The smooth, constant exchange between our bodies that week, the overwhelmingly tactile memory of it, has been a blessing to me in jail. In prison, I have had to be so guarded about human contact (an accidental brush-up against someone in a chow line can provoke a riot) that perhaps I exaggerate the degree to which we were, in New York, enthralled with each other. But it does seem to me that, after that first night of post-Quarry lovemaking, we moved around the city as a single unit. Our bodily smells commingled, and our other senses—sight and hearing, in particular—responded to stimuli in unison. We did not, however, become one of those couples who hold hands, as if bound by fetters, as a sort of implicit rebuke to passersby: We're in love and you're not.

I was warier of public displays of affection than you. From a culture where men more regularly touch each other, and emerging from a period of life, adolescence, when arms flung round shoulders are an unsuspected sign of buddydom, you felt free to grab me affectionately on the street and direct my attention to an outlandishly dressed, or ridiculously behaving, pedestrian. You were vaguely aware that there were loose rules in effect all throughout Manhattan, even downtown, if one did not want to be thought a *faggot,* and you could be a little afraid of unleashing the full force of your horniness, at least in public, but your hormones were racing faster than any externally imposed code.

You relished the liberty conferred by anonymity. In New York, no one knew you; you had an almost unimaginable freedom of association, and the fact that your mother was preoccupied with diplomatic functions, and Zeus with his floozies, only increased your resolve to enjoy yourself.

Just how much was made clear to me the night we went out with Andrea. She had phoned me on our second night together; we were in bed, holding each other and watching reruns of *The Mary Tyler Moore Show*. You laughed each time Rhoda called her friend "Mare."

"Theodore," Andrea said, "I want to invite you and Eduardo to dinner and the opera tomorrow. I feel as if you've been keeping him under wraps."

"An, we only met three days ago, and you can't blame me for wanting to have him to myself. He goes back to Cuba the day after tomorrow."

"I still think you two should get out of bed for a minute. Where shall I take you for dinner?"

"How about Café des Artistes?"

"Not too *vieux jeu*?"

"No, An, it's become smart again."

"All right, then. I'll make a reservation for 6:30."

We arrived first and idled at the bar, allowing Andrea to make an entrance, wearing a black-and-white beaded jacket over a dress of tweed and iridescent teal cloque.

"Andrea," you said, "you look"—I liked your word choice here: I had no idea where you'd picked up such a term—"smashing."

"Smashing?" Andrea replied. "It's Valentino!"—a set of cadences which for some reason reminded me of an old joke, the one about the Texan who sidles into a Paris *vespasienne*, casts a cruisy eye down at the equipment of the Frenchman pissing next to him and says drawlingly, "Say, bo'," a come-on that drew the derisive: "*C'est beau? C'est magnifique!*"

"You look great, Andrea."

"I had a lively discussion in the taxi over here, one that you, Eduardo, would have enjoyed. The driver was from South Africa; he was black, a situation which for some reason always makes me feel like Miss Daisy."

"Who's Miss Daisy?" you inquired.

"A Southern lady in a play that's off-Broadway. You haven't time to see it, which is just as well, since the actress in it at the moment is all wrong for the part. It should have gone to me. Anyway, the driver kept talking about 'the revolution, the revolution,' and other vivid concepts. Right up your alley, Eduardo."

"You know, Andrea," you said, assuming a serious, scholarly mien of which I felt paternally proud, "we Cubans do not think about the 'revolution' 24 hours a day. We feel just as passionately about American culture as we do about the 'revolution.' Even when we try to separate ourselves from you, we cannot help but be defined by you. Our bond can be antagonistic, but it is unshakable."

"My God, John, he's not only handsome, he's eloquent. Although he could use a little help in the wardrobe department. Eduardo, did you borrow the jacket from John's closet?"

"Yes."

"I knew it. It hangs too loosely on you."

"I think it looks fine."

"You would. But your sister would agree with me. And she's the one with the good eye in the family."

"Oh, I don't know about that," I said, looking at you. You seemed oblivious to my indirect compliment.

"We were seated by a maitre d' whom Andrea had known for years. He slid her and then you into place, facing the room, so that Andrea could sit conspiratorially next to you. I didn't mind, since we kept up a game of footsie through the entire dinner, a series of kicks and taps that responded jointly—slyly—to Andrea's near-monologue.

"How is your wife, Tony?" Andrea asked the maître d'. "Still singing?"

"She's still singing, but she's no longer my wife. We separated last month."

"Sorry to hear it. How long were you together?"

"Six years."

"Just a hot minute, as one of my old suitors used to say. She seemed so charming when I met her here that night. No way to salvage the thing?"

"No."

"A wise woman once told me that couples should live by one rule: Murder, yes; divorce, never.'"

"Yes, ma'am," Tony muttered, disappearing.

"Who said that, Andrea?" you asked.

"Clare Boothe Luce, Eduardo. Someone whom I'm sure you've never heard of."

"I do know that name. She wrote that movie John and I watched on video last night. *The Women*."

"I'm a little alarmed that John is exposing you to the pernicious influence of camp so early in your relationship. What did you think of it?"

"I thought it was funny. All those crazy dresses and the women acting so—I'm not sure this is a word—bickersome. It reminded me of some of the old movies my mother and I watch on Cuban television every Friday night."

"Well, I must say that I never liked *The Women*. Ladies acting like bitches. Such a stereotype. And Rosalind Russell is a little too outrageous. No one is that outrageous in real life."

You kicked me under the table. My foot nuzzled your ankle.

"Boys, I think we should order, or we'll be late for the opera."

By the time we reached the Met, it was only 10 minutes before curtain. I hurried you and Andrea through the front door so that we'd have time to read the program synopsis before the overture. But the experience was quite new to you, and you wouldn't be rushed.

"Wow," you said, "this place is huge. The opera building in Havana is much smaller. And much, much older."

"Have you ever been there, Eduardo?" I said.

"A few times with my mother."

"Where is that stunning-looking mother of yours tonight?" Andrea asked.

"More U.N. business."

And she doesn't mind that you're swanning about with John?"

"Well, to tell you the truth, I think she may have found a friend herself."

"Ree-ally," Andrea said, arching an eyebrow and the resisting the urge to pry.

"Eduardo," I said, "do you remember which opera your mother took you to?"

"Verdi, I think."

"*Otello?*"

"No, we read that play in school, though."

"*La Traviata?*"

"Is that the one with the champagne at the beginning?"

"Yes."

"That one."

We passed through the lobby, and were about to have our tickets torn, when a baritone boomed, "Andrea!"

Andrea turned. "Augustine, darling, how are you? You know John, of course, and this is our friend Eduardo Garcia."

I tried to limit the conversation there, but Andrea, knowing my history with this particular investment banker characterized by disheveled hair and Brioni suits, and wanting a little malicious fun, kept the exchange going much past what would have been cordial. I had had a date with Augustine, because Andrea knew he was rich and practical and thought those attributes would appeal to me. No dice: When Andrea called the next morning for a report, I remember saying, "His feet are on the ground, all right, but his legs were in the air."

Augustine's date was a young woman from his office; she seemed nice enough, even though the Lacroix-like pouf skirt she wore—so in vogue at the time—did not flatter her spindly legs.

As we walked down the aisle to our orchestra seats, a scowl took control of your face.

"Eduardo, what's wrong?"

"Man, I can't believe you did it with that guy? He's such a queen."

"How do you know I dated him?"

"Well, you did, didn't you?"

"Yes. But only once."

"Yeah, right. You're such a *putana*." If we hadn't been at the opera, I swear you would have spit.

I tried to make light of your outburst, but the jealousy was not an act. You took your seat in a minor huff.

I had looked forward to that night's opera, *The Magic Flute,* but I was caught up in your mood. When the overture was almost over, I tentatively placed my hand on yours, but the gesture was rebuffed. During the opening, my mind wandered to Josh, because this had been his first opera with me, too, and I felt a little guilty that in the three days I had spent with you I had barely thought of him at all. He would never have let a little pique affect his enjoyment of that first scene, Tamino's love song to the portrait. Josh was much more the opera expert than I. I once heard him offer a reading, briefly, confidently, of not just the first scene ("Love not as physical passion but as spiritual solemnity") but the entire score ("*The Magic Flute* does have its sweet serenities and its insistence on belief, but finally it is about irony, the irony of the magic flute itself: Given to Tamino as an instrument for evil, it becomes a vehicle for good.")

Neither irony nor spiritual solemnity were on my mind that night, though. I not only wanted to alleviate your mood; I wanted to fondle you, right there at the Met. By the second act, as the lovers are facing their ordeal by water and bright sun, you relented. You did more than relent: You let me jerk you off.

I suppose that the idea of masturbation at the Met would be shocking to most people: in the temple of high art how could one sink so low? But for me it was another seal of the bond between us. When we made love the night after the Quarry, the interaction had been much more complete, for sure. Though bold at the bar, you had turned teenager-shy (yes, you had: admit it) when we got to my apartment. I had almost to coax you out of your clothes. Once freed from these restraints, your hormones had taken over, so alarmingly that I was afraid you'd come in a minute. But you held back; you edged recurringly, unpredictably, up to release, and waited until I had cli-maxed before coming yourself. What stunned me from the start of our lovemaking was how well, physically, we fit. Jigsaw tight. And not just the obvious pieces but the often overlooked ones, too. The length of my arm, for example, when flung diagonally across your torso, reached exactly to the sensitive spot on your waist, and in repose your head set itself neatly against my neck, without your chin driving into my collarbone.

The sight of you standing in front of me, with your clothing removed, was thrilling. Nothing quite matches the first glimpse of someone's flesh, so allow me, as the prison ceiling drips and snoring threatens at every moment to overwhelm my concentration, to savor it for a second. To delight in the scent of stale beer, cigarette smoke, sweat, and your waning cologne. There's always something one has misread through the clothes, and with you it was your skin. I thought it would be hairless, but there was a patch of dark on the chest, and your legs were quite densely matted, too. Your skin's texture, though, was smooth, much smoother than might have been extrapolated from the roughness of your hands. Your ass I knew was relatively small, but I was stunned by its upper ridges, by how curved they were. Everything else—from the subtle definition of your pectorals to the deep recess of your navel—was as I had imagined.

So as the orchestra got to act 2, scene 7, of *The Magic Flute* and discretion dictated that I could do no more than touch your lap, I did not feel frustrated, or that I was settling for second best compared to our initial night together.

The coat on your lap, not to mention the dim lighting on stage just then, concealed my action, but still you flinched when my fingers touched your upper thigh. I could tell that you were no longer angry with me; you made no effort to remove my hand. Our attention was fixed on the opera, as if to allay any suspicion that we were up to something.

At first, I intended only to cop a feel. But when I noticed you were immediately hard, I decided to go further. I did not want you to return to Cuba two days later and think that I lacked audacity. This wasn't merely about boldness, however. In removing your dick from your trousers I also removed my self-control. As I massaged your penis very, very slowly, almost imperceptibly, I realized that there was absolutely no way, once you went home, that I was never going to feel this hardness again. As you came a minute later, I resolved that in order to have your uncircumcised penis—of average length, impressive width, and near-perpetual stiffness—in my hand and mouth and ass again I would do whatever was necessary.

Onstage, the lovers' ordeal continued. We sat quietly, my hand semen-sticky and your dick at half-mast. As the lights came on, you turned to me and said, "Hey, Johnny, when I take you to the opera in Havana, will you do that again?"

✳

On your second-to-last night in New York, I must admit that I was a little glum. You had to accompany your mother to a U.N. function, and I wasn't invited. I shouldn't read anything into this, you assured me. Your mother was happy that you had met someone to show you the city, and since she assumed Zeus was accompanying us, you were sure she was not suspicious.

At least, on that crisp, sunny autumn afternoon, a Saturday, you were coming over for lunch. Jackson and Sarah would be there, too, but only for the meal; I had made it plain to my sister that the afternoon was reserved for the two of us. I returned from the grocery store around 1 o'clock to find my front door ajar. Since I had given you a spare set of keys, I assumed you had arrived. But as I reached the doorway and heard cartoons blasting from the television, I began to revise my assumption.

"Watch out, watch out!" Jackson screamed. "The monster's in the closet!"

"No, it's not, you'll see," you said.

"Always watch out for the monster in the closet," I announced as

I walked into the front room. Jackson was slumped on the sofa next to you. He immediately got up and turned off the set: Such was the polish of his manners that he would never have had a chat with me while the TV was blaring, not unless it was a program everyone enjoyed. The boy came up and gave me a hug.

I walked over to the sofa and gave you a kiss on the lips.

"Oooh," Jackson said. "Uncle John!"

"Did you like that, Jackson?" you said teasingly, pulling my head down for another kiss and causing the boy to giggle in delight, as if he had been allowed for the first time into a secret clubhouse.

"Where's your mother?"

"At the U.N.," you said, getting up and exposing the fact that you were wearing a pair of my jeans. Josh had never conducted raids on my wardrobe, but then, unlike us, he and I were not the same size.

"No, not *your* mother, Eduardo. Jackson's."

"She went out for juice boxes. She says she doesn't understand why you don't have them."

"Well, that's typical. My refrigerator is supposed to have what she wants."

I put the groceries on the kitchen counter, which bumped up against the back of the sofa.

"Uncle John's kinda severe, isn't he, Jackson?"

"Yes. I mean, no. I mean, sometimes."

I put the perishables in the refrigerator.

"Uncle John, what happened to all your *nice* furniture?" Jackson was an observant boy, and his attention to interior decor made me hopeful for his future.

"I cleared some of it out. I got tired of dusting it."

"Did it remind you too much of Josh?"

"Because Jackson was also a sensitive boy, the tenor of his question did not throw me. He had not yet reached that age (8 in the city, 9 or 10 in the heartland) when unaffected honesty was seen as a sign of sissydom.

"It did a little, yes," I said, wishing to avoid the subject. Your eyes, however, suggested that you wouldn't mind a little more information on the subject.

"What happened to the picture of you and him that was on the kitchen wall?"

I didn't feel quite up to explaining that I had put the picture away, because it was an annoying drag on my recovery process. I could spend a whole day out of the house removed from thoughts of Josh's onerous last weeks only to return, see the picture, and be unhinged for hours. In the same way, I find I cannot look too often at the photo of you that is hidden under my prison mattress.

"I put that picture in my photo album, Tiger," I said.

"The one that Grandpa gave you?"

"Yes."

"Can we look at it?"

"Yeah, Johnny boy, can we look at it?"

"Sure. It's in the bottom drawer of my bedside table. Why don't you fetch it, Jackson?"

As he did, I panicked a little. "Oh, shit, Eduardo, that drawer is full of condoms and dildos."

"He has to learn about life sometime. And who better than from you?" You walked into the kitchen and gave me a hug.

"You weren't with Josh when he died, were you, Johnny?"

"How'd you know? No one—Andrea, Sarah—knows that."

"I'm surprised they haven't guessed. I felt it as soon as I walked in. The way you've removed his photos from your home told me. Man, it's almost as if he never lived here. And yet, when I see pictures of you and Josh together in that photo album, it's clear how bonded you were."

"I'd only left his hospital room for a minute. To tell the nurse there'd been a change in his breathing. When I returned he was gone. His spirit fled without me."

"No," you said, kissing me, "his spirit fled within you. Here." You touched my chest, hidden beneath a tattered gray Dartmouth sweatshirt.

"What's all this talk of 'spirit'? I thought you were a materialist."

"Even nonbelievers can talk about spirit and find things to worship." You touched my shoulder, and all atavistic worry that my lack of religious observance doomed me dissolved. A capacity for reverence remained.

Jackson returned, and the two of you sat back on the sofa, placing the album again in your laps. You put your arm around the boy. In my years with Josh, I had never seen him so cozy with Jackson. Josh treated him like a miniature adult, and when he fell ill, he found the boy's high spirits a drain on his energy.

I stood behind you, making sandwiches, kibitzing.

Jack immediately found a snapshot taken when I was almost exactly his age. My family was fishing on the banks of a Missouri River tributary. My jeans were turned up unevenly, I had on a straw hat, and a coffee can with bait lay next to me: I can still see the worms wriggling.

"Did you catch anything that day?" Jackson asked.

"I'm not sure. Grandpa was the expert fisherman in the family."

In the photo my father was only a few years older than I am now; yet the responsibilities of wife, children, and family business had already taken quite a toll on his face. How he doted on me then: A taciturn man with a rigid code of manhood, he nonetheless never returned from a trip without something generous—a toy soldier, a baseball cap, a boys' adventure story.

"Eduardo," piped Jackson, "did you ever go fishing with your Dad?"

"No, he died when I was too young to remember him."

That's exactly what you had told me about your father on our first date. I wanted to find out more about him, but on the first night I was preoccupied with you sexually, and that afternoon I did not want to disturb your communion with Jackson.

"Did Grandma catch something that day, Uncle John?"

"I expect she did, kiddo," I lied. My mother never snared fish or much else. In that respect, Eduardo, she is so unlike your own, high-powered mother. My Mom—Beverly—was not lucky; all her life a dark star seemed to shadow her movements. Finding my father at the University of Montana had been her only stroke of fortune. Otherwise, she spent her life ruing the fact that she had not pursued a career in physics, a field in which she had shown promise.

"You look like your mother, Johnny."

"My father thought the same." He thought that not only my mother's fair coloring but her strong nose and sloping cheekbones had been passed on to me, but I have always resisted the comparison, thinking it marks me out as more feminine than I, sensitive about stereotypes, wish to be. As I remembered the woman in the photo, however, in love but slightly lost, I realized that my father was right.

"Why did Grandpa Sam always wear black hats?"

"His father before him had done so, and I suspect he wanted to carry on the tradition. Grandma thought they were snazzy."

"I don't like black. I don't understand why Mommy always wears it."

"Your mommy has to look chic, Jack. Black is the way. Personally, though, I'm with you. I agree with whoever said that people in black are in mourning for their lives."

"What's mourning?"

"Feeling sad when something, somebody you love, is gone."

"You mean like Josh?"

"Yes."

"Oh, look, here's a photo of him!"

"That's nice," I said nonchalantly as you looked at me and nodded, as if to confirm our kitchen discussion.

The boy contentedly turned the pages of the album and squeezed your fist with certainty when he found someone he recognized. You allowed him to dictate the pace of the page-turning, though I swear you lingered at every shot of Josh.

If I thought that Jackson would tire of the pictures after a few minutes, even after I had placed sandwiches on the table, I was mistaken. He flipped the leaves as if he were absorbed in some larger feat, trying to figure out the relationship between the adults he had seen and those he hadn't.

"Who's that man?" Jackson asked, staring at a picture of my freestyle relay team from my senior year of high school.

"Yeah, man, who is that handsome dude?"

"Terry Press." He and I, along with Bill Samuels and Chuck Dolan, were posing together on a starting block. It was early summer, and as if in silent exultation of the season (of the year, of our lives), we held onto each other in exaggerated affection. The joke, of course, was that my affection for the boy Jackson was pointing at was not merely matey. I had developed a crush on him sophomore year when I played football, a sport in which I was ridiculously sub-par. I don't need to tell you that such crushes are dangerous, since it was the exposure of just such affection that provided the lawyer at our trial with the basis for a prosecution. For some reason, Terry kept me around. Despite my gridiron ineptitude, he made sure I was included in all the private, post-game celebrations. In return, I lobbied for him to be placed on the swimming relay, even though he was not a gifted freestyler. Our friendship was strong enough, in fact, to outlast the drinking-buddy shallowness of high school athletics, continuing until I was 22 and wrote him an alcohol-induced confession of affection. We have not communicated since.

Unhappy with photos of unfamiliar people, Jackson plowed through my school snapshots, alighting only when he found one of Josh's brother, Jake. The brothers were so similar—jet-black hair, olive eyes—that they were often mistaken for each other.

"Was Josh's brother a homosexual, too?"

"Why do you say that?"

"He looks happy and healthy. And mommy says he's cute." The boy's equation of happiness and health and handsomeness with homosexuality made me think that an urban version of the 4-H Club would be a viable possibility.

"You know, Jake is married and has a boy about your age. I seriously doubt that he's a homosexual." The perplexing possibility of being married and queer, I felt, could not be introduced to Jackson until he was at least 10.

"Mommy says that all the boys at her office are homosexual. Do you have to be like that to work at an office?"

"No, sweetheart, you know you don't. At your daddy's office all the boys like girls."

A few more photos were discussed, and Jackson reached the album's end. He closed the book with terrific finality, causing a loose snapshot to fly onto your lap.

"Oh," Jackson said with surprisingly aware emphasis. "It's you with a *girl*."

"Yes, it's me with a girl. Nan Gustaffson. Senior year."

"Did you like that girl, Johnny Baby?"

"Yeah. I did."

"I'll bet," you smirked.

"But I thought you liked, you preferred, boys."

"I do. But no matter whom you marry, you can love people of both sexes"—a watered-down version of something I had decided a few years after Nan moved away: If I had to decide which sex I was more attracted to, I would have to say that women and girls were more beloved by me, but men and boys riveted my attention.

"Eduardo, do you have a girlfriend?"

"Not right now, Jackson. But I used to."

I was not nearly so interested that day in finding out more about your high-school sweetheart as I was in quizzing you about your father. I took it for granted that neither of us had had a gender-exclusive history.

Talk of girls led Jackson to another subject.

"Uncle John, what are those little packages in your bedside table drawer?"

"Which things?"

"Those gold packages?"

"Those are things boys wear on their ding-dongs when they're snuggling up to someone they love."

"I wouldn't like that. What if one of them didn't come off afterward?"

"That's a very good question," I said, hearing a noise in the hallway. "I think your mother has come back. Be a good boy and promise me you won't tell her we talked about the gold packages. That stuff should stay just between us boys."

"OK, but Eduardo has to promise, too."

"I promise, Jackson."

Thrilled that I had entrusted him with a secret, Jackson sat up straight and giggled. His mother—the woman who could conceivably be in Havana right now, ready to liberate me—walked in.

Sarah wore a calf-length, side-slit silk skirt and an asymmetrically cut black jacket and blouse. Around her neck sat a scarf so bright, it almost wrenched my eyes from their sockets.

"John, when are you going to move into a building that has an elevator?"

"It's only two flights, Sarah. Just think of it as a StairMaster." I thought she would rise to my kidding, to prove to you how combatively close we were, but as soon as she saw you and Jackson on the sofa together, she relaxed and smiled.

"Yes, John, you'd better watch out, or your nephew will steal Eduardo right out from under you.

"Pheromones must be genetic. Why else would Eduardo be so attracted to all the men in your life?"

"He hasn't met George yet."

She deposited the juice boxes on the table next to the sandwiches and walked over to kiss you and Jack. Her scarf grazed your chin, and you looked over at me, amazed, I sensed, not at the rustle of the silk but at the glare of its color. It seemed as if the doorways of our minds stood completely open and we could walk in and out with utter liberty.

You sat at the table, sandwiches beckoning, and opened a juice box for Jackson.

Lunch was over in a few minutes and after an offer you made to do the washing up was rejected by Sarah, you and Jackson retreated to the bedroom to play a video game on my TV.

Sarah was in an expansive, gossipy mood, and she shared stories about a colleague of hers, Phillippa Carrington, who was having an affair with her much younger assistant.

I laughed, but was not about to make light of this office liaison. I had listened to enough friends' troubles to know that an affair retains a farcical quality only when you aren't involved. As my mother used to say, quoting a phrase, the force of which has pressed on me fully only in prison: Love is a comedy, and so is life, until you have to play one of the parts.

"You know, Sarah, maybe we should change the subject."

"Oh, God, I'm sorry, John. I wasn't making fun of the age difference between Phillippa and her employee, only the way she's been handling it. You and Eduardo, that's different."

"It sure is: Phillippa's guy at least lives in New York."

"Don't lapse into self-pity. Enjoy your time with Eduardo. He's an angel. And you never know: Perhaps you'll go to Cuba. Maybe we all will."

She touched my shoulder and winked, reminding me that of everyone I had in the world she was the only witness to everything in my life, or nearly so.

Sarah opened the refrigerator to extract the dessert I had made. "How do you keep the fridge in such impeccable order? Even when your apartment's a mess, everything in here is ship-shape. My icebox is hopeless: If it weren't for George, I don't know what I'd do."

We took the dessert into the bedroom. I'm sure that at that moment we were the only people in downtown Manhattan sitting four abreast in bed, playing Pac-Man and eating lime Jell-O.

"So where is he now?" Andrea asked on the phone, your last night in New York.

"In the bedroom," I said, "listening to some music through headphones."

"Where did you take him?"

"To a café in the neighborhood. The Little Lamb."

"Right to the slaughter. What did he order? Cheeseburger? Milkshake?"

"You think he's such a baby. He's not that young."

"Theo, to me, anyone who doesn't know who Jo Stafford is, is young."

"You should get out more."

"Less. If I stayed home and watched TV, I'd recognize all these kids' references."

For me, as you know, the main gulf between young and experienced is not who knows what TV show Marlo Thomas starred in. The main difference is loss. And loss of an old pet, even loss of a parent doesn't always count. Loss resulting from choice—spouse, lover, friend—counts. (Loss of a child I can barely fathom.)

"So what grade of relationship is Eduardo now?" Andrea recognizes three grades: those who get Christmas cards, those who get birthday presents, and those who get a place in the will.

"I'm ready to deed him the farm."

"I won't allow it. You've promised it to me. I'm not about to relinquish that set of silver cloisonné spoons without a struggle."

"Don't worry. You'll get them before I go."

"By the way, how was it?"

"How was what?"

"The restaurant."

"We ran into that fat stage-manager ex-friend of yours—Stanley, the one you call 'Full Helpings.' He breezed by the table and issued a smirky look. Thank God he didn't stay to talk to us."

"What new stuff have you found out about Eduardo?"

"He told me about his little sister, who was killed in a car accident when she was 6. And his mother's had a harder time of it than I thought. At least when Eduardo was younger."

Andrea listened intently to your personal history, then suddenly rang off because she had a late date with a Senegalese cab driver.

After putting down the phone, I walked down the short corridor that connects my apartment's two-and-a-half rooms. I remember looking at the art on the corridor walls and thinking, *Why have I never studied this stuff?* It was all Josh's, and was noticed only by visitors, mostly his friends or family, who recognized them as patrimony. That night you had noticed them, too. There was a small oil of an Edwardian mother with two children, the sentimentality of the subject vindicated by the skill of the painter, and a still life of stargazer lilies—the texture was so rich, I swear the flowers exuded fragrance. Passing through this mini-gallery, I had the enveloping feeling that you were also a work of art, finely etched, chiseled just right, so well-planned and executed that I had the whimsical thought of placing you on a plinth. It would have been difficult to do: I entered the room and found you in bed, music bleeding through the headphones.

"Hey, John, you have a great stereo system," you yelled at me, looking up. You grabbed me into bed, removed the bonnet of sound, and motioned for me to come down and have a listen.

"Man, you are so lucky to be able to get every new Prince album as soon as it comes out," you continued. "So lucky."

"Isn't most American pop music available in Cuba?"

"Are you kidding?" you said, fashioning your face into a slight sneer. "You must really be naive if you think everything in your country is allowed to infect our way of life."

"I wouldn't be too critical if I were you. You seem to be enjoying America well enough right now."

"I guess so, I guess so," you said, softening your expression a bit.

You placed the headphones over my ears. They were warm. A bead of your sweat trickled down the rubber casing on the right side. Headphones still on, you shoved my face into your chest, which was a little sweaty but odorless.

"Have I ever told you, Eduardo, how much I love your armpits? I didn't know such overwhelming love for armpits was possible. What texture! What taste!"

"Cut it out, man. You're starting to sound like one of those novellas my mother reads."

I ran my tongue over your torso and laughed when your muscles contracted, like an animal's.

If you're going to start that, why don't you remove the headphones?"

"Yes, chief."

"And why don't you massage my shoulders a little bit?"

"Yes, chief." I sat behind you, kneading your flesh, marveling at the tautness of your skin. My hands seemed to release the essence of your flesh's fragrance.

"I can't believe that I'm spending the whole night tonight, rather than running back to the hotel before my mom gets in."

(As I read these fragments over in prison, the idea that staying up late could be bliss rather than torture seems perverse.)

"Where is she tonight again?"

"Someplace called Westchester. Is that far from the city?"

"In some ways, yes. Geographically, no. Is she with the man she met?"

"I think so. I'm surprised she's willing to take such a risk."

"What's the risk?"

"I dunno. Having an affair with an American. But I have been, too.

"At least we haven't been taking other kinds of risks."

"Well, you've made us use condoms even though you're HIV-negative. And even though you know how much I hate them. I appreciate that. On the news last night, they made AIDS in New York sound like total hysteria."

"Yeah, it's been rough. Josh and I were pretty panicky when the syndrome first came to light. It just made us more determined to be faithful. Then he got sick, and I was so preoccupied with him all the time that AIDS seemed less of a pressing personal issue. For a while at least."

You turned your head around and kissed me on the lips. "If Josh were here right now, what would he say?"

"He'd say, 'Normally, John, I don't like threesomes, but tonight I'll make an exception.'"

You rolled over, in feigned hurt. "That's twisted. I think we should respect the memory of your dead boyfriend. I think—well, I think I should make a little shrine to him on the beach on Havana."

The mention of Havana sent me into a momentary tailspin, reminding me that you'd be leaving the next day. I rolled to the other side of the bed—in real hurt.

You crawled over, placing yourself provocatively behind me and rubbing my ass. "Johnny, you're going to come visit me. Soon. I know it. It will happen."

"Do you know how difficult it is for an American to travel to Cuba?"

"No more difficult than it is for a Cuban to travel here. And I'm here."

"But your mother knows Castro. I don't have connections."

"You can join one of those 'political study' brigades. I've met a few of the Americans who come to Cuba that way."

"But that can take months to arrange."

"I'll write you in the meantime. I mean, I'll try to write: The mail boat to the United States goes by way of the Soviet Union, I think. But do me a favor: Just to be safe, when you want to refer to us romantically, talk about 'Prince and his girl.' OK?"

"OK. And don't worry: I promise to write you, too. But can we get off the profession-of-devotion thing? And not start saying good-bye already? And, please, no long goodbyes tomorrow morning."

"Yes, sir. You want to stop talking about us now?"

"Yeah. Please."

"Then tell me some more about Josh."

✳

We awoke early and took a shower together. We took our time toweling off. Despite the need to return to your hotel before your mother, you wouldn't be rushed.

You asked if you could shave me. I was surprised and pleased by the originality of your request.

Wearing a loosely draped white terry-cloth covering, I sat on a chrome stool in that bathroom, trembling a little. You put on one of Josh's old robes, leaving it open a little suggestively. I told you that the shaving set could be found under the sink. The implements had belonged to my grandfather and consisted of a soft brush, a wooden bowl, a straight razor, and a leather strop. I mentioned that my father had given them to me shortly before he died, and you mentioned that you used to watch your father shave before he moved away, kicked out of the house by your mother when you were still so young. You removed the implements from their soft case and laid them so surgically on the sink that I gasped, a little afraid. When I complimented you on your precision you said that you had volunteered the previous summer in a Havana hospital and had sometimes been called upon to shave people.

You stood between my open thighs, dipped the brush into some lather, and spread it rapidly across my stubble. I drew my head away, wincing at the foamy texture. Cupping the back of my head in your left palm, you drew me closer. Since you had already spread lather across my cheeks and chin but had not yet picked up the blade, I could only guess at your next movement. I was trying to operate on instinct, to follow the lead of your gestures unthinkingly, but the closeness of your skin, visible only patchily through the robe, sent out a sweet smell, a smell as unmistakable as the cadences of a good writer's prose. It was citrusy, as if the cologne you had worn to the opera had not yet been scrubbed away. I was making very strict efforts not to look at you, fearing that a loosening of our almost professional restraint might annoy you. For your part (I hope I don't attribute too much to you), you were trying to focus on the task and concentrate only on the spread of lather: Was it warm enough? Even enough? While you made this assessment your left hand slipped a bit, and foam drifted into my eyes. I pulled away. Before you could wipe off the substance, which you did with alacrity, you were forced to look straight at me.

You slapped the blade a few times over the strop, which had weathered with the years and had reverted to a crackly hardness owing to lack of use. I could feel the lather continuing to seep into my skin, softening the whiskers. You suspended the razor for a second over my face. You were deciding where to begin, though I wondered whether you were having second thoughts about proceeding at all. You had said little since the operation started, so I was left to speculate about the source of your hesitation.

You slid the razor across my right cheek, and I was surprised to feel very little of its sharpness. My racing thoughts were inuring me to its edge. In other situations where I'd been similarly exposed, I'd tried willing a reversal of values, to make hot cold or sharp dull; in the dentist's office, for example, with the burr of a drill ringing in my ears, I would close my eyes and transform a harsh setting into one that was as clear as noon and as soft as dusk. There was to be no such transformation that day. The tension between us was unslackening. Any effort to dismiss it only increased its hold over me.

You grabbed a towel off the rack behind the basin, to wipe some foam away.

"No, not that one," I said, a little too sharply. "That's just there for display."

"What?"

"Sarah got that for me at Raffles hotel in Singapore." I pointed out the towel's monogram. "See?"

"But why do you have it out then?" Your voice rose, and I thought we were going to spar. The prospect excited me. Hadn't we tiffed at the opera, and hadn't that fight increased our intimacy? And hadn't your ability to get me to fight forced me, paradoxically, to display the obverse of my post-Josh personality? I felt myself again able to show a soft side, something I had put away in a back bureau, like winter woolens.

You didn't want to fight, though. After making your way across my cheekbones, you paused before shaving my chin. Your thigh nearly touched my groin. As often happened to me on a masseur's table, a brief brush against a delicate area threatened to incite an erection.

Only a few minutes before, when climbing out of bed, I'd had a very visible hard-on, but, counting on your buddy-like understanding of my morning missile, I had suffered no shame. This time, however, more excitement loomed: You were acutely aware that I hadn't come yet; you exploited that fact a little maliciously.

You shaved the lower regions of my face, and I began to enjoy your sensuous sweep along the ridges of my chin and along my neck.

Satisfied with the razor's regular rhythm, you were now free to break it. With a toreador's flourish, you tossed lather into my grandfather's bowl. The third time you did this, I let out a little laugh.

You laughed, too, and as you did you seemed to shed what was left of your protective armor.

The laugh exposed a few creases near your left eye, wrinkles that allowed me to forget the difference in our ages and to envision you 40 years hence, when you would be old enough to be not my son but my father. Your dark eyes would be bloodshot, the soft hair of your lashes would be overshadowed by gross vegetation sprouting from inside your ears, and the hard flesh of your torso would be replaced by doughy masses collecting along your sides. It is a sign of your hold over me then that as I stared at your youthful beauty, immensely grateful for your perfection, I was struck by the way in which your unflinching nearness allowed me a vision of future imperfection, and by the even greater gratitude brought on by that.

Your presence triggered in me not only immediate pleasure but ample evidence of both anticipation and recollection: I had fallen in love.

When the shave was complete, you wiped off the residue with a sponge.

"This reminds me of the kind of sponges, or sponge-like things, I used to find along the beach. I remember one time—I was probably about 6—I found a really nice sponge—man, it was beautiful—along the shore. This kid showed up and asked if he could take a look at it. I said, 'Sure.' We ran along the beach, tossing the sponge back and forth like a ball. The sun was going down, and it was getting harder and harder to see the sponge. Then, all of a sudden, the kid ran away with it. I went home and cried all night. My mother said, 'Don't worry; we'll find the boy. We'll find the sponge.'" I didn't see how that was possible, but the next morning the sponge was sitting next to my toast on the kitchen table. That was the first time I realized the power of my mother's connections."

As you told me the story, you stopped shaving me. I shivered a little, like a toddler just out of the tub. You threw a towel over my shoulders and resumed the shave.

When my face was free of foam, you covered it with some cologne you found in the medicine cabinet. You must have sensed that our little shaving session, which had taken only a few minutes to perform, had opened a sluice of memories in me. You touched a hand to my cheek.

I was thinking of Josh, of how he didn't like to take showers together, or share the bathroom in the morning. In this respect, in so many respects, the two of you are so different. When I was living with Josh, we got along so well that I could not imagine there could be any two people on the planet remotely as compatible as we were. And then there you were, so different from him, and able to move me as deeply.

"John, did Josh ever shave you?"

"No, he never did. But I shaved him many times when he was sick."

"Why didn't he shave you?"

"It is a little unusual, Eduardo."

"Did he think the blade would slip? Yes, that's it. He thought the blade would slip, and you didn't want a bloodbath all over the floor."

"No, that's not it," I replied. "With a little blood, Josh and I could have sword an oath—do you know about blood brothers?"

"Man, that's a practice I learned about at a very young age. But it's a little—how would my Latin teacher put it?—a little *puer*, isn't it?"

"Is it?"

"You shouldn't answer a question with a question. Swear to me you'll stop doing that. Swear!"

"I swear. I promise."

"And promise you'll come visit me within six months."

"I swear."

Finally satisfied, you finished our ablutions—and some other things. A few minutes later, you were out the door.

✳

I had always imagined Havana to be a Tropicana riot of color, and had written off reports of grim, crumbling exteriors as yanqui propaganda. So I was disappointed when my vessel, a rickety *paquebot*, entered the city's harbor and I found a quite colorless city, one made grayer by a lightly falling rain. I saw in this no portent: It was February, well outside the hurricane season. About the rest of the scene before me I was more ambivalent: Would you be at the dock to meet me? You and I had exchanged numerous letters in the three months after you left New York, letters full of warmth, jokes, promises. The surest sign we were growing closer was how easily we had learned to make fun of each other: Among men, isn't it true, the language of intimacy is insult? As the boat pulled into its berth, I took one of these letters, the last one, from my knapsack, and read it. Like all of your letters, it was written with a number 1 pencil, making deciphering difficult. Legibility was further weakened by the Havana mist. I pressed on, but not before glancing at the postmark. It was dated almost a month before, January 6, 1987, and although it acknowledged with joy my decision to visit, it did not confirm my date of arrival. It is difficult in prison, since your letters to me were confiscated, to recreate the document with exactitude, but memory has been such a steadying friend to me behind bars that I hope you will forgive me if I misquote it.

Dear John,

Hey, my man, my Johnny Baby. Your last letter was great. I mean, it went on for pages, and it was full of that historical information you know I like. I have this history professor at school, and he never goes into enough detail in his lectures. And all he's done so far is cover the same stuff I learned last year when I was still in high school. The other day, he said that Manhattan Island was "stolen from the Indians." Hey, it was stolen from the Indians, but it's not like the Spanish came to Cuba and found it uninhabited!

Anyway, school is going fine. The good thing about university is that they don't take attendance. I can miss a few classes, borrow notes, and not fall behind. But you've been to college, so I don't need to tell you this. Man, here I am going on about me. How are you? Have you been thinking about Prince and his girl lately? I hear they are closer than ever. Just because Prince is separated from her (he's on tour) doesn't mean he doesn't think about her ALL THE TIME! Whenever there's American music playing somewhere (in Havana, that's not many places), I think of my girl, too. That tape you made for me before I left New York has gotten a real workout!

I play it a lot, except for the Duran Duran shit, when I'm studying economics, a course I don't really like. My mother thinks I should major in economics, because it would help me in the government career she's hoping I'll pursue, but I'm tending toward history. (Mom just walked into the bedroom, where I'm writing this. She says hello, and that she's sorry she didn't have a chance to see you again before we left.)

I'm still wearing the New York T-shirts you gave me. In my Mets shirt, I'm the envy of all my friends. Most of them are Yankee (but not always yanqui) fans, but they think it's cool that I have a new shirt from the team that could win the Series this year. I still have the shirt I brought back for my friend Carlos. As I mentioned in my last letter, he was killed recently in an auto accident. I am keeping the shirt to honor his memory. A little like the way you've kept a few things of Josh's. It's been strange and sometimes sad since Carlos has been gone. I'm starting to understand what it's been like for you without your friend.

I miss Carlos the most when I'm working out at the gym. He was my training partner in...no, I'm not going to tell you in what sport. I didn't

tell you in New York, and I won't tell you here. Not yet. I want you to
see me in action and be surprised at how good I am. I want you to be
proud of me, and surprises are important.

Your last letter said people at your office were skeptical of your com-
ing here. How narrow-minded! Do they think that the American
Revolution was, as one of your Supreme Court justices put it, "the last
great one"? Do they think that everyone who comes to the Caribbean
has to lie on a beach all the time? I'm not surprised Andrea was happy
about your travel. Man, what a sense of adventure she has! Give her a
big kiss for me. Don't worry that your sister is a little worried about you.
At least Jackson isn't concerned. So he asked to stow himself away in
your suitcase? That he, too, wants to visit "Uncle Eduardo"? That's
great! I already have some souvenirs for you to take back for him.

Well, I'd better finish this letter and return to my studies. I have an
exam tomorrow on Basic Socialist Principles of Economics. Karl Marx,
here I come!

Your friend,
Eduardo

I put the letter in my knapsack, grumbling about the coffee stain
on the envelope. This residual ring had been imprinted by a waitress
at a Cuban café in New York, who, when pouring me a refill, set the
pot down on the letter.

"Oh, I'm so sorry!" she explained, picking up the envelope gingerly
to dab out the stain. Noticing the return address, she exclaimed,
"You know someone in Cuba!"

"Yes," I replied coolly, "I know someone in Cuba."

"I was born there," she replied. "My family had a big house." Before
I could even glance up at the café's decor—oilcloths on the tables,
floral prints on the ceilings, Republicans on the walls—she added,
"And we had many, many servants."

"Really?" I continued.

"I hope you're not thinking of going there. As long as Fidel is in
power, the island is a very bad place."

I had gone to the restaurant to order a Cuban meal and, by imbibing its flavors, perhaps to feel closer to you. I had missed you so wretchedly that I had begun scouring New York for any vestige of your country—music, movies, books on politics and culture. I had even taken to watching *I Love Lucy* reruns, as if laughing at Ricky might also bring me closer to your essence.

I scanned the Havana quay uncertainly. That you had neglected in your last letter to say whether you would attend my arrival had, to put it mildly, made me anxious. What if I had spent all those months pining for you—banishing all lustful thoughts toward strangers as an affront to your honor, turning aside all attempts to disparage the present state of Havana, practically entombing myself in my apartment every night reading Cuban plays and listening to Cuban records— only to find myself alone at the dock?

In prison, I have wondered if there were other reasons for me to leave New York. I told myself that my desire to get out had only to do with you, that I was not one of the many guys I knew who, shell-shocked from AIDS, was seeking refuge in warmer cities where no one knew them. I was pretty naïve, I guess, about my desire to escape reminders of Josh; pretty unconscious, too, about my restlessness— about any desire to escape that may have been buried in my makeup. In my mind, I had never been grandly reckless. Even my nights of abandon had usually been controlled, and only Josh had been allowed to witness them. But there I was, coming to Cuba for several weeks: The tectonic plates in me had shifted. (To paraphrase one of my prison authors: I was only just then beginning to realize how these layers of our lives rest so tightly one on top of the other, that we always come up against earlier events in later ones, not as matter that has been fully formed, but absolutely present and alive.)

I am astonished my curiosity drove me so ridiculously during that first separation. Perhaps if you had stayed another few days in New

York the passion would have embered out. I would have spent a few weeks bereft because of the inability to touch you again; reflected how much bitter fermentation there always is at the bottom of all sweetness; and of course cursed my stoicism—my penchant for burying despair underneath abnegation. Instead, my need to see you again only grew. Sarah and others told me I was stupid to undertake a quest in which to reach my goal—seeing you—I would have to endure so long a period of *not* seeing you. I would have to endure six backbreaking weeks cutting sugarcane with a left-wing brigade and undergoing "political education"—the only way I had found to gain entrance. But I had laughed at the scoffers: I had lived for so long in a city where barriers to sex were few that I perversely relished the opposite scenario. Moreover, I had already made it through months of your absence; what would a few more weeks be? And so what if I had to engage in strenuous manual labor and profess radical politics? Harshness mingles with passion like sand with gold: All is borne along by the stream.

The ship's passengers moved back and forth like cattle, anxious to disembark. The boat had docked, the moorings were secured, and guards had emerged from shoreside sheds, along with a few customs types. Most of the passengers had gathered near the exit, and they suddenly grew quiet, perhaps wondering whether we would be subject to elaborate questioning, as we had been in Mexico, before setting forth. Perhaps the somber-looking city worried other people, too. I decided to put on a brave face. It was Sunday, after all; perhaps even Communist Cuba retained the habit of retiring on that day.

I could not have stayed grim. I had dreamed so long of that day, fantasized about its contours daily as I shaved, and no weather was going to ruin my mood.

I had been surprised to find the boat so loaded with passengers, Mexicans mostly. I somehow imagined that our political group would be afforded a separate vessel, as if every party of *compañeros* would be treated like saviors arriving for the harvest rather than yanquis truffling after political correctness.

The first passenger off the boat, a man with an English accent, made a fuss at customs. Anxious to pass, and prevented from doing so, he mumbled something about the damp, arrogantly heaping contempt on a small country. I tried to remain upbeat, even though I myself soon had grounds for complaint: Amid the small crowd of well-wishers near the dock, there was no sign of you. I read the fine print on my passport and questioned my sanity at allowing such a drab mug shot to be used for my photo. I studied the façade of a building near the water. I chatted with Richie, a guy from Boston I'd befriended on the boat, and rationed the number of worried glances I cast at the bystanders.

"Can you believe this weather, Richie? I thought Havana would be nothing but blue skies."

"No," he replied. "I knew that it could rain here sometimes, even now, when we're out of hurricane season. My sister was down here a couple of years ago on a similar trip, so she gave me the lowdown."

I didn't hear anything else about Richie's sister, because just as I was going through passport control, I saw a pair of hands flutter up from the crowd, like awakened pigeons. "Johnny Baby, Johnny Baby." Next to an old woman holding a child, and a rather grizzled man, stood you. I was afraid you might have altered significantly. When I had gone to Montana the year before, for my father's funeral, I had found the town's buildings as I remembered them from annual visits, but the streets had changed somehow, because the trees along them had either doubled in size or been eclipsed by Dutch-elm disease. Your color and contours had also changed, but structurally you were similar. The jeans and long-sleeve shirts of New York had given way to light-blue cotton trousers and a fatigue-green tank top, and your light-brown skin had been deepened considerably by the sun, making you blend in with the blacks and mulattos and copper-skins among whom you waited. Your eyes were as clear as centuries.

I waved back at you vigorously, then prepared myself for customs.

Sandy Bjorkman, my brigade leader, had told our group of 15 what to say. My dockside official had been rough with the passengers in front of me, a young woman and her two kids, and I thought how unfeeling it was for a lowly functionary in an out-of-the-way harbor to behave in such a manner. After nine months in prison, I no longer find the indifference of such functionaries exceptional.

The customs official looked at my passport photo, compared it to my face, and squinted a little. I understood his confusion. In the photo, taken three years before, my hair was long, curly, and artfully unkempt; now it was ruthlessly cropped, and my face was a little fuller. (Taken today, with my scruffy beard, greasy hair, and prison pallor, a photo of me would be almost unrecognizable.) I was still a decent-looking man, or so I was told, and I had used my looks when new in Manhattan to gain entrance to trendy nightclubs, but handsomeness was no passport here, where my literal passport was suspect. The official checked my papers against a list of names in a ledger-large notebook, and for a moment I panicked, my paranoia assuring me that the high-school summer I had spent campaigning for Nixon had somehow found its way to the Cuban dockside. The official waved me on.

I could not join you just then; I had to wait while the rest of my group underwent inspection. At any sign of delay, the official would be besieged by Sandy. She was a fuzzy-haired philosophy teacher from Madison, Wisconsin, and she approached any problem with the fervor of an old-fashioned Midwestern populist. She fancied herself levelheaded and untrickable, but I realized when we met in New York that she was lonely and thus susceptible to the least scrap of attention. I flattered her, made a few perfunctory noises about the revolution (well, more than a few: I was so desperate to see you), and the next day received my acceptance for the sugar brigade. (Gaining clearance from my government was a more difficult process.) I had looked into other ways to gain entry into Cuba, but unless I were a journalist or politician or had family members in dire need, there was only the one alternative.

I hated having to linger dockside that day. I kept looking over at you for encouragement, but before long, more sinister scenarios of detention, regarding gay men in Cuba, appeared to me instead. I preferred to ignore these. I was not naïve about Castro's cruelty—and was aware of the irony of signing up to cut cane in order to pursue a homosexual attraction, when such labor had once been assigned by Castro to men as punishment for same-sex behavior—but even with my country's vaunted laws of due process I knew of so many American instances of unjust imprisonment that I hardly considered tough treatment of gays reason for staying home.

Richie came over to sit with me.

"Is this the revolution?" I asked him. "A constant state of expectation?"

"If I were you," he replied, "I'd enjoy these moments. When you're under a hot sun cutting cane this will seem heaven." Richie's elimination of the word "like" before "heaven" made me laugh. Andrea employed a similar locution. In fact, she had used it on the telephone the night before I left New York.

"Teddy," she had said, "the vice-consul from Togo whom I saw tonight told me I looked heaven. We went to the Rainbow Room, where he spent more money on me than his country produced in GNP all of last year."

She went on to encourage me to take the trip, however much she suspected my motives. "Teddy, you're about as much a zealot as I am. I may not know much about Communism, but I do know that 'deviance' is definitely not part of the program. I'm worried you're going to end up behind bars. Or thrown out to sea, like one of the great unwashed in some boat lift."

"An," I told her, "nothing's going to happen. I'm going as a political observer, a friend of the people. Nothing's going to happen."

"Nothing's going to happen to you until the day that someone taps you on the shoulder and says, 'Come with me.' Then you'll feel the way my father did"—her father was Jewish—"when his second wife cajoled him into visiting Germany. On the third day, as they were touring King Ludwig's castle, he started screaming, 'Get me the fuck out of here!' I hope that's not you, Teddy."

Just then, a customs official tapped me on the shoulder.

I wasn't sure what was happening, and would have panicked if I hadn't noticed that everyone else in my group was also being asked to go with the official. I looked over at you, gave you a thumbs up, and collected my bag. I'm sure you don't realize how ashen your penny-colored skin went. Sandy Bjorkman came up to me and said, "Isn't this great?"

"What's great?"

She said that we would be bypassing Havana. Officials had arranged to take us to a place near the sea for several days of indoctrination before the hard work began.

Desperate to see you, I used the only excuse I could. I told her I needed to use the bathroom.

I got your attention, pointed in the direction of the facilities, and you nodded and disappeared.

I made my way, hurtling through puddles on rough ground, the quayside water awash in refuse of every kind. I set my backpack outside the facility, a one-toilet affair with a latrine-like, unlatched door. I opened it because, before you arrived, I really did have to pee.

But you were already inside. I tried for a little "Hello, how are you?" decorum, a ridiculous approach, given my time constraints. You reached round to lock the door. The tentative child had been replaced by a very determined man. I didn't have to tell you what was happening. You knew.

In both of us lurked four months of pent-up conversation, but you spoke first.

"Shit, Johnny, I can't believe you're here."

"You didn't think I'd really make it?"

"I wasn't sure, wasn't sure. Anything can happen en route."

"Well, here I am. Are we going to waste this moment on small talk?"

You touched my shoulder and kissed me, a little hesitantly at first, as if you were checking the gauge of my desire. Finding it intact, we kissed each other harder. Your skin's fragrance, like its color, had altered. The sweetness I had remembered from New York had not entirely disappeared, yet it was joined by a saltier taste, a taste sharpened by the briny smells of the dockside and the earthier aromas of the latrine. My left hand moved up your torso under your shirt, even as my right hand gripped your neck so you would not stop kissing me. Your body felt more muscular than before. I slid a fingernail, in a quiet glissando, up the middle of your back; you tensed.

"Have you been working out?" I asked.

"Yes. I've been preparing for weeks, training super-long hours. And now you're going to miss my bout."

"How did you know about the change in our plans?"

"One of the officials on the dock told me."

"Yeah, it's terrible news. But what's this bout you're talking about?"

"My boxing match. Tomorrow night. It's the regional final. In my weight class."

I touched your hands, seeking proof of your statement. The palms were as rough as ever, and there was a cut healing on your right ring finger. I kissed the hand, shoved the finger to the back of my mouth, until I reached the knuckle.

"I can't believe how stupid I was not to realize why your hands were like this. But why didn't you tell me?"

"I wanted to surprise you. I wanted you to come down to Havana and, after you'd been here for only a day, to see me in the center of the ring. Winning! And now you're going to miss it. You've been one of my main motivations to get me through the training. And now for what?" You turned away from me, petulantly, like a child just barred from licking the cake-batter beaters.

In the confines of the latrine, you couldn't turn far. I placed my mouth on the back of your neck, nuzzled the dark hair there. I turned you toward me; you were skittish. I maneuvered your face toward mine, and our kisses of reacquaintance turned into kisses of solace, of entreaty. My technique had an effect: You began to kiss me back. Your teeth tugged at my bottom lip. You pulled it back and looked up at me, suggesting that you were about to bite it and that there was no way to prevent that. But you didn't bite me; you shoved your tongue down my throat and then sucked mine down yours. I detected very faintly the taste of nicotine.

"You've started smoking?"

"No. I just had a few puffs of one. To calm myself down at the dock."

I placed your hand on my trousers. Why don't you puff on this?"

"Whoa! You've been in Cuba for five minutes, and you've already turned into macho?" You bent down, laughing, and planted your face next to my crotch. "Are these the jeans we saw on Canal Street?"

"I can't believe you're more interested in the jeans than in what's inside them." It was my turn to break away, but I did so theatrically.

You hugged me from behind, kissed my hair, said how much you missed me.

A voice not far off cried, "Webster?" Hey, Webster? Where are you?"

"Who's that?"

"Richie. He's in my group. I have to go."

"Wait, I've got something for you."

"Oh, shit, I almost forgot: I've got something for you, too."

You reached into your knapsack, and I reached a hand outside the latrine momentarily to pluck something from mine. We exchanged small, wrapped packages. Their similar sizes made us eye each other suspiciously. We tore off the paper ferociously, and when it became apparent that we had gotten each other the same thing—thin, supple-leather wrist bonds in a double strand, we both burst out laughing.

"After you left, I went back to that leather store on Bleecker Street and got this for you."

"I meant to give you this before I left New York, but I forgot."

We affixed them to each other's wrists, uttering tribal-like incantations over the gift exchange. Richie's voice was creeping nearer.

"Eduardo, it's going to be really hard for me to get through the next six weeks without seeing you. Six weeks of hard work."

"Well, I'll be working hard, too. Preparing for my next match. If I win tomorrow night, that is."

"You'll win, Eduardo. You're a warrior."

We embraced, and as I breathed in your fragrance, inhaling a six weeks' store of it, I told myself that the trip had been worth it, even if I was being wrenched away from you and carted off to do a duty in which I didn't quite believe.

"Johnny Baby, you'd better leave. *Ahora mismo.*"

I raced out the door, leaving you in that wet ramshackle toilet. I felt very full—not the least because I still had to pee.

✳

We were taken to the remnants of a resort about two hours east of Havana. It was difficult to believe that the compound had once welcomed wealthy travelers from all over the Western Hemisphere. I wondered if my great uncle Alex, the only rich member of my otherwise quite humble family, who for several winters made a triangular cruise to Port-au-Prince (French), Nassau (English), and Havana (Spanish), had ever stayed in this area, and, if he had, what he might have thought of his grandnephew visiting it as part of a left-wing brigade. My grandfather, even when his business had failed under Eisenhower, had maintained the Republican prejudices of his disadvantaged youth. I remember him one winter Sunday, after he had returned from the Caribbean, tanned and glowing from a week's worth of attention from underpaid locals, telling one of my cousins, then in her Young Socialist phase, "When I was your age, there was also a lot of talk about 'the people.' No one realized that 'the people' would one day mean 'the public.'"

After the third day of seaside speeches about "the Struggle" and movies like *The Life of Lenin* ("killingly funny": *Pravda*), I began to long for some of my grandfather's dry wit. I did not share his politics. Far from it: I admire the fire of the revolution and have been inspired by the early hardships of its instigators. What I have never

71

been able to bear about extreme politics is the lack of irony. Humor is to the firebrand as the cross is to the vampire.

Why, then, did I put up with the situation? Simply, I did not think I could have left the island until the tour of duty was up, and would have been afraid to in any case. I was afraid not just of the Cuban authorities, but of the reception back at my part-time job in New York. I had been granted a leave of absence with great reluctance; a blue-chip firm does not generally smile on revolutionary politics, even for its underling employees. How humiliating it would have been to crawl home five weeks early. And what relief it might have given Sarah. Though she adores you, a premature return would have dissolved her worry about my safety.

Even amid the anxiety, I was beginning to notice the consolations. Between the lectures and the movies, we were allowed to bathe in the Caribbean. Walking along the beach at twilight, watching the sun fall into the sea and breathing the salt air, observing the waves attempt to reach your feet, I understood why all the Cuban writers I read in preparation for the trip, and later in prison, return so often to the sea.

I went swimming every day with Richie. One afternoon, after a lecture and a consciousness-raising session, we waded along the shoreline. Richie was conspicuously brainy and combative and by his own admission "an almost stereotypical Jew." Still adjusting to the tropical heat, I had learned right away to listen to his views, rather than challenge them, to conserve energy. I even held back when he started asking me further questions about you.

"So, Webster, I assume it was love at first sight. It would have to be love at first sight for you to throw your possessions in a backpack and come here. Despite what you may think, I don't disapprove. The passion you evidently have for this kid almost makes up for the lack of passion you have for Communism."

"I wouldn't make any assumptions about my politics if I were you. You may be surprised."

"Oh, Webster, don't be so fucking nuanced. You keep the fire burning; let me look at it objectively."

"Why put my lover under a microscope? That will hardly repay examination."

"On the contrary. If you examine your passion you can manage it better."

"Why would I want to manage it?"

"For one thing, you're in a country where you need to watch yourself very carefully. Too much romance could lead you astray."

"Lead me astray? I think you took today's lecture on 'Deviance from the True Path of Revolution' too seriously."

"Not at all. In fact, I was sitting there thinking how 'deviance' never turns up in Marx or Engels, only in their later corrupters. I was thinking how 'deviance' is a very bad term to toss around when your macro-vision should be one of social justice. Because again, despite what you may believe, I would argue that the revolution must become more inclusive if it is to continue. For my parents' generation, their struggle was to include black people in the vision. My father used to yell at my New Deal Democrat uncle—and in my family, New Deal Democrat counted as 'deviant'—that he, my father, hadn't served in the army for three years, watched friends die, seen families torn up, to sit quietly by while country-club Democrats, to say nothing of Republicans, defiled soldiers' blood."

Sensing that his climb up to the bully pulpit was losing me, he reverted to you, indirectly. "For my father, the question of integration centered on blacks. For me, it's about women and, yes, homosexuals. I don't want to live in a world without gay people. I wouldn't want to leave the decoration of workers' paradise, once it's achieved, in the hands of heterosexual men." Richie guffawed, and I laughed, too, in spite of myself.

"I think we'd better send you back to consciousness-raising— the session about sexual orientation."

"Humor, humor, Webster! I thought you guys were born with acute irony built-in."

"Not always. Not when it comes to love affairs."

"But why not treat them a little more lightly? How old is Eduardo again?"

"Eighteen."

"Eighteen? He's barely out of short pants. He's got a lot of living to do yet, don't you think?"

"And why can't that living be with me?"

"Excuse me, but where are you going to set up house? As far as I know, Fidel doesn't allow many Cubans to study in the U.S., and I doubt you'll be allowed to set up shop here after our trip is over."

I had given a lot of thought to this question in New York, deciding that our relation was a romance rather than a courtship with nuptials in sight. But why couldn't romance last a while? It seemed to me unsophisticated to think that all valuable relationships must last a lifetime.

"Richie, why are you fast-forwarding everything? Are you so cynical that you think romance is never worth pursuing? And are you so unrealistic as to think that love never encounters obstacles?"

I continued in this vein, opening myself up to Richie. Something prevented me from divulging too much, even though Richie turned out to be tremendously reliable: a mensch times three. The beneficiary of a Brandeis education, and suffused with an idealistic commitment to teaching, because he thought nothing nobler than the opportunity to influence others, he was a throwback, a reminder in fact of Josh: one of those assertive, self-educated Jewish boys whose illiterate immigrant fathers determined their brusque emotional style. Josh could also be conciliatory. He was the peacemaker in his family, and though I liked my late boyfriend's diplomacy, I never loved him more than when he stood at holidays, or weddings, or bar mitzvahs in the midst of his father and two brothers, beaming as they squabbled around him.

"Earth to Webster? You're drifting off here. Thinking of Eduardo?"

"I'm thinking of a lot of guys."

"I'm thinking of Emma Kramer myself. An ex-girlfriend with the most beautiful tits you've ever seen."

In the weeks to follow, Richie's directness won him my respect and a joshing affection as well. It would be amusing to report that his human qualities also elicited some cloistered crush on my part, but given his short stature and baldness, two of my least favorite attributes, they did not. Richie's was a friendship neither complicated nor enriched by desire.

We were bussed to our destination, "Workers' Wonderland," on February 14, 1987. Arriving at nightfall, it was difficult to see the exact layout of the place. We were shown to our barracks (split by gender) and led to a cramped refectory for a supper of rice and beans. I don't know why, but I somehow I expected that our hosts would mark our arrival with more festive fare: plantains, at least. It had not quite sunk in that, whatever its achievements in the social sphere, this country was still quite poor, and what exotic foodstuffs it had were not going to be lavished on American *compañeros.*

Staring at all us workers at a long square table that night, I thought that no matter how bright-eyed we looked as individuals, our group formed a sorry sight en masse. The women, for example, did not have the sharply cropped hair you would expect for those who were about to undertake strenuous labor but looked as though they had all had the same perm before departure, resulting in locks electrically elongated, like Carole King's on the *Tapestry* album cover. The men generally sported beards, as if believing that it was not enough to follow Fidel's ideals; one must adhere to his grooming habits as well. In such company, with my short hair and clean-shaven features, I was an anomaly, and I wondered if other distinguishing aspects of me were noticeable, too. Even though I trusted Richie's discretion about you, it wouldn't be long before others might make assumptions. And I somehow assumed that American revolutionaries would be no freer of certain prejudices than their Cuban counterparts.

As always before the first day of anything—school, job—I had trouble sleeping that night. Mosquitoes were thick. Inchoate dreams invaded what rest I did manage.

Damn, the prison guard's coming round again, so I must interrupt my consideration of Eric Haas. The guard's gone now, but rather than cross out Eric, whose only relevance to this narrative is his slight resemblance to one of my fellow sugarcane workers, I'd rather linger on him for a minute. The guard's appearance has caused a shiver of anxiety, and only the thought of Eric, and other beauties I have known, can compose me. Eric, a junior-high friend, and I had a difficult relationship. Once, we even got into a fight. The source of our conflict was trifling, but for some reason my honor had been questioned, and I had to act. (Even then—decades before yesterday's decision not to see you—honor sometimes took precedence over love.) It was no accident that I had picked the fight with Eric. Even now, looking up at the near-darkness of my cell, the Tom Sawyerish beauty of his face almost pulverizes me, and when I think of his platonically perfect white ass, which I glimpsed a few years later in the shower of my father's country club, I think (cue voice of John Wayne), *Truly this was the face of God.* All through seventh grade I had longed for uninhibited bodily contact with Eric, and I realized that an altercation would be the only way to gain it. I envied the girls in my class, who could openly embrace and touch, and who fought only when absolutely pressed; among us boys, fighting erupted at a glance, simply because we—or at least I—wanted contact with other male bodies, and only by fighting could this be achieved. The contact on the ball field—the fanny-pat after a touchdown, the embrace after a victory—seemed more accidental, less satisfying to me. I bring up the subject here not to remind you of what may lurk in the hearts of your fellow boxers or to inveigh against the latent homoeroticism of sports in general (a tired notion.) I'm interested in this theme for quite contrary reasons. From a dramatic point of view I think that men's twin obsessions, sports and sex, are in fact the most understandable ones: In neither do you ever know securely in advance the timing of the outcome. As far as sports and sex and homosexuals are concerned, I have often thought that gay guys can be more murderously competitive than straights because they perhaps don't as often physically fight, burning off rage, just as they can be more enviously compatible than a pair of straight buddies because they can casually fuck, eliminating sublimation.

Warrior-like athletes were few among my brigade counterparts in Cuba. I'd never heard so much talk of peace in my life, which was strange, since our quarters reeked of the rhetoric of war. "The revolution requires armed struggle!" and "War on the ruling class!" were two of the slogans that shouted down at us from posters in the mess hall, and we were exhorted in the political literature left in our barracks to "take the fight for socialism to the streets!" Our Cuban foreman, Ramon, assured us that by contributing to the cause we were helping bring about the downfall of the imperialist oppressors, just as we were taking part in an important working-class tradition. Every Cuban, he said, had cut cane at one time or another, and the backbreaking stoop and slash of it would bring all of us in touch with the national character.

Backbreaking was right. The next morning, we awoke at 5 and, armed with machetes and water bottles, trudged to the fields for a full day's work, unrelieved by even a small siesta. Outfitted in long-sleeve shirts, baggy trousers, gloves, and hats, we 15 gringos and a few token Cubans cut sugarcane, the leaves of which cause skin to itch terribly. I understood immediately why forced laborers under Castro preferred desertion and a potentially long jail term to continued toil. That first afternoon, looking across the fields at all us laborers, I forgot what century I was in, so unchanging seemed humankind's hard lot under the broiling sun.

I had to adjust not only to the work conditions but to the state of our quarters. On the second or third day Richie called me to the other end of the men's barracks.

"Look at this, Webster."

"A floorboard had been cracked, exposing a vast subterranean world beneath the building. Out of a sputtering pipe came little centipedes that curled up at the slightest alarm, lying motionless like tiny copper spirals.

"God, this place is riddled with critters, Richie. Have you noticed the activity in the closets?"

"No."

I took him over to stand in front of one of them. "Listen."

There were almost imperceptible noises—scratching, mostly.

"Watch what happens when I open the door. See?"

There was a scurry of insects; a column of ants tumbled off a bottle of Coke that someone had forgotten to throw away.

Richie shuddered. In his best superhero voice he cried, "If we aren't careful, the denizens of slime will take over our beleaguered stronghold!"

I somehow made it through that first week, buoyed by encouraging thoughts of you. I imagined you at the end of my cane row, with your shirt off, sweaty, beckoning me with your eyes. My muscles ached at night, but it was a good ache, like the fatigue I felt in high school after a scorching pre-season football practice. That others shared the soreness made it more bearable.

To vary our routine, on the eighth day we were pulled from the fields. We were loaded on a bus and carted to a nearby town, Niquero, which was awash with the scent of the sugar harvest.

At one of the town's mills, we were given a talk about its history, and shown books and sepia photographs. In one of the volumes circulated among us, an 1854 work called *Gan-Eden,* I read about slave-era procedures there: "Wild-looking, half-naked hordes of Negroes," the book geysered, "many of them roaring out jokes to each other in savage dialects of the African coast...[thrust] armfuls of the cane between the ponderous rollers of the crushing machine." Such scenes would have made Andrea swoon, and I myself was caught up in the erotic force of the mill process, at least in this historical version: the "milky stream of cane juice...endures all manner of transformation, simmering here, foaming there, here moody and sluggish, a brown and turbid pool, there tossing and bubbling, an uneasy sea of liquid gold, sending up its wholesome vapors in dense white wreaths." As if to complete the picture, one of the boys who tumbled out a mill door as we were leaving was bare-chested and crusted over with crumbly white. He looked a little like you—dark hair and eyes, full, slightly uneven lips, about your age.

By the second week, however, it was hard to entertain sexy thoughts at all. One afternoon I cried out, "Richie, come quick." A sharp plant had torn a gash in my left palm.

"Jesus, Webster, you're bleeding." Red ran down my arm, combining with the stream of sweat present all over my body.

He helped me get patched up, but the bandage kept tearing against the cane, making me worry constantly about infection. At least this concern took my mind off the litany of pains I experienced. My head ached from the heat, my skin sizzled from the sun, my hands itched from the cutting, my back throbbed from the bending over, and my feet kept getting caught in the underbrush. Hard labor was beating Eros from me. At the end of a day, I had no energy to fantasize floridly. And if I had felt randy, group living tended to subvert the usual outlets. Bathrooms were communal with neither doors on the stalls nor curtains on the showers. The thought of sneaking outside at night to seek release was dispiriting: There were mosquitoes everywhere.

As for reverting to a summer-camp ploy of "just helping out a buddy," luckily none of my *compañeros* were attractive to me, not even under duress. They were an odd lot, these seven guys. You'd have expected them to be hearty, as full of physical fire as they were of ideological fervor. Instead, with the exception of Richie, they were nerds. The women in the brigade turned out to be more varied. Two were unregenerate leftists, three were academics in search of "broadening" experience, and three wanted to imbibe radical chic a couple of decades late. With the exception of Sandy, I tended to avoid them.

If I did not always relish the politics of my comrades, at least I appreciated their table talk—especially early in the day, when the coffee tasted strong and the heat was still at bay and we had a few minutes calm before our muscles began flaring again. Talk usually turned to the brilliantly plumed birds we'd seen in the field or lush flowers we'd glimpsed behind the barracks. At night, when physical fatigue dictated economy of movement, everyone chatted more rotely, reproducing the slogans that covered the compound's walls, the same slogans that, on billboards, form the backdrops for this entire nation.

One morning at the breakfast table, Sandy suddenly cried out. "Look, look!"

All 15 of us moved en masse to the window where our leader was standing.

"Did you see them?"

"See what?" Richie asked.

In the east, where the sun should have dominated the sky, a strange cloud—like a dark pollen—had arisen.

"My God, it stretches from horizon to horizon," I commented.

When the cloud moved overhead, it began to rain butterflies on the roof. We moved outside and gazed up.

"I can't believe how small they are," Richie said.

The butterflies were deep amaranth, striped in violet.

"They're moving in a kind of frenzy," someone said.

"Yes, as if they'd been driven away by some kind of cataclysm."

"Cataclysm?" Richie repeated.

"Do you think they're fleeing something?"

"Oh, God, Webster. Suddenly, our socialist band is becoming biblical, scanning the skies for portents." But even he was awed by the morning burst of color.

I wrote you letters about those first few weeks, and your responses were heartening: lots of sweet things about Prince and his girl. I began to rely on the rhythm of their arrival every few days to carry me through the toil. One day, when I should have received a letter, nothing arrived. I went through a rash of moods: I was stoic, paranoid, heartbroken.

Rather than lose heart completely, I embraced fate—not in too tragic a fashion. I saw myself neither as a prisoner of love nor a prisoner because of love. I told myself I was someone who had been shipwrecked within sight of shore, someone who knows that salvation will require exertion but is eminently achievable. Were there three weeks to go here? In New York some people wait longer for restaurant reservations.

The next day, however, your letter arrived. It was short, but sufficient to lift my mood.

Johnny, Johnny, Johnny,

So sorry, man, for not writing you yesterday. I had a little accident. Well, not an accident. Something happened in the gym. I've been training hard for my next match. (I'm still pissed—not really!—that you missed seeing the last one. I cleaned that guy's clock!) I slipped on some sweat in the ring when I was working with my sparring partner. I hit my right hand on a corner post and sprained it. Don't worry. I should be fine by the time of the final. But since that is my writing hand, and since I had to have it bandaged up, I couldn't do a letter to you yesterday. Also, you can see from this scrawl that I'm having to use my left hand to write. Which is very awkward. So forgive me if I end this letter here. I hope your cut is healing, and that the work is not too terrible. I'm still awaiting more news of Prince and his girl. Apparently, they've still got it baaad for each other.

Your friend,

Eduardo

I was of course concerned about your injury, but so happy to have a letter I told myself you must be fine. I read the letter before work the following morning and had a good day.

I began once again to enjoy the work-induced exhaustion, the way it cleared my vision of everything except the landscape. I breathed in the volcanic soil and the mountains of blue rock nearby. Sweaty as I always was, I took solace in the occasional airiness of the landscape, the unyielding light, the thin breeze that was so similar to the one that wafted off the rivers of my boyhood. I enjoyed the simplicity of the camp and the slave-like barracks where I slept, with bunks piled on top of each other like crowned checkers. So many of my possessions, I realized, were considered luxury items here, none more so than the pens and notebook I had brought along to sketch the flora. As it happened, I did very little sketching, having more ambition than talent in that area, but I did keep a diary of who in the group cut his finger, who shammed sickness.

As part of my renewed attitude, my thoughts about you were slowly transformed. They were no longer painful but sweet. Straining in the fields, unable to lift my machete another instant, I would feel your hand lifting mine. Lying awake in bed, trying to masturbate myself to sleep (no privacy be damned!), I would suddenly feel your fingers slip in next to mine, and your voice whispering, *"Here, let me help you with that."*

You began to follow me around more diligently. My love, I realized, had made me memorize everything about you—your quick manner-isms, habits, humor; the blinding lilt of your brown eyes. I called up these images when desperate, and you complied graciously. You could be helpful but also hostile: my support and my scourge. You were never indifferent.

One morning, with less than two weeks to go, while you were chiding me for my slack work pace, a black sedan made its way along the plantation's improvised roadway, and all of us in the field looked up to measure its progress. The car's crunch of scattered gravel was accompanied by a thick cloud of swirling dust, which was joined in turn by a dull throb along my temples. The car alarmed none of us. Two or three times a week, an official or sanctioned visitor would show up to observe us and talk to the foreman. He would usually leave with a forlorn look on his face. Perhaps we were not doing enough to help the region reach its quotas.

As I watched the auto slow down, an outlandish fantasy took shape in me. I imagined that the sedan would come to a halt exactly alongside where I was working. The rear window would glide down, and a white, elaborately gloved hand would emerge from it. The hand would wave tremulously in my direction. I would wonder what deranged dowager had made the journey to that forlorn place. Suddenly, your eyes would appear, majestic, like the features of a surfacing sea mammal. The car door would open, come-hitheringly. Then the voice, stentorian: "Johnny Baby, get in. Before the beer gets warm." You.

In reality, the auto stopped near where I was working, and two men got out to speak with the foreman. I resumed my tasks. I had worked my way from the periphery of the field back to the center when I heard boots rustling the plants behind me. A second later I heard Richie's voice: "Ramon is being arrested."

I was sorry to hear this. He was a friendly sort. Only the night before, the foreman had overheard Richie and me talking favorably about the women we had seen briefly in Havana.

"You enjoy looking at our women?" Ramon had asked. "They are world famous for their big, round asses. Cuba is a factory, my friends. It turns out human beauty on a conveyor belt, and with much more success, some say, than it does sugar."

As he was led away by the police, Ramon's expression was anything but hearty. The pull of the muscles over the surprisingly aristocratic bones of his face resembled an instrument tightly strung.

When, in prison, I now think of Ramon's arrest and how it was an indirect sign of what was to come for me, I turn philosophical. Anyone who says that a visit from the police can ever be insignificant or nonthreatening knows nothing about threats or significance. Even the most casual of visits carries with it the hint of aggression, the need for information, the veiled promise of implication as well as a blunt reminder that the police have the power at any time to upend our lives, to say nothing of the currents in the atmosphere. So when I turned to follow Ramon entering the police car in handcuffs, and both a sheet of rain and a curtain of fear descended on me simultaneously, I was not surprised.

That night, I asked Richie what Ramon was charged with.

"Petty theft."

I couldn't sleep that night. At 3 A.M., I sat up in bed with a vague sense of dread. Trying to give shape to it, I stared at the barracks ceiling, which had been soaked through by the afternoon rain. I thought of a line of poetry I had once read: "Landscapes opened on water drops and dragons crouched in stains." The dragons were suddenly staring back at me, threatening to breathe fire.

The sight of the policeman's car kept coming back to me. It would be easy to say that it affected me so powerfully because the vehicle enclosed our foreman, reinforcing the sense of confinement that has been my lot in your country. But in that sleepless night the automobile represented something very different: freedom. Churning up the dirt pathway leading off the plantation and spewing dark sporadic gusts, that 1962 Chevy was an emblem of liberty. It was all ridiculously simple now. To achieve freedom, all I had to do was walk off the compound and make my way to the road that had deposited me there. In a flash, I would be reunited with you. *Why the hell*, I asked myself, *should I wait two more weeks?* My skin was cut and bruised, I was unbearably horny, and I ached for you terribly. The rural scenery I had drunk in for a month had, it's true, been sometimes stunning, but the policemen's arrival reminded me of how quickly butterflies can turn into locusts. I saw no downside to curtailing my tour of duty. On the contrary. To split just before dawn struck me as headstrong and romantic. In Havana, just before my boat departed in late March, I would alert the authorities that I had left the plantation early and was now prepared to go home with the brigade. Meanwhile, I would have spent two wonderful weeks with you. And why should I wait till morning? To tell Sandy I was leaving? For all I knew, I might have been required to ship out immediately. No way.

I gathered my belongings, being careful not to wake Richie, who was a light sleeper. I felt guilty not extending him a proper goodbye, but was confident that we would see each other again and that he would keep quiet about what he would know was the reason for my departure. I made my way off the plantation to the accompaniment of only a few whirring insects. I was 300 kilometers from the capital, and on the two-lane road near the plantation there was no traffic in sight. But I was going somewhere.

✳

After so many months in prison, I am amazed that I acted so impulsively: I had less than two weeks to go, so why didn't I complete my tour? On the other hand, coming to Cuba at all had been much more reckless than my decision to leave the sugar fields. I was driven to leave them by fear, fear and joy, and maybe a little by compulsion, too, though who in love has not come to feel the fusion of those three states? I wanted—had to—be with you. I was in such good spirits that morning that I had to share my mood with someone. I called Andrea.

"You did what?" she said when I rang her.

It was early morning, and I was calling from an outdoor post office about 50 kilometers from the plantation. Few cars rumbled by. I heard various background noises through the receiver. Human noises. From where did her latest overnight visitor hail? Ghana? Kenya? Gabon?

"It's fine," I insisted. "I had less than two weeks left, anyway."

"If you say so."

"I haven't done anything wrong."

"No, but it sounds as if your brigade leader, not to mention Cuban officials, might be unhappy to hear you're on the road. Undoubtedly, they already know."

"Hmm."

Andrea coughed, and she sounded so nasty, so glottal that I told her she should see a physician. She brushed aside my concern. Andrea hates hearing about doctors so much, you'd think she's a Christian Scientist, which she might have been, had she not hated hearing about religion even more.

"I assume you're planning to hotfoot it over to the child's house?"

"Absolutely. Although I'd like to find a place to stay first. And not at a hotel, where I might not be able to have Eduardo as my guest."

"At least you know where he lives."

"Yes. Just a few blocks from the Malecón. So if things get complicated, I have an easy out—I can dive into the water and swim to Key West."

"I'll be waiting for you there on the dock with a pitcher of daiquiris."

"Daiquiris are Cuban. At that point I think I'd rather have something more American. Bourbon, maybe."

"Speaking of bourbon, do you want me to notify anyone at Harrison, just in case? The old law firm might be able to help, if you need it."

"I've already called them. By the way, how's your Angolan consul friend?"

"We did it, and it didn't go well."

"Couldn't keep it up?"

"God, no. He was hard as hell. Something else."

"What?"

"He wouldn't eat my pussy."

Andrea, as you've probably guessed, is always trying to shock me into silence when I pry too burrowingly into her love life. It wasn't vaginal aversion, however, that forced me to cut off our conversation, but an automobile slowing near the roadside phone where I was chatting. I had been holding out my thumb for a ride, and it appeared I had a taker.

Since my escape from the fields two days before, I had become an expert at hitchhiking. I hadn't expected to rely on that method of transport. Green to the facts of Cuban travel, I assumed I would just walk into the nearby town, hop on a bus, fall asleep, and reach Havana in a matter of hours. Instead, I sat for six hours at the first bus stop, trying not to attract attention, until a passing motorist took pity on me and asked if I wanted a ride. He ferried me to the next town, where I waited at the outskirts for the next chance chauffeur. Opportunities were few. The paucity of private automobiles meant that when one did appear I would, quite often, be joined by other people plying the thumb trade. My rivals were not subtle. They would whoop it up on the roadside. Whole families carried on in this manner, oblivious that their numbers alone might scare off drivers. By comparison, I was lucky, even if I often waited for aeons on the shoulder in the rain or blazing sun with nothing to read except strident billboards and with only my memories and my thoughts of you for company.

The trip wasn't a total waste, however. For one thing, I received a crash course in the provincial Cuban idiom. Like their counterparts the world over, motorists who picked me up were often spoiling for a chat. They were also eager to pass on jokes they had picked up during their travels.

✳

My ride from the Havana outskirts began typically. The driver was a man in his 30s, and we had been in his car for no more than five minutes when he started a story so famous that I'd even heard it in the United States. Reagan and Castro meet after death at hell's gate. After the devil pitchforks them in, they both yell, "I've got to call my office and let them know *he's* here." Reagan uses the phone first. After he makes his call, the devil says, "That'll be $100." Then Castro rings up and says, "Reagan is here!" Afterward, the devil says, "OK, that will cost you 5 centavos."

"Five centavos!" Reagan complains. "I had to pay a hundred dollars!"

"Well, yes," the devil replies. "But your call was long-distance. His is local."

I'm sure you've heard this joke, Eduardo. Perhaps you groaned just now as you read it. The teller, Raul, however, shook with laughter at the punch line, and his smile so lit up his face that I could not believe he was the same man who had stopped for me. Before, he had been one more plain-faced guy who picked me up to supply some idle conversation. Now his looks were evolving. He had dark, close-knit eyebrows, devious sparkly eyes, and a wide bow of a mouth that parted sensually when he laughed.

Raul asked me where I was from. I found myself tailoring the truth. With previous drivers along the road, I had shared an authentic autobiography. But I told Raul that I was a semipro American baseball player visiting the country's ball leagues during my off-season. I played for a team in Arizona. That I chose baseball, your country's national passion, to outfit myself, did not surprise me. Feeling tenuous in a new land, I was trying to fit in.

(Goddamn it—the guard is in my corridor again, and he's got his transistor going: Pachelbel's Canon in D. This may be my last night on earth, and I have to listen to the most overplayed fucking piece of classical music ever!)

I had hoped my baseball identity would impress Raul but not lead to detailed talk about the game. He was discussing the St. Louis Cardinals, a team whose history I barely knew. I was underinformed by choice—by love, really. Josh had also been a Cards fan, and that was the turf on which he and my father could shake hands. The Cards constituted a kind of freemasonry between them. I had no wish to join their club.

As Raul launched into a long story about his childhood baseball days, I found myself, for the first time in a while, thinking about my dead lover. I was not ashamed at having thought of him so little at the sugar fields. We are surprised at how quickly intense loves can fade, but we shouldn't be: Perhaps the organism is programmed to forget in order to continue surviving. In truth, I was really rather grateful that Josh wasn't with me much when I cut cane. He would have hated the barracks' food, to say nothing of the color scheme.

I was reminded of Josh not only because of baseball but because Raul was exactly his type. (Josh would have liked you all too well, I'm afraid.) I wondered if the twinge of attraction I felt toward him was not a sign of just how insidiously Josh had incorporated himself into my makeup. It was one thing, after he died, to start buying his brand of toothpaste. Now I was acquiring some of his taste in men.

As Raul told me a long, not very engaging story about some of his baseball-playing friends, my mind stayed stuck on Josh.

LAST NIGHT

I've given you only scattered details about my life with him, so in the spirit of disclosure, let me tell you about the night we met. It was in Chicago, where Josh had grown up and where, after Dartmouth graduation, I had gone to visit a college friend. On my last night in town, I had broken away from him and his girlfriend and sought out a gay bar on the Near North Side. The place was almost deserted, and what patrons there were all seemed ancient: over 30, that is. I had just left the place, when guy wearing a Supertramp T-shirt was entering. I turned, hoping against horny hope that he would, too, but he went through the door without wheeling around. I didn't keep going. A voice told me to stay put and keep staring at the door. I must have stayed there for at least a minute before the guy returned, and as he reached the sidewalk, I called out cockily, "You really thought you'd find someone in there better than me?"

"I had to find out, didn't I?"

We shook hands. "My name's John Webster."

"Josh. Josh Roberts."

He removed his cap, not out of politeness but to scratch his head. His dark, curly hair—his thick, magnificent hair that I would spend eight years running my hands through happily—was especially long then. A streetlamp suddenly caught the gleam of his brown eyes. With a rather small hand, he took a puff of a cigarette (it took me years to wean him of that habit!), and he reminded me of John Garfield, the star of the all-time greatest boxing movie, *Body and Soul*.

"From the way you're dressed," he said, "I'd say you've been to a nightclub." I became self-conscious about my black rayon trousers and blue wide-collared shirt.

"Yeah. Went with some friends but wasn't into it. I guess I felt—"

"Horny?"

"Yeah."

"I know the feeling. You're not from Chicago, are you?"

"No. How'd you guess?"

"Just a hunch."

"Since you've taken the liberty of critiquing my outfit, let's turn our focus to yours. You in your butch phase?"

"It's not a phase. I went to a Cubs game this afternoon. They only play in the afternoon."

"I know. Where do you think I grew up? Red China?"

"Where did you grow up?"

"Montana."

"That's where your all-American good looks come from."

I must have blushed, making me appear vulnerable.

"I'm apartment-sitting for my sister on the lake. You want to come over?"

"Sure."

Josh's sister, Alice, lived in a tall 1920s building off Lakeshore Drive. The lobby and elevator were a little shabby, but the apartment itself was charming, with a small balcony with a sideways view of Lake Michigan. Josh was ruthlessly aggressive when we arrived there that night, dispensing with the house tour. He tossed me a beer, grabbed my hand, and led me onto the terrace. Water slapped in the distance and couple of ships could be glimpsed far out.

Josh sat me down on a wicker chair. I unbuttoned his shorts and pulled them down over his thick hairy thighs. He wore no underwear. I pried off his shirt and shoes, and he undressed me as I surveyed his nether region. Your equipment compares favorably, although he was circumcised. I made myself intimate with his dick right away. Josh stood quite still, except for his face, which grew more and more rapt, reaching a kind of Saint Teresa–like ecstasy. Concerned about what this heralded, I stood up and, in those long-ago condomless days, turned my back to him. He fixed my hands against the metal terrace fence and pried my feet apart. He silently went about his business. I concentrated on the sensation. I surveyed the dark avenue and wide water below. A dog darted in and out of the shadows, and one of the ship's lights flashed. And then the rap began.

"Bottom of the ninth...two out, two strikes...Mark Clark unwinds...a low fastball...Sandberg swings and misses...Clark pumps his fist...the side is retired!"

"Hey, Harry Caray," I said, twisting my head around. "Do you think you could turn off the sound?"

"Huh?"

"I said, nix on the play-by-play. You're...taking the...pitcher-catcher metaphor a...little too far."

Josh complied, but something went out of his ardor after that. Just then, luckily, I noticed his cap resting on another chair. Disengaging, I picked it up, put it on, and resumed the position. Josh's ardor returned, and a minute later he collapsed on my back, spent.

We stayed like that for a minute, catching our breath. I enjoyed the street scene below with the incomparable intensity brought on by fully opened senses. A Harold Melvin song escaped from a passing car, completing our postcoital tenderness.

We went inside and took a shower. As I was soaping his back, he asked me not to leave Chicago. Two months later we moved to New York, where he went to law school. Until his death eight years later, we spent only three days apart.

But back to the ride to Havana with Raul. After he finished his baseball stories, he sat silently, cocksure behind the wheel. I willed him to be unappealing. No use. He smiled at me again, and I found myself admiring his eyes and his mouth as well as his deep, slow-paced voice. I tried to resist his allure and felt resentful that he engendered such resistance.

"Where are you going?" asked Raul. It was odd that my destination, which should have been his first query, was coming so late. We obviously had decided that a businesslike approach would be inappropriate to the hoped-for friendly outcome of our encounter.

"Vedado," I replied, which was merely your neighborhood, not a street address.

"But where are you staying?"

Even during all my roadside layovers, when I had little to think about except where I would stay in Havana, I had arrived at no clear decision, other than I didn't want to check into a hotel. ·

Raul asked, "Why don't you stay with me?"

I admired his boldness. To be seen taking a foreigner, an American at that, into his house, posed a risk to his reputation. The neighborhood watchdog group might report him.

I said nothing.

"Don't worry; my mother and sister are out-of-town. The apartment is quite spacious." He added that he lived across town from Vedado but would happily take me there the next day.

We sat in silence for a minute, me deciding and Raul cursing cars that tried to cut him off at intersections. He exuded control. This, too, I resisted and resented and therefore found sexy. But the idea of crashing in a stranger's apartment violated the unspoken fidelity between the two of us and, strangely, any lingering fidelity I have to Josh's memory. I thought that death had freed me from all moral obligation to him; I had been so moral—so constant—during his illness that I never again wanted to believe that the word "Josh" was a synonym for "duty." Suddenly, however, I again felt his specter next to me in the automobile, reminding me of the beauty of spontaneity. His spirit was pressing me to live Live LIVE! So what if this was merely a play to ensure that no one would so rapidly replace him in my affections?

I succumbed: "OK, Raul. I accept your offer."

"OK, OK," he replied, happy as a birthday boy and squeezing my thigh with his right hand. "Let's go."

His happiness caused him to speed through the streets, which were amber in the late-afternoon sun. They were emptier than I'd expected, nearly bereft of cars but filled with bikes and motorbikes. The vintage automobiles that dotted the countryside were only slightly more prevalent here. A '56 Chevy Bel Air hardtop sped by, succeeded by a Ford Thunderbird from the same year. Was this a movie set or a real city?

Raul's vehicle, a 1970 cherry-red Chevy Malibu, seemed plain by comparison. I asked him to slow down so that I could get a more leisurely look at the neighborhoods we were passing through. There was a crumbling beauty to much of the city's architecture, though I suspected that this wear was more charming to the outside observer than to the denizens within, who had to cope with the accompanying leaky roofs, rotting pipes, and intermittent electricity. The melange of building styles and colors (baroque, colonial, Communist blok) mimicked the human blending on the street: the brunettes, mulattos, and noirs, whose racial mixture I had encountered in only one other city: Rio.

I peppered Raul with questions about the scenery, and as he answered them, I found myself smiling almost as idiotically as he was. The stresses of my journey fell away for a moment as I awakened to the sights and was reminded of just why we undertake travel. Like sex, it takes us out of ourselves, helps us forget. And it teaches us to be modest: We see what a small place we occupy in the world. The lack of routine awakens our senses to the beauty of the trivial.

Raul said he lived only a few miles from Vedado, but as we drove through district after district, I felt as if we were traveling through a far galaxy, and that I, suddenly concerned, would never get back to Earth and see you again. Raul kept up a lively chatter the whole way, tossing in English phrases here and there.

Finally, we reached his apartment building, a bland low-storied edifice, and parked on the street. We got out of the car, and I was impressed by just how tall Raul was: at least 6 foot 4. As he led me up to his flat, I took in further perspectives on his ass: impressive.

"We have a very nice apartment, you'll see," he said as he led me up a disconcertingly narrow flight of stairs. Maybe it was because I'd lived for so long in New York, where anything more than a maid's room seems luxurious, but I found his assessment pretty accurate. Two bedrooms, dining area, comfy kitchen. I popped into the bathroom to piss. It was Times Square–bright and had photos on the walls of what must have been Raul's mother and sister. Both of them were tall, dark, bright-eyed. For a moment I was stabbed with nostalgia for my own family scenes, so much so that I had to remain a minute in the john, composing myself. Just because I have not written of my relatives for a while, do not think I have ceased to think about them.

"Everything OK?" Raul asked when I emerged at last into the living room. "Too much Cuban cooking?" He gave me some coffee, as if that were a stomach-settler, and sat down on the sofa.

I sat next to him, and as I did he drew away imperceptibly. For a moment I had the horrible thought that I had misread his intentions. I saw myself laying a soft hand on him and him turning into Charo in *Airport '79*, screaming, "You misconscrew me!"

Hardly. After another minute of chat, I yawned, and he seemed to accept this as proof of his failure to seduce me. He showed me to the spare bedroom, and I, tired of travel—too tired even to have thought of racing over to you—fell asleep.

The next morning, as Raul drove me over to your apartment building, he asked, "Were you and your boyfriend faithful?"

I was in no mood to debate monogamy, but since Raul was giving me a lift and putting me up, and since I had told him about Josh briefly, I felt obliged to answer. "Yes."

"You were never jealous?"

"In my gene pool we feel it but don't talk about it. What are your views? About monogamy?"

"I'm pretty jealous, but I don't believe in monogamy."

"What does that mean?"

"I believe that, when you're in love, you shouldn't do it with two at once. You can do it with 10 but not with two." Raul gave me one of his big baritone laughs and dropped me off on your street. I took my place at the outdoor café directly opposite your building. I pulled out my agenda to make sure I had your address right; I did. It felt odd not to be rushing right up to your doorstep, to enjoy your undoubtedly surprised reaction. My adrenaline was rushing, but in a nervous direction. Though impulsive enough to have bolted from the plantation, now that I had arrived I was suddenly an insecure, pimply schoolboy. I ordered a café con leche: We need strengthening before the acts of life.

✳

I sipped the coffee and wondered how often you had been thinking of me; wondered, too, what you were doing right that second. It was 8:30 A.M. Were you just rising from a long, bear-like sleep, trundling to the bathroom and brushing your teeth? Were you berating your mother for not having your breakfast ready in time? Or had you already left the house for class? If you were anything like I was during my first year of college, you would be in no hurry, the outlines of your academic career having already been sketched. I imagined for a moment that I was your girlfriend accompanying you to school, and the whole world stared approvingly at us as we strolled down the boulevard. Your *girlfriend*: Was I loco or what?

I had a second cup of coffee and studied your building further. For some reason, I expected plainclothesmen to be standing sentry out front, protection being necessary for an official as exalted as your mother. Perhaps I needed them to be there, the way a marauding crusader in front of a castle requires a moat, barriers conferring meaning on our adventures and tension on my narrative. (I am now so accustomed to the presence of police, or guards, that I am sure I minimize just how terrified I was of them then.) Then it hit me: I had your house under watch. It was difficult to square my act of surveillance with the morning scene around me: The sun was bright but not yet unsparing, and birds chirped—always a soothing sign in a city. Caffeine coursed through me, and for the first time since Josh died I was purely happy: This was my first full, solitary moment since I arrived in Cuba. I was ludicrously tourist-looking— fair-haired, ruddy skin, wasting time in a café—yet I fancied that I blended in here as smoothly as the sugar I was stirring into a second coffee.

I had not been sitting long when a woman emerged from your building. At first I could not get a good look at her. But just before she blended for good into the pedestrians on the avenue, I made out that the woman was your mother. She didn't look threatening at all. She wore a little ladies-who-lunch suit and had her long dark hair pulled back in a semi-chignon. When Chanel said that nothing is more chic than a Latin American woman wearing couture, she had beauty like your mother's in mind.

Once your mother was out of the way, my decision to enter the building was not joyous. Before paying the bill I asked the waiter if the bar served alcohol: I needed another quick nerve-straightener. He said no, so I took a deep breath and crossed the street. The salty scent of the sea blew in from nearby.

I was surprised to see no doorman. Was that a position that had been abolished by the revolution? There was a row of buzzers to the left of the entryway. I pressed your apartment, which I had memorized from addressing so many letters to you. No answer. My heart beat faster. I pressed the buzzer again. Still no answer. One more time and that would be it. I did not want to loiter conspicuously there.

"Johnny Baby?" the intercom responded.

"Eduardo? Eduardo? How did you know it was me?"

"I've been watching you at that café the past half-hour. My bedroom faces the avenue. I couldn't believe it was you. I told my mother I had a stomachache so I could wait for you. Just a second. I'll let you in."

What is it about the prospect of a live encounter that sends extreme emotions—joy, fear, especially fear—to the surface? Even as I bounded the stairs to the third floor and a feeling of affection welled up in me.

You did not, you must recall, immediately embrace me. You ushered me in gently and politely, and I thought, *So this is his home.* In your domestic lair—two small bedrooms, living room, kitchen, and terrace, all sparely decorated: elegance as refusal—you were sleek and agile, very much the young lord.

We stood in the entryway, not touching. You grinned, then threw yourself into my arms, so vigorously that I was slid into the foyer wall. You were wearing a T-shirt smelling of the unwashed laundry pile. I sniffed your collar conspicuously. "Nice to know you put on a new suit for me."

"C'mon, Johnny, you know I didn't expect you for at least another two weeks."

"Don't you know?"

"Know what?"

"Why I've come?"

"Oh, man, something's happened. Tell me."

"No, nothing's happened. I've come to see you."

"Of course you've come to see me. Did they let you off duty early?"

"No, I just left."

"You lazy son of a bitch. You should have called me."

"I wanted it to be a surprise."

"Well, it is."

"Was that your mother I just saw leaving?"

"Yeah. She's gone to work."

"So we have the place to ourselves? No maids, no goons, no Zeus?"

"No nobody. Just Prince and his girl."

With that you broke into a grin and punched me playfully.

I air-punched you back. We fake-boxed our way over to the sofa and collapsed, laughing.

I took your right hand. "Have you healed well enough to fight?"

"I'm still a little sore. But the fight's six weeks away. I'm sure I'll be OK by then."

You wouldn't let me stay on the sofa. Like an experienced seducer, you took my hand and led me into your bedroom, where I observed that the walls were plastered with posters (Ali, Stallone) and the tables were heaped with books (García Márquez, Stephen King). We reclined on your twin bed, and then something extraordinary happened. Instead of my tearing off your clothes and measuring myself against the demands of your adolescent libido, we lay clothed and still for several minutes, touching each other, whispering to each other, occasionally switching positions, but only to prevent limbs from falling asleep.

"So, Eduardo, have you been saving yourself for me?" I asked, burying my head in your T-shirt, resigned perversely to your dank odor.

"Johnny, I haven't jerked off in at least a week."

"More like a minute."

"To be honest, an hour."

"I'm not making out with anyone who's depleted. Before I even think of taking off your clothes, I'm going to make you study for a while."

I grabbed the García Márquez and reinterpreted the first sentence: "As he looked back over his life—"

"As he faced the firing squad..."

(The water still drips, my fellow prisoners still cry out: Need I comment on the horrible aptness now of that morning's recitation?)

"Very good, Eduardo. How cultivated you are!"

"I'm a very educated young man!"

We were quiet again. If intimacy depends on stillness—the ability to spend hours in the same room with someone, reading or working, with no words exchanged but a steady current nevertheless running between you and the loved one—then these seconds were proof that we had an authentic intimacy that had not vanished during our time apart. I had not been so happy since I had lain almost as quietly and as long with Josh in the hospital not long before he died. But in that moment he and I were absorbed sadly in the past; in your room I shared palpably the present: the refrigerator humming in the next room and the occasional muted car horn from the street.

I must have dozed off for a moment, because the next thing I knew you were pressing yourself against the wall and squeezing me out a little as you climbed under the covers.

For a while you lay motionless, with my knees against your belly. You seemed reconciled to your discomfort, to the impossible position of your body. You didn't squirm. Resting your head on my shoulder, you began to breathe quietly, even puffing and wheezing, as if trying to lull yourself to sleep.

(If you think I am lavishing too much detail on this moment of almost-slumber, keep in mind that much of our time together, to say nothing of my time tonight, as I read over these fragments, has been spent bumping up against the borders of sleep.)

Suddenly, you let out a growl and pulled your arm out from under my neck.

"Just wait," you said. "I'll show *you*."

With that you yanked the blanket off both of us, pushing yourself away from the wall, and slipped off the bed.

You got undressed. I heard the whoosh of your shirt, and pants being unfastened. Then you fumblingly undressed me.

You planted yourself firmly on the soft, slightly sagging bed and, with your knees spread wide apart, leaned over me. I breathed in the smell of your body, which compared to mine—already exposed to the heat and air outdoors—was still a little gamy. It was such a contrast to our first meeting, when your skin smelled as fresh as early morning at a flower market.

I kept my eyes shut. After Josh died I wondered if I would ever lie this way with someone else.

Staring up, I swore I had seen this particular ceiling before, the way the late-morning light, arching toward noon and divided by the window pane, was chasing the small shadow cast by swaying palm branches outside. For a moment, everything seemed already to have happened.

Your hand covered my face and the sight of it started to trigger something in me; maybe its limpness struck me as corpse-like. At Josh's wake, I arrived first so I could have some time alone with him, only to notice, as I entered the funeral parlor, that his right hand extended over the casket, the light blue of his shirt-cuff matching precisely the blossoms on the bier.

Suddenly, I let out a howl. I lay there, moved but not moving. I lay there not moving because I was frozen by your beauty, and I wondered if I deserved it.

I whimpered.

You whispered words into my ear, trying to console me. "There, there; there, there." Minutes and minutes and minutes of this. Then the pauses between my sobs grew greater, and you wiped off my snot-dripping nose with a handkerchief you had plucked from a nearby dresser.

My face clean, you held me, like a child nestled in his mother's arms. You held me. *Ah, yes,* I said to myself softly. *Now,* this *is what I wanted.*

Then we did something very unmaternal: We fucked each other.

✳

Forgive me if I keep reverting to my chats with Andrea. I'm sure you've figured out by now that these vignettes are necessary to help me eventually, explain my stated theme: why I wouldn't see you yesterday. You must pardon me if I, say, realize that there is a distracting chorus of coughs emanating from my ward just now, and I need to amuse myself for a moment. In addition, relaying my conversations with Andrea will, I hope, remind you that during all the time of our acquaintance, whether we were together or not, I did not give up completely on all my friends, at least not my best friend—the mistake so many people make during a love affair. I didn't want to find that you had abandoned me and that I had nothing to go back to.

Despite the emotional chaos of her existence, Andrea's daily habits are really quite settled. She rises at 10, makes coffee, does the crossword, calls her agent. She plays with the cat. When I telephoned her that next wet morning from a Havana post office, she was still struggling with the puzzle.

"What's a four-letter word for 'difficult'? she asked, dispensing with a proper greeting.

"Cuba."

"No, no, no. Oh—I know what it is." Without telling me, she scribbled something onto the newsprint.

I listened to the rain on the asphalt roof of the Havana post office; it resonated like pebbles in a pan. I had waited in line for an hour to use a telephone, and there had been a brief power outage. During it, I cursed the gods. Waiting for her to pick up, I cursed myself—for humoring her.

"I've met the most fantastic guy through a matchmaking service," she said, as if I had inquired directly about her love life. As if I ever needed to. "He wants me to send him a photo, but I said I was an actress and my portrait was being redone. Which is true: It *is* being redone."

"What's the guy like?"

"Sounds yummy. Has a very good job. In his mid 40s. Seems genuinely to like women. Divorced, Italian-American. He has an East Side duplex and a home in the Hamptons—oh well, nobody's perfect."

I listened to her description of him. (Why did the image of a piano roll come to mind?) I changed the subject before she had a chance to describe his vitals.

"I talked to Sarah," I said.

"I know. She called the other day to discuss you."

"What did she say?"

"She's still a little nervous about your being in Cuba. But I think she honestly understands your reasons for going. Of course, Teddy, she's your older sister—your only sibling—so she feels the need to look after you."

"Did she mention how Jackson is?"

"That's about all she talked about. Little Jack's having quite a time in his gymnastics class."

"I miss that little guy."

"I'm sure. But you must have your hands full with Eduardo."

"Actually, he has his hands full with me. Showing me around the city, missing classes."

"Have you alerted the officials to your being in Havana yet?"

"No, I'll do it next week, when my visa is up."

"Don't wait too long. You don't want to get in trouble. Or have to flee the city until the coast is clear."

"Actually, I think Eduardo and I may be going to the country. To visit some adopted grandmother of Eduardo's."

"What will Mamacita say about that?

101

"She doesn't know this old lady. It's a relationship he formed through a teammate on his boxing team. A teammate who died."

"That kid's got some secrets from his mom."

"She's a higher-up in Castro's government. I suspect she's got a few of her own."

The connection was breaking, so I hung up, but not before giving Andrea your address and phone number, to be used only in an emergency. She must have called you a few times by now; your never mentioning it I attribute to your discretion. I would thank you for it, if that quality hadn't proven modest consolation in the end.

✳

As you know, I stayed on at Raul's not only because it placed no burden on my thinning wallet, but because a hotel would have required surrender of passport. I relished the irony of lodging with a cop, with any kind of official, even though by the second night, having taken the bus home from your house, I thought the situation might prove awkward. I was not anxious to be in a situation where there was even a chance that I'd have to put out. What vanity to have worried! A sheepish-looking Raul let me in. Would I mind staying in the second bedroom, he asked; he had "company." The next night it was someone else, and then another. I began thinking of him as a Cuban quasar: He glowed only when swallowing up new material.

Not that I spent much time in his apartment. How pleased I was that you cut school on Thursday and Friday that week to show me your city.

Was there anywhere we didn't visit in those palmy, balmy days? So preoccupied was I with you that only a few of the tour specifics have remained in memory. The cathedral where the body of Columbus had once lain and where the explorer's rebarbative gray-stone statue stood outside, withstanding aerial assaults from gulls, assaults that must be more humiliating for him than not finding the East Indies. The small park called Plaza Hemingway, where a bust of the writer is surrounded by princely columns and where, as if in defi-ance of his lifelong celebration of machismo, I planted a big wet one on you.

"Johnny, do you know that after you kiss me you always lick your lips?"

"It's because I want to savor your taste."

"Yeah, I know, man. What I like is the taste of your feet."

"Don't tell me you're going to turn into a foot fetishist. I had a date with a guy like that, my first date after Josh died. A model/writer type. An hour of foot obsession felt more like a marriage than a fuck."

"How many men have you dated since Josh died? Be specific."

"Four, I think."

"You're so experienced!"

"And you? How many guys have you had?"

"I told you. Just the one friend in high school. We fooled around in the locker room."

"Very porno-movie."

You gave me a little shove. "Get your mind out of the gutter. We're in Plaza Hemingway. Show a little respect."

"I'll show you respect," I said, kissing you again.

"Did you know that Hemingway won the Nobel Prize in 1954? And that he was a fan of the Havana baseball club?"

Although you acted as the tour guide that first week, I was hap-pier when we just strolled up and down the Malecón, your slightly shabby but still romantic seawall promenade. I was awfully impressed when I asked about the promenade's name and you launched into a little soft-shoe about Malecón's etymology (uncer-tain), a subject you had studied at school.

I was astounded by how much history you knew. (People who don't find knowledge sexy must have impoverished love lives.) Accustomed to the ahistorical mindset of young Americans, I found your intelligence splendidly anachronistic, like the shiny Studebakers I occasionally saw slither down the streets here. (I hope you found useful the information I offered in return, especially the description of MTV videos that I'm sure lasted longer than the videos themselves.) How wondrous it was to find someone who could tutor me in a subject—history—I had long claimed as my own. I was so eager to shed my own history that to find someone so beautiful to whom I could entrust not just the past but the Past that may have connected me to you more than anything.

But of course, we couldn't exist forever in the insularity of mutual tutelage and attraction. That night, my fourth in Havana, a Saturday, had to happen. I'm sure you have replayed that evening in your head as many times as I have, and not just in court. Your memory may diverge from mine mightily. I only ask you to consider my version for a moment.

We were to meet, as you know, a few blocks from your apartment. I was feeling high that night, the first that you and I would be able to share completely. I had visions of smooching in the shadows somewhere, maybe getting a little drunk off rum. I stood under a streetlamp like some seaport slut, and as you arrived the light caught the chemical sheen in your hair.

You rubbed your hand across my chin in what I took to be a greeting but what was really an inspection of how closely I had shaved. You did not, I suspect, want to return home with a face rubbed raw by stubble.

"Hey, my main dude," you said, "your skin is like a baby's. Although I would like to see you sometime with a mustache. Yes, I would like that very much."

I replied that I would look better with a beard, which would be "more revolutionary." Inwardly, though, I cringed, remembering photos of me blond-barbed in college and another image of me in my mid 20s, afflicted with a three-day male-modely growth.

"I'll bet Josh saw you with a mustache. I'll bet—yes, I'll bet, that he liked it."

"He said: 'You and facial hair are not an obvious match.'"

"Fuck obvious matches. All kinds of them. Who wants to talk to the couple at a party who've been betrothed since birth? The pairs who present a baffling first impression are the only ones with any mystery."

"Have you held this view for a long time, professor?"

"Only since I was 13 and found myself always wanting to sit next to Hector Gonzalez in class. I didn't know why then. Now I think it's because he was already tall and had facial hair, and I liked measuring the difference between him and me."

"Were you good friends?"

"Not really, although a kid once called him 'faggot' after school, and I beat the kid up. Hector got a sadistic kick out of that."

You landed a playful punch on my shoulder, and we set off. You became so animated as we approached our destination: Coppelia Park. You had talked all week of taking me there, and since I knew only its reputation as Havana's outdoor festive center I resisted at first. It was one thing to walk about the city by day, wearing caps and sunglasses and harming no one. It was quite another to hang out in a spot where police would surely be out in force to control the carousing crowd. How easily I accepted your reassurances: that so many people showed up at Coppelia on the weekend that we would surely not stand out.

"I feel lucky tonight," you announced as we approached the corner near the park.

I grabbed your left upper-arm, thrilled to its instant Popeyed hardness, and replied, "Muchacho, you were born beautiful: *That's* lucky."

Something in you chafed at the compliment. You placed a hand on my ass and said, "I'm not so sure. When I was a boy, my grandmother Clara, my father's mother, told me, 'Eduardito, when you were born, a very chatty angel, one of God's silliest, said, "Go, go, be a little loco in life.' I'm trying to fulfill the prophecy." We laughed, setting the initial tone for the festive atmosphere that greeted us as we rounded the corner and came into full view of the park.

I drank in the hundreds of people milling about, dancing in the streets, singing, screaming, joking; music-ridden cars stopped for minutes to let muchachas by, despite calls from police to proceed.

There were beautiful boys and girls everywhere my glance alighted, and I felt a deep sense of homecoming. I had had a similar feeling only once before: when I had moved to New York, drawn inexorably to the city yet sure that its most vital privileged life would always remain elusive to me, always pulsate just outside my grasp. A college friend had taken me to a—the—gay disco. I walked onto the dance floor, took one look at the hot muscle-bound men around me, and realized, as I threw back my head and whooped, that ecstasy was possible and that I was not alone.

To express the magnitude of my joy I would have had to toss you back in a dancer's dip and kiss you as indiscriminately as would a Victory Day G.I.; instead, I merely touched your forearm, thrilling at its tautness.

I couldn't believe the park was the same quiescent oasis we had ambled through two or three times already that week. It was not only the addition of crowds and noise that amazed me. The colors had changed, too. The grass and trees had shifted from a lime and brilliant-emerald to a green more like that of a forest: The park was a watercolor by day and an oil by night. In the evening the loudness was not in the palette but in the pulse: Salsa music blasted out of every other car radio. It was impossible to square the scene with the Soviet-grim images of Cuba that I had been force-fed in my youth.

So carnivalesque was the park that it was difficult to know just where to wade into it. As we walked across the street and into the park's main plaza, a young voice solved the problem for us.

"Eduardo!" A face popped out of the crowd and approached us. It belonged to a boy of about your age, a lad who despite his diminutive height and stocky figure was cute in a knuckleheaded sort of way.

From the lack of a handshake between you, it was clear that you were more than mere school chums. You exchanged an allusive few words. I was silently wondering whether you and he had ever done it.

"Carlos, this is John. He's visiting from America."

I expected that all your friends would find me exotic and ply me with questions about life in the States. Carlos, however, shrugged me a bored-teenager greeting and went back to you, shooting forth a rapid-fire volley of questions in Spanish that he must have hoped I'd have difficulty following. I felt a bubbling resentment. My love of the carnival apparently depended on my utter possession of a partner. The salsa around me grew louder, harsher, less inviting. Your neglect did not feel deliberate; it was as if, intuiting my sense of déjà vu, you assumed I'd find a soul there who corresponded to someone I'd known in a past life and just begin babbling.

It was only when Carlos noticed my sneakers that your attention returned to me.

"*Sus zapatos: muy* cool."

To me they looked rather worn, having pounded the pavement of both New York and Havana. Their red-and-white stripes had dissolved into a faded suede blur, resembling, very roughly, a late Rothko. Nonetheless, I wanted to rebuke Carlos's surly manners with my own superior ones, so I accepted the compliment with exaggerated grace.

"How much?" he asked.

"Fifty dollars."

"Where did you buy them?"

"New York." Assuming Carlos's English was minimal, I added in my native language, "From a Cuban street peddler whose ancestors were probably your family's employers in a previous century."

"What?"

You laughed and mistranslated my phrase back to him with the necessary emendations.

Carlos laughed, too, and, deciding my shoes if not I were worthy of greater attention, lassoed some nearby friends over to take a look at them. There were five or six kids, including a beautiful café-au-lait-complexioned girl, Maria, and two boys whom I must assess as "lookers." Scarlet O'Hara never had so many suitors.

One of the boys dropped to his knees for a closer inspection. "What's Reebok?" he asked.

Reebok was the brand of choice for me and my friends in New

York and, I assumed, even here, where certainly copycat brands existed. Not so. Those kids wore Keds-like shoes that were as vintage-
looking as the country's autos.

"Is it an American brand?" the girl asked.

"No. English."

A round of aahs: of course.

"How much?" Carlos inquired again.

"Fifty."

"No, no. How much do you want for them?"

"They're not for sale." I rolled back and forth a little nervously on
the front of my sneakers, causing them to pinch a little.

"Too bad!" Carlos said, not completely resigned to the turndown.

"Poor baby!" you said to him in taunting tones that made clear
who was the alpha male here.

We said goodbye to the group and went across the street to one of
the park's ice-cream vendors. The line was long, not, you said,
because of the confection's scarcity—in Havana ice cream is as pro-
saic as pizza is in New York—but because of this particular vendor's
quality. I prayed you were right, because when we reached the front
the only flavor for sale was my least favorite: pistachio. We bought
our cones, and I balked at the thought of trying this green stuff. It's
funny how a twinge of initial disgust can heighten one's pleasure: by
the third lick you would have thought I was lapping...

You and I made a circuit round the square. From time to time you
would call out a greeting to someone ("Hey, Manny Man, how's your
sister?") and I would ask you to provide the profile. ("Manny's a
buddy of mine from high school. Dumb as shit, but you'd want him
in your foxhole.") You seemed to know a lot of people. It was impressive how many of them were aware of your boxing.

"Hey, Eduardo," shouted a pretty petite girl named Teresa. "How's
your hand? You going to be ready to fight in the final?"

"Of course. You think I'd miss a fight because of a little injury?"

I never noticed you favor the hand much and wondered that night
if you were feigning injury because you had lost your nerve. I guess I

had a hard time reconciling the sweet polite beautiful boy I loved with someone who was said to have a lethal left jab. I also had difficulty looking at your tall, lean physique and seeing it as boxing material. On the other hand, the boxers I knew were not physically large, either; Tony, a champion pugilist at my gym, had an unimposingly scruff torso. Tony was quick, though, and bounced around the gym floor throwing clipped jabs at imaginary opponents and darting in and out of reach: Perhaps speed was your advantage, too.

A guy wearing makeup and tight jeans crossed our path.

"Robertito! Where you off to looking like Alicia Alonso?"

"Where do you think, Eduardo? To a party. Do you want to come with me, oh handsome one?" The boy shook his hips a little.

"If I did, I would be in danger of compromising my reputation." Your bantering tone—proof, I thought, that you were secure enough in yourself to be seen talking to this guy—I found admirable.

"What reputation? If you don't win your next fight, you'll *have* no reputation. Who's the friend?"

"John Webster. From New York."

"He's very cute," Robertito said, as if I'd walked away. "When he tires of you, give him my address, will you?"

"Find your own friends," you counseled. "Now you'd better be off, or you'll be late for the ballet."

Only in prison have I realized that, though you were comfortable around queens, not once during our Havana idyll had you taken me to any kind of specifically gay gathering place.

I was happiest that evening when you and I could break away from the mob and stroll around the park's periphery. I could daydream about the scene. So much lilting humanity unencumbered by Walkmans suggested centuries not our own. The salsa from the radios could have been a live band dressed in 19th-century cottons, the political leafleteer at a corner could have been a preacher atop a soapbox during the Spanish-American War, and the palm reader in the center of the square could have been forecasting futures there since the time of Columbus. As for you and me, we could have been a Jesuit and his favorite student walking back from Sunday Mass and talking not about Prince and Michael Jackson but about Aquinas and Loyola.

Though I was just as happy it was "1999" you were singing just then, with me chiming in on the chorus. Shared references were crucial, weren't they? And if ours were to consist mostly of Top 10 lyrics, so be it.

"Johnny Boy, let's go back to the other side. Macho men are in modest—no: scant—supply here."

"Except for us, of course."

"Yeah. Who's more macho: Eduardo Garcia or Johnny Webster?"

"Neither. Lloyd Bridges is."

"And Fernando Lamas."

We returned to the side of the square where we'd come in. There, in what they must have thought a semi-secluded corner, a young couple was making out. They were both mulattoes and, as they kissed, her body seemed to scale his as if she was an alpinist attempting Everest. Although they were certainly escaping cramped conditions at home, there was no way they would find any more privacy here. Onlookers alighted like birds on the car next to us, hooting the couple on. To show pity for the pair, in my imagination I sent them back a century. They were in a garden under a lime tree, making frenzied siesta love until—what's this?—servants gathered on an nearby balcony and greeted their carnal triumphs with approval. Back at the contemporary scene the boy reached round to knead the girl's *culo,* and the gawkers gave him a stadium ovation.

This floor show was making me horny, too, anxious to exchange voyeur's robes for randier raiments. Where, though, would you and I go? Since that first morning we had been making do with a hurried wank here and there, but I did not want to take you to the cop's place and you had not been able to secure your house for further sex. As you know, I was still wary of hotels. You and I were not better off than the mulatto couple. In fact, things were worse for us: At least they could make out anywhere without drawing suspicion or causing ire.

We left the park by a street different from the one we'd entered by. It was a dim avenue that promised privacy. The festivities faded from our ears as slowly as the sound of a just-ascending jetliner, and I looked forward to the promise of gropes and kisses. We had gone about a block when a noise like a snapped stick made me look over my shoulder and realize that two young men were following us. One of them had a huge, thick, bare branch in his hand. At first I assumed they were your friends, but I became fearful when I realized that you did not immediately greet them. They didn't look old enough to be policemen, but they presented a menacing picture. *Wouldn't it be ironic,* I thought, *if after worrying all week about a visit from the authorities, we were waylaid instead by a couple of juvenile thugs?*

I quickened my step, contemplated breaking into a run; from jogging together along the Malecón I knew that we were both pretty fast and could probably outrace them. You, however, had to stop and stare down the pursuers. Though overcome with apprehension I found a second to admire your courage. Standing on that dark street with your torso arched, your head held high, and power stored mortally in your hands, you were magnificent.

When the pair came closer, I thought all might be put right. The first boy, tall and rather rough-hewn, looked like one of the kids who had hovered around Carlos in the park. The second boy was shorter and even more brutish.

"What do you guys want?" you said.

"We're not here to cause trouble," answered the tall one. "We just want your friend's sneakers."

"And how is my friend supposed to walk home?"

"Perhaps you could carry him," the short boy hissed. "Like a good husband."

Your voice grew hushed. "Why don't you leave us now, and we'll forget the whole thing?"

"Why should we do that?" said the tall one. "We could sell the shoes for a lot of money. My mother is sick and we need the cash."

For a split second, I was touched by so basic a family need. I considered taking my shoes off and handing them to him, or at least to give him some money. Why now, in my cell, do I think of Aristotle's definition of drama—a story in which both sides are partially right?

Any sympathy disappeared, however, when the tall boy suddenly hauled off and whacked me on the shoulder with his stick. Pain— adult this-is-the-army pain—enveloped me: first sharp, then throbbing, then a long slapped burning sensation. The night had been joyous, yet it is these few seconds of physical discomfort that I remember most clearly.

The aftermath of the aggression was swift.

You grabbed the assailant by the shoulders and wheeled him around into your direct line of attack. The other boy and I did not try to assist. We became spectators. I was going to see the boxer of whom I had heard so much. Suddenly, however, the boy flashed a knife at you; with a swift kung fu–like kick, you knocked it away.

You charged in for a succession of swift blows—left, right, left— that sent your opponent onto imaginary ropes, half-tripping as he lurched backwards. I conjured up a mock-referee between you, issuing an eight-second standing count. The tall boy, a real schoolyard pummeler, managed to place a couple of good body shots under your guard, punches that you did not expect. In retaliation, you viciously struck the boy's face, and I heard not only the muffled smack of your fist but also a squinching sound. As the boy stumbled, you followed up with a blow of lacerating accuracy. You moved your hand away, and it caught what little street light there was. Across your paw were smeared traces of blood.

I should have felt pride then, pride that such a fierce young warrior was defending me, or a smidgen of shame that I was not fighting my own battles. But I didn't have time for more feeling: Things went too fast. You stepped up your assault, raining a downpour of blows on your opponent's head. The blows did not abate.

"Stop," I cried. "Eduardo, stop. Stop. Please."

By the time you did cease the short boy was racing back to the park, screaming for help.

You stepped back to survey the damage, panting, panting.

I couldn't wait until you caught your breath before I walked over to where the beaten boy lay on the ground. I knelt down next to him and delicately touched his neck, onto which facial blood was pouring. I searched for a pulse. I prayed that he was still alive.

"I couldn't stand back and watch him hit you like that," you said, in a frenzied near-shout. "I couldn't. I couldn't. I love you."

How I believed you then! How could two men, whatever the nature of their relation, express love more nobly than by vanquishing the other's foe?

I stood up and felt the color rush from my extremities, even as the boy's blood trickled down my examining hand. I smeared red across the sidewalk, as if it were the wall of a cave.

"Eduardo," I said in a voice nearly hoarse from shouting. "I think he's dead."

We were stopped at a service station, waiting for an attendant to pump our gas, when a woman suddenly appeared. Do you remember? We were so skittish in those days after the death that anyone's abrupt appearance caused us alarm. Certainly, in that first week we proceeded with much more deliberation than we had that night, when events flowed so quickly. Vestiges of our argument remained as the subtext, strangely unspoken, to our conversation.

"We've got to wait and see if we can save the guy's life," I had said.

"No, Johnny," you said, after examining the boy yourself, "he's dead. We can't stay here. Trust me: There'll be trouble. Especially for you."

"For me? But I didn't do anything wrong? I'm in this country legally."

"I know. But whenever there's a foreigner involved in anything, things can get ugly. Oh, man." You crossed the boy's arms over his chest, as if you were a mortician. A look of remorse washed over you—but only for a second; the shift from contemplation to action was terrifying.

When you grabbed my hand to pull me down a dark street, I was revolted at the notion that we were fleeing the scene; in prison, however, where I have had time to try to forgive myself—writing letters to the boy's loved ones, begging their forgiveness—I recall the touch of your arm then as arousing. Danger accelerates the pulse.

In a sign of our on-the-lam punchiness, nervous humor suffused our days. Laughs papered over the pain. Especially laughs about passersby. Once we were convinced that the service-station woman intended no harm, we were free to make her a figure of fun.

"Hey, Johnny, her buttocks are like choir stalls."

We had noticed many prominent derrieres along the way since you and I left Havana three days before, in a red '72 Chevy that I had purchased hurriedly with dollars. Women's big bottoms were so much a part of the scenery that you and I began to hold butt contests to pass the time, not only giving them ratings from one to 10 but composing elaborate, florid descriptions to go with them. It was our fugitives' version of the family travelers license-plate game.

None of our comments, however, could out-purple descriptions I have noted in some of my prison books, especially the batch that my trusty guard Demo smuggled in.

Lezama Lima sketched a Havana woman with: "The neat outline of her back stretched down to the opening of her solid buttocks like a deep, dark river between two hills of caressing vegetation."

Such quips remind me why no ideology will ever outstrip Cuban eroticism.

These sexy moments were fleeting, however, given our circumstances. Our flight made my own exit from the plantation seem what Raul would undoubtedly call "bush-league." Sandy and the brigade were due back in Havana then, having written me off, I supposed, as some crazy dilettantish fellow traveler who was in over his head. Someone incapable of a real commitment—or a real crime.

But commitment and crime were fueling me forward. I still can't believe how quickly we hit the road; something transgressive in me, long buried until then, hummed hotly. A psychoanalyst might have said that my "shadow side" was in the ascendant, yet it sometimes seemed to me the reverse. Racing down bumpy country back roads, honking at stray animals crossing our path, waving at strangers, singing at top volume to songs on the radio, I returned not to the past, to my car-crazy, gas-imprudent teen years in my tan Chevy Camaro, but advanced onward giddily to some unknown precipice, from which I hoped to have a clearer view.

Jagged emotions kept flashing before us, but in self-protection we often ignored them or tried to. A boy had died; we had left a bleeding body untended on a dark sidewalk. It was an accident, and certainly any investigation would find as much. Yet here we were, fleeing. A preoccupation with our senses had forced us paradoxically to lose them. We inhaled fear with every breath, or so I can say now, when I have the luxury of hindsight (and a fear of the morning).

Your seeming embrace of joyriding should have surprised me, but it did not. You were primed to gallop away from your proper life, where the day had been set rigidly by your school, mother, and boxing coach. In a country where idleness was discouraged, you had decided to embrace waste—of fuel, time, opportunity. I had expected you to rely on your mother's position to exonerate you for your killing; instead, you left all that behind. You didn't even mention the possibility that she could have sorted things out for us. That would have made the boy's death banal. By running, the death became tragic, thrilling. In Havana, sitting through an inquest, we might have been bored; on the road, we were bonded.

"Don't think about that son of a *puta*," you said callously, when I mentioned the dead boy for the first time after we'd hit the road. "He tried to hurt you. I could never allow that."

Your disregard, I decided, was excusable: You were a kid. But I was—am—a grown man. I knew the recklessness of our flight, its likely consequences for me and its possible repercussions for you. So why did I flee?

I beg you to show sympathy if all I can say now is what I thought then: *I did it for you.*

We told ourselves that we were not joyriding altogether aimlessly. We were working our way toward Cienfuegos to visit your adopted grandmother, Alma. I marveled at how your relation with her was all epistolary. How your mother seemed to know so little of it.

Maybe because I didn't want to face the boy's death just then, I was grateful for the many stories you told me on the road. I particularly loved the ones about Alma. She lived on a farm, you said, where for decades she had gotten up at dawn to tend the animals, despite the fact that night was her true domain. In the infinite dark of the countryside she was at home. Alma, you assured me, was very wise; she had the wisdom of a peasant woman who had given birth to eight children, four of whom had died. She had suffered the trials of living with an alcoholic wayward husband. She was poor and in need of much help on the farm, but she made all her children go to school. As a result, all of them had decent jobs in Havana.

After such a buildup I wasn't sure if I was fit to set foot in Alma's house. Would she see through my calculations, the false pretext that had got me to the island? Would she suspect my motives toward you and wonder if I was a corrupting influence? Would she make me rise at 5 and milk the goat? Of all these fears, only the last did not undo me. Although I grew up in a small Montana city, I'd had sufficient contact with the countryside to have a good idea of what farm life entailed. Andrea never quite believed me when I told her that as a child I had kept goats and chickens on a friend's farm. She imagined my time there as a kind of *Green Acres* comedy or a summer interlude bathed in pastoral romance.

Your constant descriptions of Alma made me feel I'd already been to the farm we were still a long way from. I was excited to be going there, and this anticipation helped damp down memories of our violent night in the park. (At least during the day; at night I would wake in horror, even vomiting once or twice.) I was cheered by your almost wifely generosity—how every morning and every night before bed you asked me if there was anything you could get me—as if we had a kitchen and stocked fridge to draw from.

I was also buoyed by your running commentary on the sights we passed—insignificant ones mostly. One day it was roadside bales of hay under a canvas awning next to two rutting bulls, the acrid smell of alfalfa blending in with earthier odors to assault us through our rolled-down car windows. The next it was a group of workmen, hoisted high by a crane to adjust a political billboard. Until then, I had never had a full discussion with you about our positions on contemporary Cuban politics. I feared it might expose unbridgeable differences between us, and I was still at that stage of romance when I was praying foolishly that we would get along for years without much verbal fighting. (Such an attitude, of course, neglects the possibility that discord can deepen a union, exposing tensions that can be the source of a more complex kind of pleasure.) My disinclination to discuss politics also had its roots in a strange mixture of snobbery and guilt: snobbery because the ideology in which I was raised was, despite its limits, the superior system, and how could you and your country be so blind not to see that; and guilt because my government, through decades of ill-advised action, had caused such deprivation in Cuba that as an American I could only be seen as emblematic of such injury.

"But I don't see you," you said one afternoon as we were stalled behind an ancient sputtering van, "as an emblem of anything. That's the mistake you Americans make. You assume that all Cubans secretly blame you for the economic blockade. That's not the case at all. It's the American government, not the American people, that we detest."

I was reassured to hear this, even though something about the formulation seemed catechetical: Hate the sin but not the sinner— and if the sinner suffers as a result, oh well, it's all for someone's greater glory.

Before our politics seminar had quite ceased, we pulled into a service station in the middle of Palmira, a small town to the north of

Alma's farm. You started to pump gas, and I got out to stretch. As I
walked to the curbside, a minuet came in on the breeze. The music
came from a small band practicing in the town park across the street.
I stood for a moment, absorbed in the music; I flashed to one of the
few lines of poetry I remembered from high school. Wordsworth,
from "The Solitary Reaper":

The music in my heart I bore
Long after it was heard no more.

Struck by the ability of feeling to collapse time (I wonder what time is
it right now—2 A.M., maybe 3?), I was reminded how eras cannot just
dissolve, but overlap: A horse with a young man astride clopped down
the street as a roller skater, a young girl, held on to the left stirrup.

I turned around to share the scene with you, but you were chatting with the station attendant. He was a wonderful-looking young
man with deep-set brown eyes, an angular nose, and architecturally
swept-back hair. The two of you were having a laugh. The attendant
looked even younger than you, though you were both old enough, I
guessed, to be conscripted into Castro's army. The gentle camaraderie of the scene, in fact, suggested soldiers just off guard duty
and sharing a tension-relieving cigarette. In the wake of your joke, the
attendant touched you amiably on the back, and I flashed to the
thought of the three of us in bed together, and what I might like to
watch the attendant do to you. When the guy's touch moved up to
your shoulder, however, I was stabbed with jealousy. Was our relationship entering a new, more dangerous phase?

I tried to bury the feeling and got back behind the wheel, taking
a deep breath as you lingered with the attendant.

We drove out of town onto a country road, empty except for billboards. I couldn't keep quiet.

"You know, when you have a conversation like that, I'm afraid
you're going to slip and give us away."

"Give us away? How would I give us away?"

"Back there. With that attendant. You told him where we were
coming from."

"Havana's a big city, Johnny Baby. That was no clue."

"No clue? Really? You were a heartbeat away from telling him our destination and that was no clue?"

"You're wrong. I was a heartbeat away from telling him that you worked for the CIA and that you had blackmailed me into entering your plot to assassinate Castro."

You laughed, thinking that mild irony would diffuse my irritation. My tetchiness, however, only increased, and with it my desire for you. I wanted to fuck you right then to punish you for your sarcasm.

I continued to stew, and we passed a billboard that shouted "We must fulfill the roles that the armed march of history assigns us." I mused on the military theme. We were captain and adjutant, going forth on epochal campaigns. Under Caesar we could have been legions subduing Teutonic tribes; in medieval Spain, Christians repelling the infidel; and, at the Somme, troops leaping out of our trenches. And who is to say that in past lives we had not taken part in such offensives? When Andrea had, for my previous birthday, given me a session with a past-lives shaman, I was told that the military had in fact been a theme throughout much of my spirit's history. I would have found the information more persuasive if my lives had not all taken place in renowned imperial settings.

"Tell me again what you told your mother," I said as the road entered a billboard-free stretch and my cloudy thoughts cleared.

"I said I wasn't going to class yesterday. I was going to the boxing academy in San Luis de Sangre."

"Didn't she think that unusual? You're recovering from an injury."

"She knows how hard it's been for me not to compete. She's not about to deny me the chance to hang out in the gym and soak up a little sweaty atmosphere."

"And what do you think happened when you didn't come home?"

"I doubt she panicked. She's been through much worse."

"You don't think she called the police?"

"By the second day, undoubtedly."

It was good that you and I could joke about the cops, because we were both ill with anxiety about them—anxiety that we kept trying to conceal behind our road-movie high spirits. Ordinary sounds that hinted of the authorities were taking on a dangerous tinge. The simple honk of a boy's bicycle had caused you to press the metal and almost get us arrested for speeding. Overhearing an off-duty officer at a roadside *pollo* stand talk about his arrests had sent us scurrying for the car. After every getaway, we hooted and whistled and high-fived pathetically, but eventually the hoots were going to abate, and I had no idea what would replace them.

I kept waiting for you to profess second thoughts about our leaving Havana and was surprised that you avoided such a declaration. You killed someone accidentally after he had threatened us; surely you would be pardoned for that. But you pretended not to care; you kept saying you were being loyal to me. My situation might have been seriously compromised had we stayed, you insisted. I was touched by your loyalty, even if after a few days the adrenaline rush of running away struck me as another motivation for your action. The adrenaline of fear—so addictive!—was roaring through us at such a rapid rate. Perhaps you rationalized that you were a simple runaway, whose return would be met with a slap on the wrist and the withholding of TV privileges for a week. Perhaps you were puzzled (I know I was) that the woman who could give advice to Fidel had not yet tracked down her fugitive son. Were you an actor, I'd have said that you were so in-the-moment that you transcended the need for motivation. I, too, tried to relinquish everything but the sense of right now: the surge of tropical air, the throb of the engine, the tightness of the country roads where the billboards seemed to close in on us, the wind-caressed palm trees that were no sooner visible than they dissolved in a bright blur, white lines disappearing endlessly under our wheels.

Driving fast complemented perfectly our afternoon naps together. We may have been forced to crash every night in the backseat of the car, hunched together awkwardly, but oh, how I liked our siestas outdoors. Savor with me again day 2. We had spread towels in a discreet field of freshly cut hay. At first, afraid of being observed, we lay in our jeans, but later, when no one seemed likely to bother us, we got naked. We put sunscreen on our bodies—mere dabs for you but all over for me. I insisted on lots and lots of it, not only for protection but also, when our desultory stroking and rubbing of each other turned purposeful, to aid release. Sex provided our only respite from anxiety.

We'd been trying so hard for three days not to attract attention that I was surprised on our fourth day out, very near Alma's farm, when you spied an athletic facility on the outskirts of Cienfuegos and insisted that we stop for a little exercise. I protested only feebly. What a coward I was! The thought of seeing you in gym trunks dissolved my resistance.

The Che Guevara Sports Center must formerly have been a Roman Catholic school and chapel, and this realization did not shock me: It seemed entirely appropriate to an age that has replaced the worship of the spirit with the worship of the body. The bulk of the facility was made of drab gray tile; tacked on at the front and sides were modern extensions in concrete and glass with metal-frame windows and peeling white trim. We entered through the back. You explained that your "youth athletic card" would suffice to gain you admission, and that you could probably talk me in. The front-desk guy was mock-offended when you asked if my fee could be waived. "This is a Cuban facility," he said proudly. "All are welcome at no charge." I thought of the hundreds—thousands—of dollars I had surrendered to private gyms in New York over the years and felt an immediate increase in revolutionary fervor.

The locker room, a former sacristy, was mildly derelict in mood. The echoes of rush-hour crowds lingered, but at this hour, 2 P.M., it was deserted, like the chapel it had once been. Only a few young men were changing, and though not one was handsome, I was reminded palpably of why I like changing rooms: not for obvious ogling reasons but because they are places where people so purposefully strive for transformation.

From my backpack I took out a T-shirt and a pair of shorts, which, like most of my clothes at this point, had a faintly rank air.

I started undressing. Watching you shed your attire and display your taut body did not excite me immediately, maybe because the smell of our unwashed clothing dampened desire. It was only when you had completed your transformation that my bowing to your beauty took hold. In your baggy, shiny trunks and shirtsleeves rolled up in tight bands around your globed biceps, you were what my grandfather would have called "a splendid specimen." You caught me staring at you and smiled, and my willingness to ruin myself for love seemed a choice that only a bitter man would disapprove of.

Before rushing onto the gym floor, you and I nipped into the bathroom for a piss. I finished first, and while waiting for you I looked at a glassed-in bulletin board on the bathroom corridor wall. I scanned the announcements: baseball practice times, the schedule for political youth-group meetings. In the glass I also studied your reflection at the urinal. Your legs were wide apart. You had one hand on your hip, twisting back the wrist, and your other hand holding your penis.

The way you so calmly stood there, with the urine cascading in streams onto the porcelain, made me revert to an image of my father in a similar stance, in the upstairs bathroom of our Montana house, when I was about 4. It was a warm summer night, when wearing anything was a burden, but, my family's proprieties being what they were, we all walked around quite clothed. I was taking a bath. My father, however, thinking he was alone on the second floor, entered the bathroom naked and started urinating before he noticed my presence behind him in the tub. It is my main memory of him undressed. As he turned around I saw his body from the side: it was long, not very hairy, and though there was a slight spare tire around the chassis, it looked wonderful to me. And if I say that from the side his body looked well-proportioned and attractive, I also have to add something that natural modesty makes even more difficult to articulate, which is my strange desire at that moment to couple with my father because I thought him—and at the time my mother, too—the only perfect creatures on earth, even though they were of course flawed physically. I do not think it was an odd memory to be having in the bathroom of a Cuban gym. If I could not abandon my yearning for perfection, I have learned from this memory of my father's form that everything seemingly perfect also contains a tendency to be twisted. That day, however, thoughts of my father were suggestive not only of perfection but of protection: If Dad—who as he noticed me that day in the bathroom gave a wink of absolute assurance—had been in Cuba, I might not be in this mess. He would, I fantasized, have marched to the police station and cleared matters up.

"So what do you want to do?" you asked as we walked onto the gym floor. "Play some basketball?"

For years the only athletic activity I had pursued was weight lifting, and the thought that there might be other things to do at an athletic facility was a throwback to high school.

"Do you want to lift weights?" I proposed.

"To be honest, I'm not much for weight training. I've done some light work with barbells, but only after my boxing workout is over. But I guess we could lift."

The idea that weight training could be a small part of a regimen preparatory to competition rather that the entire regimen struck me as odd, so long had I been going to the gym to do battle with only myself.

The nave of the church had been converted into a basketball court, and the side chapels into gymnastic areas. We did some perfunctory stretching near a bank of pommel horses. We looked for the weights area. Walking into the building's addition, I smelled the slightly noxious combination of chlorine and soda ash that had characterized my boyhood summers. We soon saw the pool. I longed to dive in, to show you that I, too, excelled in a sport, but we had no bathing suits and, according to a list of strict regulations posted in the entryway, any makeshift attire was forbidden. A whistle-happy lifeguard sat nearby, glowering hard at the swimmers with the air of an informer.

I started telling you about my careers in both swimming and water polo. For some reason, I wanted desperately for you to feel proud of me just then, and if only you'd seen the match I played sophomore year at Dartmouth, a league quarterfinal against Yale, you would have. I was a goalie. I made a record-setting number of saves that match, a couple of them quite spectacular. But it was neither these nor the outcome (we won, 4–3) that stirred in me just then. Nor was I remembering all the conditions of play: the cool, early-evening pool; the mist collecting along the gutters; the bobbing of heads at the other end; muffled sounds; a scream, a whistle, the splat of a collision. No, it was what happened next that came back to me: The ball propelled in my direction, where, heart knocking and spray blinding my eyes, there was another collision, and one of my opponents was immediately hoisted onto the pool deck. Blood coursed from his face to his neck, and he passed out, and everyone feared that he was dead.

As the memory of the match faded, I felt ridiculously old, a spent athlete whose glory days were pathetically behind him—someone powerless to mend the mess of his current situation. I needed you to touch me, to reassure me that I was still vital, but of course, not having shared the memory, there was no way you could guess my mood, and to convey it would have indicated a vulnerability I did not wish just then to express.

Besides, you were onto other things. A boy in pugilist's gear passed by us and you tugged at my arm with little-boy excitement.

The boxing ring was in the next room. It was slightly raised, supported by thick wooden pillars. The air in the room was much closer than in the rest of the facility. Standing on the sidelines, I could see that you were anxious to enter the ring, but when I asked why you did not, you replied, "We're trying not to attract attention, remember?"

You would have had to wait regardless. Two boys were sparring under the watchful eye of a grizzled trainer. You began a commentary on their deficiencies. It would have been easy for me to believe that boxing wasn't brutal, if I hadn't watched you beat someone to death just a few days before. How you could fail to associate the gym scene with the death?

"Eduardo," I said, interrupting your analysis, "isn't it a little sick for you to be enjoying fisticuffs after what happened the other night?"

"Why? That kid got what he deserved."

"You keep saying that, as if a life hadn't been taken."

"When you attack someone, you take a risk. That guy took the wrong risk."

"I can't believe how fucking callow you are."

"Well, if you think I'm so fucking callow, you can always hitch back to Havana. Me, I'm watching these guys spar."

I would feel freer, all these months later, to excoriate your chilling insensitivity, if I had not, by staying, exhibited such a lack of courage. To have abandoned you then might have saved my situation, or at least inhibited later escalation of the action, but separation would also have destroyed our connection. We shared a bond stronger than sex or money or a million raucous Saturday nights: deep complicity.

From what I'd heard in Havana, I thought that your pugilistic prowess might have made you identifiable at the gym. This fear was activated when a young man who'd been hanging about near the ring came over and said hello to us. He was tall and pretty dense, with a light-skinned baby face. I was relieved when he asked you if you'd ever boxed and you said no. I was a little insulted when he told me he was sure I'd never boxed because I was white, and that only blacks boxed in my country.

I thought of enumerating all the great Caucasian champions but decided to keep silent.

"Muhammad Ali was not the Greatest," the boy asserted. "He could never have beaten Cabron."

Since I had seen Cabron on a poster in your bedroom, I knew his name would ignite your interest. You jumped into the discussion with such connoisseurial vigor that I was again a little offended by your enthusiasm for an activity that I could then associate only with death. As you argued Cabron's fine points with that surly gym boy, I started flashing back to the aftermath of the killing.

I had run, terrorized, from the dead body. Though you didn't say so, I suspect you thought this girlish, unseemly. You caught up with me and insisted that we walk slowly.

"If you don't slow down, you're going to draw attention to us."

"The police will catch up with us if we don't run."

"No, they won't. I know a little street where they'll never find us."

We reached that thoroughfare with its narrow cobblestones that seemed to amplify our every move. The street was eerily dark, and though it wasn't that late, not a soul crossed our path.

Forgive me in retrospect for panicking again when we reached Old Havana. I was sure that this brightly lit, crumbling, sinister-after-dark area was exactly where we didn't want to be. Credit me, however, for saying nothing, for having confidence that you must have had a plan. Even if I suspected slightly that you might phone your mother or the police or even implicate me.

I was relieved to see that the old quarter's sidewalks, so narrow that custom allows strollers to spill onto the street, were nearly deserted. When we ran into those two young women camped out near a store on Obispo Street, it suddenly occurred to me that we were now homeless, too. I had had no idea where one went to be homeless in Havana. Few panhandlers worked main thoroughfares.

Even those two women turned out not to be homeless. I was amused when you stopped for a moment to chat them up—acting unflustered is a good way of pretending that even under duress life goes on—and discovered that they merely wanted to be first in line for goods at this shop, which sold housewares.

I was nonplussed when you insisted we spend the night at a little Old Havana hotel. I was sure my passport would give us away imme-diately and, moreover, that hotels were exactly the places the police would ransack once they started pursuing us. How lucky that you remembered a friend who lived in that area, a guy who used to haunt your gym. His apartment, you said, had a spare bedroom, and this man was single. I was suspicious: Just what exactly was the nature of your relationship? It was only when we reached his place and I saw how ancient he was that I was reassured.

"Eduardito!" he said. "What are you doing here with a...friend:at night?" His insinuating tone you ignored. I couldn't. I didn't like his face or his constant winks. His pupils were half-hidden under heavy lids, as if his eyes had stopped between floors.

When he led us up to the spare room, you followed him with a familiarity that suggested frequent visits there. Despite my curiosity, I had no intention of quizzing you. I told myself that respect for a lover's secrets, and the knowledge that the lover knows you suspect them but compassionately say nothing, still figured into my strategy of sentiment.

We got undressed silently and slipped quickly into the room's narrow bed. We did not discuss what to do next and we did not make love, though part of me desperately wanted to, as a way to relieve the tension. Instead, you put your head softly on my shoulder and fell asleep. Whatever terror I felt would have to work itself out in slumber. If only it had.

When I awakened you were standing at the foot of the bed, your friendly dark eyes following every little movement of my awakening, as though you'd been there forever and even had a good idea of what I might have been dreaming about. You were dressed in a new T-shirt. "A present from our host," you said, tossing a second one to me.

You asked me how I'd slept and said that I had talked a lot during the night, calling out names—"Willy," "Ralph"—of guys you were sure I'd had before you. You called me a *puta* and said that compared to me you were practically a virgin. The girls had meant nothing, and there had only been two guys. One of them had rejected you, and you in turn rejected the next one. I thought of how often the calculus of our affections has little to do with compatibility or mutual regard or even good chemistry; it concerns, rather, silent revenge for past slights. You asked if you could get me coffee, and I said you could get me something else. You said I was starting to sound like a character in one of the trashy novels your mother likes to read. The affection you attached to your mother then made me realize that, no matter what you said, you missed her. I should have known then that one day you might want apologetically to return to her. The prodigal son: Why are young men's stories never anything else? (Except the myth of Narcissus.)

I asked you if you didn't want to lie down on the bed. When you refused, I realized that you were more agitated than you were letting on.

"Don't you want to take a second shower with me?"

"Not really, Johnny. I have an upset stomach."

"Well then, I guess I'll just have to listen to your long-winded bowels blow as I wash up."

"You're really trying to gross me out, aren't you?"

"Not at all," I said, thinking suddenly of something Josh said toward the end, when he was forever barging in on me during my morning ablutions so he could yet again use the john. He said: "Sitting on the toilet while someone showers next to you is the ultimate intimacy."

You laughed, but the laugh disappeared a moment later. "Johnny Boy, your hands are trembling."

"So they are. It must be cold in here." I glanced out the window for confirmation. The light was already strong, and there was no breeze. The fronds of a palm tree hung stiff and transparent, thin jade knives against the sun.

"No, Johnny, it's not cold in here at all." Gently, you slid one of your rough hands into mine. I pulled away.

"I'm not trembling because of the cold. I'm trembling because of last night. You didn't mention anything to your old friend downstairs, did you?"

"No," you said. "You think I'm fucking crazy?"

"No. You just think you can get away with it. And that scares me."

"We didn't do anything wrong, man."

"You keep saying that. But if we didn't do anything wrong why am I sitting in some stranger's apartment instead of going to the police?"

"You want to go to the police? Go ahead. But they might not ship you home on the next boat. They might detain you for a while. And in Cuba, Johnny, there's no habeas corpus."

"Stop scaring me."

"And if they do ship you home, well, that's the last of us. And I don't want that. Ever."

My cerebral cortex transmitted one message ("Go to the police") and yet my words were a mid-brain product: "I don't want it, either."

"Before we figure out where we're going, I thought we should eat something. You ran to the other room, returning with an ice-cold pork sandwich accompanied by a small blue bowl of leftover sauce. It was hardly my normal breakfast. "Thanks, but I only want coffee."

Our mode of eating, however, had become so communal, that you habitually disregarded my refusals and put food on my plate or, in this case, in my mouth anyway. Your contradicting my wishes I found not rude but endearing.

After two or three bites you did something new. You ripped a piece of your half and transmitted it, half-masticated, from your mouth to mine, as if I were a baby bird. Your saliva had removed whatever spiciness the cold pork had had, so there was no point pretending I found the food delicious. Your mouth had luckily retained the sauce's piquancy, and since the touch of your breath at that point was sufficient to arouse me, I started getting hard.

"What have we here?"

"A little gift for Eduardito."

"But my birthday isn't for a month. Can I open your gift anyway?

"Yes, please do. Coyness is a capital crime, you know."

As you placed your mouth on my penis, I gave a little shudder. I shuddered because your mouth was wet and because each time you switched from mouth to hand you licked your lips and because your skill at fellatio was so prematurely advanced that any man might understand why, less than two hours later, I had given up thoughts of contacting the police and was driving out of Havana in abating traffic. Not long after we both came, however, I noticed that my hands were once again trembling.

✳

I thought I'd never pull you away from that guy in the gym that afternoon. I was amazed you couldn't see what a blowhard he was. When I tuned back into the conversation again, he was saying something annoying to me like, "I don't know why they call your baseball championship the World Series. There are many other champion teams in the world, and besides, I bet our national team could beat your all-stars. The last crop didn't sound so good."

We walked alongside the boxing ring on our way out of the gym; a security guard had shown up, and though he was obviously not a policeman but an employee of the facility, we decided not to work out. Looking at the sparring boys, I suddenly understood how manslaughter could really be an expression of your affection for me. What I still hadn't yet grasped was why you would leave everything behind for me. Aside from sex and an invigorating shower of attention, what possible use could I have for you? I wasn't rich or powerful, and even if I could see that you wanted, as lovers inevitably do, to absorb my aura—of American pop culture, of worldliness—how long, in our compromised situation, could that possibly last? It was one thing to have chosen flight, but you had chosen flight without a ghost's chance of escape. And then it hit me: That was the point. There I was, once again expressing everything between us as merely preliminary to some horrible future, whereas you miraculously were caught up in the excitement of the present. That was the attitude that I craved but which for months (years?) had eluded me.

You were anxious to reach Alma's farm, but when we passed a post office I had to make a few phone calls.

The first was to my sister. Getting through to Pelham was about as easy as summoning help from the *Titanic*'s lifeboats. You were impatient about this, sitting on a ledge in the post office's main room, a cross between an expectant father and a traveler awaiting news of a delayed flight. After almost an hour, I got through.

"Hello," a small voice said.

"Jackson?"

"Uncle John. Mommy, Mommy, it's Uncle John."

The child's voice conveyed excitement. I was grateful that there was someone in my life who was always glad to hear from me, but had no sense that the precariousness of my situation had been hinted at. In the background, highlights from *La Traviata* were blaring. act 2, scene 5—I'm sure you know it: You told me it's your mother's favorite opera.

"When are you coming back from Cuba?"

"Soon, soon."

"Is Eduardo with you?"

"Yes. He's right here. Do you want to talk to him?"

"Yes."

"Jackson? How are you, man?"

You chatted for a minute about some video game, and passed the receiver back to me.

"Are you bringing me something, Uncle John?"

"First, tell me, Jack: Do you smoke yet?"

"No."

"Too bad. I was going to bring you back some Cohibas."

"Those are *cigars*." The wire hummed with the boy's pride in having recognized the brand. "Daddy has some in his desk drawer in the den." Rifling through bureaus was becoming something of a habit for this kid. I made a note to speak to his father about it.

"Jack, I promise to bring you back something. But now you'll have to fetch your mother for me."

As he put down the phone, I realized that I had not spoken to Andrea since the night of the death, so Sarah would have no way of knowing about the incident.

Jackson put down the phone, and I listened to the opera, as faraway from my ears as the passing band is to Violetta at the opening of act 3. The baritone playing Alfredo's father brought a quality of superb blossoming respect to his character. The sincerity with which he overlooked the possibility of his son's continuing ardor for Violetta made me compare it to my own situation, and by the time my sister picked up the receiver, a tear was streaming down my face. The tear should not have surprised me. I had not heard my family's voices for days, for so long that I wondered if they still existed or were just figments of my febrile imagination.

"Don't tell me," my sister said. "You're in jail, and I'm your one phone call."

"I'm not sure you're allowed even one dime-drop here."

"So you're not?"

"Disappointed?"

"No. Although the thought of waging a crusade to free my baby brother from one of Castro's horrid prisons does excite me a little."

"I wish I could find your flipness funny right now."

"You're not in trouble, are you?"

"Things have gotten a little more complicated than that."

"How so?"

"There's been an accident. A death. In Havana. I was with Eduardo."

"Oh my God! Eduardo's dead?"

"No, no. He caused a guy's death. Indirectly."

"What did the police say?"

"We haven't talked to the police?"

"Aren't you in Havana?"

"No."

There was a pause, and her digestion of the news was almost audible. "It's silly for you not to talk to them. It's just a matter of time before you have to."

"I know. But I'm scared for Eduardo. What will happen to him?"

"His mother will have to look out for him. Use her ties to Castro."

"I wish I had a connection."

"Don't be self-pitying. George is a friend of Jerry Williams, or at least of his son. They were college roommates."

"Who's Jerry Williams?"

"A congressman from Long Island. Very involved in Cuban-American relations. God, I wish George were here. He's so practical about these things."

"Well, I'm not in jail yet."

"Why do I feel as if I may not talk to you again for a while?"

"Don't be melodramatic."

"It's been hard enough adjusting to Mom and Dad being gone. I couldn't bear losing you, too."

"I know." The connection entered a delayed reaction stage, making it impossible to assess Sarah's emotional tenor.

"Sarah, it's getting hard to hear you."

"Call again soon," she shouted.

"I will. I promise."

I hung up the phone, feeling wrung out and longing for a rejuvenating chat with Andrea. How often an encounter with one's family leaves one craving compensatory pleasures: You've no sooner dropped your bags from a weekend with the folks or the children than you're out the door, hurling yourself into a bad movie, a double Scotch, or an impromptu fuck. The last activity can be particularly restorative. For, unlike family, strangers do not make us feel ashamed of our animal natures, or painfully aware that we have natures at all.

You were waiting for me just outside the post office.

"Eduardo, that's your third cigarette since we left Havana. Are you getting hooked?"

"Dunno. It calms me down." You offered me a puff. "You look like you could use some nicotine."

"Yeah? Tough chat with Sarah just now."

Just as I had finished summarizing the phone call, a policeman appeared. He walked into the post office with an air of looking for someone.

"Whoa, man, let's get out of here."

Until then, I'd been the tenser of us, attuned to anything unusual. But this cop spooked you. I offered to assume driving duties, which were customarily your province.

"No, I can drive. But you need to distract me. Anything. Maybe tell me a story.

"About what?"

"Andrea."

The story I told you—how I enjoyed writing it down on these prison pages!—went something like this.

Before moving to New York for acting classes, Andrea had briefly been a housewife in her native Kentucky. She was only 19 at the time of her marriage, and she lived in a small, Li'l Abnerish house with a husband whose waywardness was churning up late-adolescent angst in her—bulimia. Like Ibsen's Nora, Andrea felt herself cheerful rather than happy; beneath the smiles lay anger she was afraid to express. She saw her own needs as reprehensible and felt guilty caring for herself. She purged this self-disgust through vomiting. The routine was always the same. Every morning after her husband went to work, she would sit in front of the television watching hen-party talk shows while downing a carton of French-vanilla ice cream and a package of Oreo cookies. This was followed by a country breakfast of bacon, ham, eggs, and pancakes. Then she would force a finger down her throat until vomit spewed forth from her mouth, continuing until she was so drained she had to lie down.

At first, Andrea would vomit into the kitchen sink. She grew afraid, though, that her husband would discover traces of her crime so, illogically, she began purging in the back yard instead. She had only one immediate neighbor, to the south, and he was always away on business, so she didn't worry that people would see her. Well, no *person* saw her, but plenty of dogs did. After the first few purges she did not notice that two or three mutts would congregate around her pool of upchuck to pick over the pinkish pieces. After a week, however, the group had grown into a veritable canine convention, which began fighting like hyenas for the spoils. Andrea abruptly moved her bulimic sessions back indoors, and was so mortified by the thought of any exposure of her disorder that she soon stopped throwing up for good. There was only one problem: For weeks afterward, all the dogs in the neighborhood would follow her every time she left the house, jockeying for position around her legs and howling plaintively in hopes of another spew. "Oh, that Andrea Mills," the town biddies would cluck on the sidewalk as the future actress and her doggie pals passed by. "Animals do love her so."

On the road that day, to say nothing of tonight in prison, how I long for the Andrea who had told me this absurd tale. I was glad that mention of Andrea eased your anxiety that day on the road. For a time, it seemed she was almost as essential for you as for me. I cannot emphasize enough how necessary she was to the emotional balance I was trying to achieve in my life after Josh died. She was the daily witness to my life, even if the vehicle for affection was the telephone. The phone, with its peerless nearness (and invisibility: If you fart you don't have to pretend that nothing happened!), provided so many of the kindnesses I needed. The fact that I saw Andrea only occasionally was part of her hold over me. Like any longtime relation, she lasted by pivoting elegantly between absence and presence.

The post office was our last stop before reaching Alma's. Night had fallen by the time we pulled the Chevy up to the main house. It was barely more than a glorified shack, a stone structure with a sloping aluminum roof. The driveway, the yard, the surrounding ramshackle storage sheds: All were dark. I suspected that Alma's witches sat perched in the trees, cackling and studying us intently.

Even before setting foot in the house, I had had a good feeling about it. A light burned in the kitchen, emanating warmth. Delicious aromas—savory chicken, cooling bread—penetrated the walk up to the front door. I gathered from your relaxed gait that you felt sufficiently comfortable there to walk in unannounced. But perhaps because you had a guest with you and felt you should thus observe a few formalities, you knocked on the front door.

"Do you think Alma will like me?"

"You'll know soon enough. Don't worry; it's not like she's my mother. Just remember to hold back a little. You have a tendency to share a bit too much, especially at first."

You gave my left hand a squeeze and patted me rather conde-scendingly on the head. I was seized with a sudden desire to flee. I silently chastised myself for a habit of developing dependencies on any one person or thing.

A minute had gone by without an answer to your knocking.

"Maybe she's gone out," I said.

"No, never."

"Eduardito, forgive me. I was on the toilet when you knocked and I simply had to clean myself up before greeting you. I wasn't exactly sure when you'd arrive."

Alma's earthy candor won me over immediately. How that friend-ly, somewhat wizened woman could have presided authoritatively over four children, let alone a farmful of otherworldly spirits baffled me at first. She was smaller and less forbidding than I had imagined, and she had darker eyes. I was amazed that she could still superin-tend the gardens, to say nothing of the house, alone. You did say, however, that she had two part-time field hands.

"And this must be your American friend, Juan," the old woman said after giving you a long squeeze. "To my knowledge, there has not been an American on this farm since before the revolution. We don't see many Americans in these parts." She winked. "You will have much to live up—or down—as the case may be."

"I hope not too much," I said.

"We will see," said the woman. Her "we" was so literal that I glanced about to make sure the three of us were alone. We appeared to be. The "we," I decided, was residual, a habit I have often observed in older women whose children have moved out but who behave as if they still expect to turn a corner and find a child in from the play-ground and in need of washing or a husband in from the field and in need of supper.

"I hope you're hungry," Alma said. "You can drop your bags over there." She motioned us to the house's two spare bedrooms off the front room, where she slept, but she was calm, a little pleased even, when you picked up our satchels and deposited them in the same place. You said that Alma would think it unremarkable if we took the same bed. It wasn't a matter of sophistication, you explained. It was just that for years her children and grandchildren had been sharing mattresses, so doubling and even tripling up was not unusual.

What a refreshing contrast, I thought, to the attitude of my parents during my first trek to Montana with Josh. They tried hard to be welcoming, but an invisible conveyor belt still managed to deposit our suitcases on separate floors.

Since you and Alma had not seen each other for months, I assumed she would interrogate you ruthlessly for news of your school, family, or boxing since the injury. I was sure you two would speak long and lovingly of her departed grandson, your friend Carlos. Instead, she let us do all the talking.

"Alma, the chicken was delicious. How do you make it?" I asked.

"The secret is to let it cook for a long while in the pot."

"The spices were unusual."

"Mostly herbs that I grow." She motioned rather creakily toward the window sill in the kitchen, where sprouts of green poked through small stone jars.

"I'm surprised you still have time to cook, Alma." Your calling her "Alma" rather than "ma'am" or "Grandma" struck me as intimate rather than disrespectful.

"Cooking relaxes me. It's working out in the field that can be a strain."

"How long have you been working this place?"

"Many years. Too many, perhaps. The land is not what it once was. When my husband was still alive…" She gave a sweep of her hand, as if to indicate that when the husband was alive everything was eternally in bloom. The dramatic gesture threw her off-balance. I found the way you steadied her touching.

"Alma, where's Maimonides?"

"Hit by a truck. It was sad, though to tell you the truth, that mutt was getting to be a terrible little beggar. And no bladder control." She cackled.

"But you must have a new dog. Eduardo and I heard barking when we arrived."

"Yes: Orlando. But he stays in the shed. Too wild for the house. You'll meet him in the morning. And the morning will be here soon enough. Excuse me if I turn in."

It was not yet 9 o'clock.

As I was undressing for bed—do you remember the wonderful curved candles that lit that room?—you walked up to assist me. I was a little startled. Many times, I had undone your shirt, removed your trousers, yanked off your shoes, and I had felt powerful doing so: Here was a handsome boxing boy allowing me to remove his first line of defense. The night was remarkable, not just because you undressed me, but because it was the first time during our lovemaking that I did not feel the implicit presence of an interrogator: the cop or cops who were certain to be trailing us before long. Psychiatrists like to point out that we are never alone during sex, that invisible parents, teachers, or lost loves always crawl in with us, but I would like think that we shed some of those specters along the way. If they were with us that night, they were extraordinarily, graciously hushed.

That night the after-sex was remarkable, too. After fucking each other very quietly so as not to disturb Alma, you nudged me into the bed's backboard.

"You know you like it hard, Johnny," you joked.

"Enough of the porn talk," I replied.

Until then it had always been the feigned threat, the small hint of violence that had fueled our couplings. Now playful force had been used. I supposed I should have seen this as some kind of omen. At the time, though, it felt quite the reverse: pleasurable, really.

Besides, after that two things happened to efface any residue of violence. First, trying to whisper in deference to Alma, we got a case of the church giggles. (Just thinking about it, here in prison reading this over, I'm chuckling again now, though not loudly: My death-row—or day-of-deliverance—guards keep checking up on me all too regularly.) Our muffled hysteria broke into high-pitched squeals as you began tickling me. We would probably have awakened Alma, had not the second thing occurred: a storm.

It was a spectacular, orchestral collection of sounds. I could go on and on about how the storm startled us like gunfire, how the lightning outlined palm trees as brightly as a Kirlian photographer, how the rain came down like an advancing army—but only one aspect had overwhelming evocative resonance: the thunder. Its echoing loudness and unpredictable rhythms provided us with a drumming exhibition reminiscent of the night we met. This time, however, I ha'd you in my arms.

Huddled there under the cotton covers, looking out the window and listening to you whistle a soft little lullaby I'd never heard, I felt we were two souls in one body. I felt so warm, so protected, so in the bosom of your love that it seemed no demons or dragons could ever harm us. Then I thought of my childhood and my much less settled behavior during storms. Until I was at least 10, I would hear the thunder crash, glance out the living-room window at the Missouri River below the bluffs on which our house sat, and tremble with excitement at the eerie, soft whistling of the wind. I would fly out the door, skip vigorously toward the river, and exult as the storm made of the sky, from horizon to horizon, an electric canopy. I would avoid the sireny songs of girls from front porches or the sailory ahoys from boys splashing in the gutters. The tempest was mine. I would let out banshee yells, emit warrior-like whoops, and disconcert dreary-eyed fishermen who, despite the lightning, were religiously tending to their lines along the banks. How could this well-behaved boy, who was so proper and polished that he was held up as a model to his resentful classmates by their mothers, transform himself into a creature more uncontrollable than a high-strung spaniel awakened by a fire whistle? If in my frenzy I had bothered to stop, I would have told these perplexed adults: "I am only responding to the river." If I had been brave enough then to dive off its shores, I might have escaped home prematurely, been carried along to the remotest reaches of the Great Plains. Instead, I was pusillanimous (although I made up for that later when I leapt off the suspension bridge downstream). Always, and until you, I would walk up to the edge, peer over, and fail to jump.

I would go home. My mother would be in the kitchen. It would have ceased raining. I would have stopped sporadically along the way to collect curbed night crawlers for bait so my parents would not think I'd run outside merely for the sheer freedom of it. I would be commanded to wash my muddy hands and change my shirt and say grace over a dinner of fried catfish or spaghetti. Hunched comfortably up against you, as your stomach made digestive sounds and the rain raged, things seemed very much changed.

We slept peacefully that night, the violence of the storm insulating us from the worry of a 3 A.M. knock on the door. I awoke first, feeling at home, hearing Alma puttering about.

The kitchen, where I found her after showering, had a warm aura, despite the cool gentle residue of the rain. Indulging in our first slumber indoors for days, we had slept until the scandalously late hour of 9. Alma had of course been up for hours, doing chores. Now she stood near the stove in a faded dungaree dress and sturdy shoes, preparing an eggless version of French toast. As I walked into the room, I noticed how much more of a workhorse she looked in the morning light. Though I offered to help her, she motioned me to the table. Saying nothing, she went about her business, but her silence did not strike me as rude. I was too busy observing, trying to decide what had sustained her all these years. (She was over 80.) In the kitchen, she never stopped moving her hands and feet.

I was amused that your appearance at the table received no greater greeting than my own had. Only when the food was in front of us did Alma speak, either to ensure no interruptions because our mouths were full or because, now that our needs were met, she could briefly indulge her own.

"Boys, let's start the day with a little honesty, OK? Why are you here?"

You and I looked at each other to determine if the other approved of telling everything. There was a tacit mutual approval.

"*Mamita,*" you said, "I told you we were in trouble and needed a place to stay."

"Tell me something I don't know."

"I killed someone. A boy. A young man."

I don't know why, but I expected her to cross herself. I guess I assumed that the only thing that could have gotten her through such a hard life was Christianity, even though I knew that this was not the case.

"Did you know him?"

"I think I've seen him once or twice. But I don't know his name. He wanted John's shoes."

"Ah," the old woman said. The fight for necessities and the violence it might entail seemed familiar to her.

"I didn't mean to do it. Really, I didn't."

"The authorities won't care about that. But that may be a good thing."

I had gulped down my toast, so Alma served me more and said, "You killed him with your fists? I assume that your weapon was your fists?" You nodded. "My grandson used to say that if he had to choose between fighting the entire Cuban army and you with your left hook, he would fight the army."

"Well, Carlos was my best friend."

"Too bad he's not here to help us. I always felt safer when he was around the house. He may've looked like his good-for-nothing grandfather, but otherwise they were entirely different."

"Oh," you replied, "I suspect he is in the house somewhere."

"When he was little he liked to hide under the bed. Not because he was afraid of anything but because, as he said, 'I like this house, and it will only become my friend if I take the time to listen to it.'"

Somehow, hiding under the bed did not seem like it would deter the authorities if they showed up for us.

"Didn't you run into any police coming from Havana?"

"A few," you said, "but no one stopped us. We took back roads."

"I bet your mother has had a hand in this."

"In what?" I interrupted.

"The death happened four days ago, and so far the officials have pursued you unsuccessfully—if they are pursuing you."

We had invested so much emotion in the idea that half the Cuban police force was on our tail that the notion that they might not be looking for us at all was anticlimactic.

"But why would they not want to arrest us?" you asked in a tone that suggested that Alma's remarks insulted your manly pride.

"The boy you killed may be a criminal, a poor boy whose parents do not matter. They'll pretend they want to find you, but they won't take any time to do it." I loved the fact that you thought this old woman was simple. She was about as simple as Stalin.

"But what about the boy who ran away after the fight?" you asked.

"They questioned him. Probably found out that he and his friend were trying to rob you. So it was self-defense. Another reason not to make your case a priority."

Every comment Alma made had been present in my head in some form. It took a friendly interrogation, however, for them to come clear. Perhaps if I had spent my boyhood reading the Dorothy Sayers or Ngaio Marsh novels strewn about our home I might have been more methodical. The only mysteries I had consumed involved the Hardy Boys, and I was so swoony over swarthy Joe and fair Frank (or was it fair Joe and swarthy Frank?) that I had not absorbed the basic tenets of their crime-solving technique.

"Should we stay here a while?" you asked humbly. "Or should I call my mother and try to explain the situation?"

"Up to you," the old woman replied. The response seemed to wound you, so Alma added, "Of course, you're welcome to stay as long as you like." An extremely kind offer, given that she might be compromised if the police showed up.

"But what about your hired hands?" I asked. "Won't they wonder why we're here?"

"They needn't come round for the moment. It isn't harvest time now."

"But what about more routine chores, the ones you can't possibly handle?" you asked.

Alma smiled. "You don't think your room and board are free, do you?"

✳

"You must take pictures," Andrea said to me on the phone a few days later.

"I didn't bring a camera with me."

"But it's too rich. You're milking goats, shoveling shit."

"The chores aren't as difficult as you might imagine. The hardest part is adhering to an early schedule."

"Morning's at seven?"

"Try five."

"I'm still watching the late show at that hour."

So thoroughly had Andrea adopted the role of jaded urbanite that you would never know that she, too, had once stepped in cow pies.

"I'm amazed at how much I don't mind the work. I don't even mind going to bed early. After cutting cane, this feels like a holiday."

"Maybe I should come down and join you. I've always wanted to do a one-woman show set in the Caribbean. I could play the wronged wife of some colonial viceroy who says the rosary by day and plots revenge by night."

"I only hope I live to see it."

"But from what you just said, you may not be in trouble after all."

"Wishful thinking on the old woman's part. As soon as I left her farm this morning to call you, I felt immediately less hopeful. It's as if she has a powerful magic that stops at the end of her driveway."

"You mean you're not phoning me from her place?"

"Andrea, you have this funny idea that all Cuban homes are stocked with amenities. This economy is big on health care and education, not consumer goods—not touch-tone Princess handsets."

"Then where are you calling me from?"

"Where I almost always call you from—a post office." I looked out the window and saw cumulus clouds built like piles of ice cream and higher above cirrus floating like feathers against the late March sky.

"John, I know you're probably calling me just to hear a friendly voice, but if there's something more I can do for you, you'll let me know, won't you?"

"Of course, but as I said, Alma thinks that—"

"John, the old lady doesn't know shit. You're in a strange country. Your little boyfriend's in trouble, and you don't know what the fuck's up. Please stop trying to pretend that everything's OK."

I resented hearing her say that. Andrea could afford such a statement, being 1,500 miles away in her cozy kitchen, while I was stuck in the Cuban hinterlands without a Dorothy Gale-like glimmer of getting home.

But it was the truth. I hung up with a feeling of guilt building inside me. For the first time since that night, I didn't resent the remorse. As I looked for you outside the post office, I began to feel grateful for the return of my moral sense, however unsettling. I felt restored to myself, to my parents. It was the truth. We like to think that as we move along the process of maturity—secular or spiritual, it makes no matter—we shed the moral reflexes that connect us, tenaciously, to our past (life as a "vast unlearning"), but then they reappear, like someone to whom we've gladly said goodbye at the station but who minutes later again crosses our path, leaving us to wonder whether we should acknowledge him or pretend that since we've already said farewell, it would be a breach of manners to resume a relation. It was the truth.

I couldn't figure out where you'd gone; your Mets cap, which you usually wore outside the house, was easy to identify. I smoked a cigarette. I looked around: palmettos, jacarandas. The foliage loomed chokingly. I longed for the elms or cottonwoods that arose out of the blank, dusty acreage of my boyhood and seemed more of an oasis than these tropical flora. Eduardo, in those crowded banks of trees I would while away entire afternoons, enjoying the altitude and sketching blueprints for forts I would never complete. How I would have liked, just then, to take us to the safety of those trees! They would have conveyed my past to you more purely than anything else.

I walked back into the post office, just inside the entrance. A woman was in line, her children running maypole circles around her. Not seeing you, I began to worry. I ran back outside around the corner to the lot. Perhaps you'd returned to the car, and I'd simply missed you. But you'd been near me in the post office nearly the whole time I'd been on the phone; you'd even said hi to Andrea. You weren't in the car. On the verge of panic, I ran back to the entrance. You emerged from the front doorway, nonchalantly. We knew each other too well by then: Your mood was a sham.

"Where were you?"

"I had to use the facilities."

But I'd become an expert in your digestive tract, too, and I knew that if you'd used the bathroom in the morning—as you had at Alma's—then you wouldn't need another pit stop before lunch.

"I was worried."

"Relax, man. Let's go to Alma's. There's more work to be done."

❋

That night Alma announced that she was giving us a day off. You asked if I wanted to go fishing. Though that is an activity that I had given up years ago, I said yes. I wanted to spend some time with you away from Alma's sphere of influence.

I got excited when Alma said that she kept a small skiff moored in a cove adjacent to the sea, about five miles from the farm. It had belonged to her husband, who supplemented the meager earnings of the farm with his weekly catch.

I was keyed up the night before our expedition, both out of anticipation and because I'd not been able to ask you why you lingered in the post office. You didn't help matters by starting to hum "Purple Rain."

"Eduardo, you're breaking our agreement."

You may be annoyed that I again bring up our agreement not to hum well-known tunes at bedtime for fear of infecting the other, because once-sounded, these songs have a habit of keeping me awake. And you may be enraged that by mentioning just the title of that Prince song I have resurrected the virus in you.

Tough. In prison the sound bites associated with you have kept me awake all too many times; have made for nights almost as long as this one. The offending snippets have been both well-known tunes and those phrases without obvious significance to anyone but us, those fragments of language that passed back and forth between us during our handful of days—the references that constitute almost all that remains to us of someone after death or separation.

You stopped humming Prince. "Have you ever wondered," you mused, "why some lyrics or melodies are so easily spread?"

"Of course," I said.

"Your conclusion, Dr. Webster?"

"There's no reason. Songs are like genes: They spread for the sake of spreading."

"Sounds futile."

"No. Natural."

We slept for a few hours, and arose in the light of a dying moon. Alma was in the kitchen brewing coffee. She gave us cups of it, placed sandwiches and bottles of water in our hands, and shooed us out the door. "If you do not catch at least two big fish," she said, "all sorts of curses and imprecations will befall you." I took the threat seriously.

Everything about the morning seemed simple, didn't it? It was as if all our anxieties were bound up with the demands of civilization, and only there, in the midst of nature, could we discard ourselves or at least try. We had no trouble finding our craft, since you had been to it before. We bought bait near the water and went down a pebbled trail to the skiff. We lifted it and slid it into the cove. You began to row out from our mooring. Other boats were going another direction toward the sea, and for a moment I felt regret that we would not be joining them.

I was glad that you observed the fisherman's code of silence as we rowed out. I was still a little groggy from waking up even earlier than usual and was in no mood to chat. I would have been content to be the young thing who sat back while her sweetheart did all the work, but I needed to quiz you about the post office. You rowed quite effortlessly: The water was flat except for a sporadic swirl of the waves. You were wise to let them do some of the work. After a few minutes of lounging back, I felt lazy, so I set about preparing our lines. Placing the bait—sardines—precisely on the shank of the hook, I was surprised how much angling technique I had retained.

I had no idea what kind of fish we would find in these waters, and you were little help. You were not sure whether the fish that swam in the sea itself, where you usually set up, would be the same as those in the cove. The names you did mention were in Spanish and meant nothing to me. Raised on river creatures—catfish, carp, northern pike—I was unfamiliar with marine species other than tuna or shark.

We rowed out toward the other end of the cove, where the water was calmest, and I planted our lines. There were three of them, which would be a problem only if they all went at once.

Immediately, we had a nibble, which turned into a bite, which, a minute later, after minimal struggle on my part, turned into a catch. I pulled a fish of about four or five pounds over the side.

"One more and we'll escape Alma's curses," I said. You interpreted the statement more as warning than encouragement and refused to high-five me. Though to avoid jinxing our luck I dampened my enthusiasm, I felt as proud as a hunter who has just dragged bounty back to a hungry camp.

"Man, I thought you said you were a lousy fisherman."

"I told you: I haven't fished for a while. That's the truth."

"You're just having a lucky day?"

"Yeah."

We spent another minute in similar small talk, till I couldn't take it any longer.

"Eduardo, who did you talk to at the post office yesterday?"

"Nobody."

"I'm supposed to believe that?"

True to your principle that the best defense is a good offense, you said, "You know, if you hadn't come to Cuba, I wouldn't be in this mess."

I had been expecting such an outburst for a while, and had even hoped it would happen so that you could release some of your stress. Yet the expectation did not make things pleasant, now that the eruption was occurring and you were lying to me. Confused, I wanted to smooth things over. I leaned toward you consolingly.

"Don't touch me." You took off your leather belt, shuttled back and swung it at me. You missed. I felt hurt. You swung and missed again. We almost capsized.

You let your arm fall, dropped the belt, and burst into bigger sobs. I had never seen you cry. Your face lost all shape. Wide-open eyes, wide-open mouth, eyelids swollen. Your mouth made croaking, throaty sounds. You sat there looking at me through your tears.

I should have taken you in my arms. I should have torn off your clothes and made love to you, even though we were certainly in view of the shore. I should have converted your anger into passion. But I didn't. I didn't know quite what to do. Throughout Josh's illness I had also dealt with sudden changes of temper. I had grown used to them. But what drew me to you was in part a lack of mood swings. Was there some future awfulness stirring in you? Were you going to prove to be as jagged as Josh? Oh, God.

"I've been so confused, Johnny."

"Me, too. But it's not going to help matters if you lie to me."

"I don't want to lie to you; I want to trust you." Your sobs abated a little. "But you're going to have to go home. Sooner or later. And I have to stay here. What good does it do me to trust you completely?"

"It's not a matter of good. It's what we feel toward each other."

"Spare me. My mother's right."

"About what?"

"She says you're a good guy but not very realistic."

"Really? When did she say that? At the post office yesterday? When you phoned her?"

"I had to, Johnny. I mean, I've had to sit by as you phone your family and Andrea. And I'm not allowed to phone my mother?"

"That's different. We're in your country. And your mother knows people."

"Exactly. She's sure she can help us. But we have to turn ourselves in."

Your statement was logical and in line with my renewed sense of remorse about the boy's death, and yet I resisted. I waited until your sobs ceased before I spoke again.

"If we turn ourselves in, do you honestly think we'll see each other after that?"

"I can't say."

"And I can't say it doesn't hurt to hear you say that. But at least—finally!—you're being honest."

"I'm trying."

We didn't speak for a few minutes. We reeled in another fish.

On the ride home, however, your mood slowly changed. You started humming, and unlike the night before, I approved. Soon we were both singing—Joan Baez tunes done in the style of distinctly un-Baez-like artists. I sang "The Night They Drove Old Dixie Down" like Nat King Cole, and you sang "Diamonds and Rust" as if you were channeling Madonna. The fish—two fat ones—sat on the back seat in a makeshift ice chest. Our tackle lay tangled on the floor beneath them. You'd have thought that we were two guys concluding a normal buddies' outing, rather than fugitives about to turn themselves in.

I held on tight to this feeling while you continued singing—an undernourished rendition of "Girls Just Want To Have Fun."

"You know, Josh liked that song."

"Do you think that he and I would have gotten along?"

"Well, I'm not sure that you're his type. Josh didn't go in much for cruising the schoolyard. But neither did I before you."

"Would he have been jealous of our relation?"

"Hard to say. He was generally pretty sensible. He probably would have ignored you at first, then adopted you as if he were your big brother."

You frowned. "I think you should have told me more about Josh before now." Then you smiled, seemingly satisfied that you would no longer have to compete with my dead lover's memory, since he himself would have approved of you.

In the car just then, it would have been easy to feel as if everything was going to work out, and I almost allowed myself to sink with relief into just such an emotion.

I stopped singing, but you kept on—a rendition of "Billie Jean" that was so loud I didn't hear it at first: the sound. It was faint but soon achieved a full, chopped rattle. Circling just over the hill in front of us and hovering over Alma's farm was a helicopter.

"Shit," you said, much more matter-of-factly than I might have expected, given that our greatest fear was being realized. We weren't going to be able to turn ourselves in quietly.

I kept driving steadily up the hill so we could gain a better view. I kept on, even though once we reached the hilltop, we would be fully exposed to the house below. Many times I had gone over in my mind what I would do if the authorities descended. I was sure that I would stealthily make an escape. But for some reason I thought they would arrive at night. Didn't the knock on the door always come under cover of darkness?

At the top of the hill, I slowed down. And then we both heard and saw. I was too alarmed to count, there were so many of them. In the clearing of the farmyard, there were at least five official vehicles and, standing alongside them, about a dozen men: men in army fatigues and berets; men in dark-blue single-breasted suits; a tall, in charge–looking man, his dark hair stirred by a breeze; and a lone woman, in sunglasses. She resembled your mother, but I wasn't sure. There they all waited, a little apart from each other, as if they had decided in advance exactly where to greet us. I was amazed they were positioned so calmly, as if we would just drop into their laps without a struggle.

And then, just as the instinct of escape flared up in me, I glanced in the rear-view mirror and saw two Soviet-made squad cars coming into sight. We wouldn't have been able to turn and flee, even if we'd wanted to.

Without thinking, I jerked you next to me, sure that this would be the last time I would feel you so close, at least for a while. Even though I was driving downhill and gathering speed, you grabbed my face and kissed me. It registered less as a goodbye than as a hello. *Hello, I'm still here next to you. Hello, don't despair: Don't freeze up.* I accepted the greeting, yet I could not return it. By now, you have read enough of this letter to know that in prison I have been able to ascribe an emotion to almost everything we did together. I can, however, find no words to describe or define my lack of response to you then. There was a lurched pounding in my heart, but you were suddenly a stranger to me. I was beyond either terror or relief.

✳

After our apprehension, it took me a long time to adjust to your absence. During the day, a longing to touch you, hold you, make love to you seized me at regular intervals, like hunger. At night, my body would arrange itself into curved shapes, as if you were there to fill in the spoonlike contours. I would awake and find myself in the most contorted of postures with tears in my eyes: the residue of deprivation.

In some American jails, a physician might have prescribed sedatives to ease me through my Eduardo withdrawal. In my Cuban facility, with pills a luxury, I was left to experience my feelings at full throttle. On the second day, one of the guards took pity on me and gave me a book from a small stash of reading material to distract me during the long hours. It was *The Iliad*. I read and reread the passage describing Achilles' inconsolable anger at Patroclus' death; the later, greater section when Achilles delivers Hector's body back to Priam I could not bear; its conciliatory tone was so at odds with my own ragged bereavement. My own friend was gone, and I was not about to forgive his takers.

I received a few other volumes, too—Gorky, Gogol, other Russians—whose literary quality was much different from my usual taste, but whose purity was, has been, restorative.

In my dreams I kept replaying our first night in custody, at that small jail we were taken to near the farm, that ramshackle pink hut next to a service station where trucks arrived all night, the steady downshift of the engines exerting a strange, grating effect on my nerves. It was no surprise that we were placed in separate cells. I was grateful that each contained many other prisoners; thankful, too, that we felt no need to stand at the bars and make eyes at each other. Oh, no: Defiance was to be our uniform. We sat back so no one would have the satisfaction of seeing us suffer, and no one would suspect that we were lovers. That was easy enough to do: The connection between concealment and survival we had both learned long ago.

Considering how many officials swarmed around us at the arrest, wasn't it strange how few of them stuck around and that we weren't questioned right away? And where was your mother, who I assumed was the cause of all the drama? I'm sure you spent that first night expecting that she would march in and deliver you. I spent it think- ing of another woman: Alma. She was sobbing at the scene as we were led away, hurling curses and witchy threats at the police. I had no idea what would happen to her. She had given us sanctuary, which of course made her an abettor. I prayed that since she was old she would be shown mercy. I doubted that would be her treatment. To consider her whereabouts was painful: I was so sickened by it that the first night I could scarcely sleep.

The loop in my brain those first few days kept saying, *How can I get out of here?* and *What will happen to us?* and *When will I see Eduardo again?* Although the question of freedom has remained paramount in my mind while in jail, the incessant replay of those recordings has abated somewhat. The disappearance of that head chatter makes it seem as if some other Johnny Baby has emerged. It must be awkward for you to keep turning the pages of this letter and

realize how much I have altered. In a sense, I am sorry about
that. It is sad to see people one loves changing; to see the way a
soul can replace another in a body that stays the same is a griev-
ous thing to behold. One feels betrayed. But take heart: In
another sense, I am the same as I have always been; it is just
that these many months in prison have allowed me to see myself
very clearly at different moments of history, following different
trades according to my luck. My present self, in other words, is
the outcome of all my extinct selves. It doesn't matter whether I
believe this to be literally true: Biologically, I understand so little of how memory is encoded in our genes. But it makes imag-
inative sense. Like one of my prison authors, "I was a boatman
on the Nile, a pimp in Rome at the time of the Punic wars, then
a Greek orator in Suburra, where I was devoured by bedbugs. I
died during the Crusades from eating too many grapes on a
beach in Syria. I have been a pirate and a monk, a juggler and a
coachman."

Of course, I didn't feel this historical flush at first. I was
awash in guilt those first few days, and there was nothing cleansing about it. At night it was a much thicker layer than the flimsy
ratted covering the jail called a blanket. Why was the guilt at last
so strong? Because I had exercised a choice and was facing the
consequences. I had run off to an authoritarian country, inhos-
pitable to my kind, to pursue an idea: the idea of love. And when
the idea became a feeling, I had pursued that, too. I was unused
to this brand of guilt. I associated that quality with much graver
circumstances. Of survivors, mostly: of a war, a camp, a plague.
Of situations somehow beyond one's control. I had had a friend,
an older woman, who had a facelift that ended up paralyzing part
of her cheek. When she spoke of her "guilt" to me—"I elected to
have this done," she wailed—I secretly scoffed. What she was
feeling, I was sure, was more shame than guilt, and shame was a
child's emotion, merely a higher form of embarrassment. Guilt?
Now that was for adults.

Perplexity took hold of me, too. Had we been trailed all along? Or did your mother set the arrest in motion? With what were you being charged—murder? Manslaughter? What about me? Was I considered an accessory? A nuisance? An American who had outstayed his welcome? A corrupter of youth? Did anyone in New York know I was in custody? Where were you being kept? Shouldn't I have been allowed to contact an American or American-allied official on the island? I didn't care what those officials would do to me. Fuck them. Where were you?

Guilt and perplexity gnawed at me for almost a week. The physical deprivation was almost as horrifying as the emotional fallout. Crowded in a cell with drug addicts jonesing for a fix and so irritable that a misplaced glance could incite violence, I wasn't sure I could stay alive. The disruption of bodily rhythms was the worst of it. Unsure if we would be fed or roused in the night for no reason and forced to endure the humiliation of only two bathroom breaks daily, no matter the state of ones bowels, I—or should I, starting to think of myself as merely one of a vast incarcerated mass, say we?—sank into despondency. Then one morning someone from the prison informed me that I would soon be questioned by two officials and that they would illuminate my situation. They would come for me in two days.

This news relaxed me. I became more comfortable in my skin. I set about observing the behavior of my fellow inmates, as if I were a social scientist. Morales, the Havana prison where I had been taken after a few nights in a country jail, was a modern fortress near the sea. It had not originally been a prison, but its endlessly meandering architecture was very conducive to the needs of confinement. I was told by other inmates that Morales was the worst jail in Cuba, and I certainly heard stories to confirm this reputation. One night a prisoner had complained about his food; the next morning his smashed body was found in a road below the building's entrance. Another inmate had screamed too insistently for a bathroom break; he was suffocated in a septic tank. I was kept in a part of the building reserved for nonviolent offenders. Political prisoners, mostly. We were kept absolutely apart from the rapists and higher hooligans. There would be little fodder for prison-rape fantasies here. Not that I had any sex hunger, at least not at first: I was too terrified.

For some reason, after a few weeks I was given a small solitary cell with a toilet, a privilege that caused resentment; everyone else had to use the communal one next to me. Anyone who emerged from that facility immediately became unattractive to me: *too* animal. The ward didn't have a shower room per se. Once a week, privileged prisoners would fill some large containers with water and we would file past them, as one of the privileged drew a jug's worth from them and poured it over us. Those dousings provided relief from the punishing monotony. I looked forward to the sight of one man in particular, whose name I never learned. His body was nothing special: He was rather short, and his shoulders slumped, as if he had spent his life bowing and scraping to royalty. His skin, however, was beautiful: the color of sand late in the afternoon, when lengthening shadows and late sun combine to form a rich, ruddy brown. His smile suggested a man who had maintained his capacity for enjoyment—which is obviously not a given behind bars. I have always been attracted to men and women who are able to honor the pleasure principle under trying circumstances.

There were, of course, a couple of outrageous guys, who were treated as in-house clowns. I never got too chummy with them. I kept my sexual orientation to myself, not wanting to invite abuse. "Ah, *mami*," cried a queen one day when someone lingered under the jug a little too long. "Hurry up! The rest of us are waiting for that hot hot man to throw that hot hot water on us, too." When his turn came, the queen leered aloud to one of shower dispensers. "Why don't you come to my cell tonight and splash my body with something else? *Chingame, chingame, chingame.*" Though naked, she was shaking all her best jewelry. But comedy was rare the first weeks: I thought I'd never laugh again.

On the eve of my interrogation, the prospect that all would be revealed no longer inspired hope in me. I couldn't sleep. What if I had to spend the rest of my life in Morales prison? And not in the country-club part but among the hardened criminals? Here I am, almost a year later, and I am still asking the same questions.

That night, I attempted to dismiss the prospect of perpetual internment as unlikely, unsound, and morbid, and force it out of my mind with other thoughts that were sound and healthy—you caressing my back, little Jackson piping up his comments about condoms, Andrea prattling on about her latest conquest. But other thoughts—dread, unspecific ones—kept coming back and confronting me. I thought of myself as equivalent to Josh in his final days: the loss of freedom and the loss of life looked the same to me.

I tried to return to the days when the thought of death was hidden from me—a time before AIDS, before illness: when Josh and my parents were still alive. But, strangely, everything I did to revert to that epoch only made clearer that there was no going back. In the small hours (this time of night when I think and, tonight, read and write), with the prison quiet except for snoring, coughing, prisoners crying out in their sleep, I lay awake, trying to remember what had once screened suffering from me, how for so long it had failed to penetrate me. In my childhood I had visited the burn ward of a local hospital; in my adolescence I had watched the television as it nightly beamed in images of bloody Vietnam battles and brutal American racial riots; in my early days in New York in the litter-laden late '70s, I would pass whole platoons of the homeless and not lose a step. In that era Josh and I would go out dancing and, emerging from a club at dawn, walk with weary contentment to some all-night diner for breakfast. We would laugh at the homeless mainlining coffee at the counter and muttering to themselves. But I had no sooner settled into that prison examination of conscience than It—the existential It: the It without an antecedent—would stand in my cell and stare at me. I would try to hide: alas, no use. Not even memory could rescue me.

＊

It was cool the next morning, April 1, 1987. Though my first cell had no aperture onto the sea, I was imagining the wind whipping impudently off the water, when a pair of guards came to fetch me. I had hoped they would be two of the friendlier ones, but the way I was grabbed dispelled that hope. I was forced to bend painfully over, and cuffs were slapped against my wrists, as if the shooting pain would numb the tight pinching of the manacling. "Take it easy, guys," I murmured, which drew a shove from the hulkier of them.

They led me through a series of narrow corridors and a small courtyard into an interrogation room. They deposited me in a chair, turned, and locked the door behind them.

I was left alone there for almost two hours. Whoever was in charge certainly knew how to make someone feel desperate: Waiting is always the worst psychological torture. I was so on edge by the time two new men opened the door that they had barely entered the room before I blurted out, "I am an American citizen. My name is John Webster, and I demand to telephone Washington."

The two men remained impassive while one of them said, "We know who you are, but you have compromised your rights. You don't even have your passport."

"I don't have my passport because it and all my other possessions were taken from me when I was put in custody."

"There's always the chance they can be returned to you if you cooperate."

The man who had been speaking motioned to his colleague, and they sat on either side of me around the room's table. The senior cop was tall, neither attractive nor ugly, around 50. He had the air of a man whose wife had refused him sex the night before. His name was Tomas Benitez.

"What have I been charged with?" My naïveté about the Cuban legal system must have touched my interrogators, for they seemed to relax a little before proceeding.

"As Señor Benitez said, you were involved in a serious matter here in Havana, and it is important to us to know why." The second man's name was Mariano Frogger. The surname was ludicrously appropriate to his fleshy mouth and bulging eyes. No doubt he had put up with painful jests about his appearance when he was young, and he had developed a tough carapace to protect himself. Perhaps he had even become a cop to bolster his psychological armor.

"Who told you that I was involved in a crime?"

Benitez said: "You have been identified from your passport photograph by the witness of the boy who was killed. And your friend has mentioned you as well."

There was no way of knowing, of course, what you had told them. I assumed that pressure from your mother might have forced you to say anything. I asked them what you had said.

"Enough," Frogger said. Neither he nor his partner would be tricked into divulging what they might use against me.

"I'd really like to know: What am I being charged with?"

"We cannot tell you," Benitez said.

I told them that unless they told me more I couldn't help them.

"First of all, we need to know why you came to Cuba," Benitez said.

"I came here to cut ," I said, "with a brigade of American supporters of the revolution."

"But you left your assignment prematurely. Why?"

"The work tired me. I wanted to visit Havana to see my friend."

Benitez complimented me on my Spanish and said, "I see."

It was unclear to me how much more I should tell them. Of course, I wanted to be discreet; to protect you, protect myself. But I have found that revealing too little can be just as damaging as saying too much. How I longed for some expert advice. Even one of the lawyers for whom I had worked in New York (I flashed to the fact that they must have filled my part-time job by then), despite the fact that my case hardly fell into their areas of expertise: estates and maritime law.

Benitez kept up questions about what you and I had done together. I was very vague. One's first inclination under interrogation is to feel resentment and then retreat into oneself. Even if there had been anything to confess—that we had planned to murder the boy that night—I would not have confessed it that day. I sensed that paradoxically what these men would have respected least was a full confession. Voluble, I might have helped them do their job; but mute, I maintained their respect.

They were, however, obliged to go through the motions, and I was bound to respond. Before long I found it difficult to focus on the questions. I could only think of you, of what you must have said under similar assault, of how I had to protect you.

Seeing that my responses were perfunctory, Benitez decided to up the ante.

"I'll be frank," he said. "The Cuban government has little interest in you. You have done nothing besides being at the wrong place at the wrong time. But we are determined to punish your friend to the fullest extent."

"I'm sure you can punish my friend however you want," I said. "I doubt that due process and a jury trial are the norm here."

"On the contrary. Everything's more complicated than you imagine. That's why we need you."

"How so?"

"We need you to testify at the trial of Eduardo Garcia."

"But why do you need my testimony? You must be in contact with the other boy who was there that night. Surely he can make identifications for you."

"But he can't tell us exactly why what happened."

I was not sure I understood Benitez, but to ask for more information would, I feared, have jeopardized you.

Frogger jumped in. "We are prepared to put you on a plane to the Bahamas with no further consequences if you speak at Eduardo's trial about the nature of your relationship with him."

I would have suspected a prurient interest on both their part, had they asked me for such information right then. But they did not. They got up to leave.

"We'll let you think about this for a few days," said Benitez, with the confidence of the veteran who knows that to have to think about anything in jail—with nothing to do and the walls closing in—is a terrible task. I assumed you were going through the same kind of psychological abuse.

"All right," I replied, before inquiring matter-of-factly, "Where are you holding Eduardo?"

But Frogger was already out the door. Benitez looked at me and smiled.

✳

I supposed I should have been seething with indignation. I should have shaken the bars of my prison cage like some junky forced to go cold turkey. I should have screamed night and day for the right to speak with my family and blubbered at all hours for you. Instead, I was quiet. It was as if I were my boyhood river, and instead of hurling into a violent ocean, I had emptied into a placid lake. I spent days of calm, feeling but not succumbing to numbness. Just as when I visited you in your apartment that morning and we spent the first hours not clawing each other but lying motionless, so did this initial encounter with the authorities leave me sedate rather than edgy. Intense, jagged days awaited me, but just then I needed to learn how to steady myself to survive.

It helped that at first prison was not the whirlpool I expected. From television and B movies, I had gleaned the notion of jail as a place of relentless brutality, where inmates did not dare glance at each other directly for fear of reprisal. Such may have been the climate of the prison proper, but in my annex there was a semblance of civility. I might have seen this as a false, lulling state, a *drôle de guerre* before the onset of conflict. Instead, I saw it as an omen that my stay would not be permanent. I told myself that patience was not the same as resignation.

Intellectually, I feared the fact that I occupied a small cell alone. With whom would I daily laugh, quarrel, exchange banalities? But solitude initially was not so bad. For one thing, the noises of the prison—the muffled clatter by day, the sleepy terrors at night—ensured that I never thought myself abandoned. For another, it became clear that in solitude one is never completely alone. Whether with dread or delight, one is always with oneself. And, as if I had just won the lottery or had my picture in the paper, voices I had not heard from in years gathered near.

I set about establishing a routine. I made sure that everything in my cell was arranged as neatly as the jewels in a casket. My cot-like bed stood at military angles to the wall. Its thin sheet was folded in Prussian-precise hospital corners. A small stand that doubled as table and dresser stood at attention in the middle of the room, all 8 by 10 feet of it. On the stand I arranged *The Iliad* and my few articles of prison clothing, as if they made up a still life.

Absorbed in my regimen, it was as if simple joys for the first time became apparent to me. I understood the almost sacred nature of bread, the thrill at the prospect of a shower, and the satisfaction when sunlight sneaked into my cell through a tiny crack on the ceiling. At still moments of evening, I could even hear the sea; sometimes, the faintest crash of waves on sand was enough to remind me that whole oceans existed.

There was no television or radio, of course, but there was music. It is the consolation of the poor and the dispossessed. In my little ward, every man thought himself a singer. At almost any hour of the day, songs could erupt Vesuvially. Since my cell was placed at the end of a corridor and therefore not directly visible to any others, I could not see the musicians, but before long I was able to match voice to vocalist. The guy next to me had a fondness for calypso, and he would follow up each rendition with a deep hearty laugh. His lyrics were frequently bawdy, on the order of:

> I gave my lady a sugarcane—
> Sweetest of sweets, did I explain.
> She gave it back to my surprise.
> She liked the flavor, but not the size!

Another guy, two doors further down, preferred Top 40. His taste was so bad it was almost touching. Between these men was an opera queen. I generally dreaded his performances. Lacking imagination, he of course fancied himself the reincarnation of Callas. Trust me: Execrable bel canto arias are not what you want to hear when you are having difficulty falling asleep.

The only real musician among us was a prisoner I called Spiderman. His cell was at the far end of my corridor. I gave him his nickname (Andrea would undoubtedly have found another) because his propensity to fantasize was so strong. Unlike the queen in the Manuel Puig novel (the one we saw in the bookshop one day), he was tall, dark, and forbidding-looking, so it did not make sense to call him Spider*woman*. Moreover, his florid fantasy life revolved not around something as obvious as old Hollywood melodramas; it centered on old American TV shows. I didn't understand this; such programs had not been shown in Cuba since the revolution more than a quarter-century before. He had many favorite characters: Ted on *Mary Tyler Moore*, Hoss on *Bonanza*, Fonzie on *Happy Days*, and Barney Fife on *Andy Griffith* among them. It didn't matter that all these were bumbling fools and that Spiderman fancied himself something of a leading man. He would recite routines from them all the time, driving his cellmate, who was slight and therefore powerless to take action against him, to distraction. Spiderman's spoken imitations were terrible. Eduardo, not even at your drunkest would you have laughed at them.

His singing roles were another matter. Spiderman's favorite character from the Yankee boob tube was Jim Nabors. He greeted any command from the guards with a Gomer Pyle-like "Yessir, yessir, yessir!" and any out-of-the-ordinary occurrence with cries of "Shazam!" His primary attraction to Nabors, however, was musical. He had obviously spent hours listening to Nabors's record albums, on which the actor presented a sincere, velvety baritone radically at odds with the pathetic, Schweik-like soldier he had played on TV. Of this Jim Nabors, Spiderman gave a startlingly authentic portrayal.

LAST NIGHT

The whole American songbook, channeled by Spiderman as Jim Nabors, wafted up and down the corridor at unpredictable moments. The renditions were rarely interrupted by other prisoners. To some, Spiderman was a great artist; to others, he was human Muzak. To all, though, he made time in jail a little more bearable. I never talked to him much, other than some philosophical chat we exchanged once during the hour we were allowed on the roof once in a while for recreation. I had too much respect for him as an artist to want to spoil it with anything so banal as chitchat. Like many performers I have known, he was privately reserved and shy, as if hoarding his energies for the stage.

I might have gotten to know him a little better if he had stayed around longer. About a week and a half after my interrogation, the guards announced that there would be an inspection of the prison by high officials from the Interior Ministry. They were trying to decide whether to open the facility to representatives from a European human rights watch group. The guard told us that we were to be on our best behavior when the bureaucrats came strolling down our corridor. We were to smile and speak only if spoken to. Any deviation from this plan would be met with loss of privileges.

The day came and, as expected, the bureaucrats walked solemnly down our hallway, pretending to be concerned about our welfare. No prisoner said anything, and the visitors mercifully asked no questions. When they reached Spiderman's cell, however, one of them decided to make polite chat, the way Her Majesty does when she deigns to pluck a commoner from a crowd. Spiderman, who was in jail because he had refused military service, took the official's question dutifully. Then he let loose a string of insults that did not stop until three guards flew into the cell to subdue him. The next day Spiderman was taken away. His removal was chilling: In a few hours, will my fate be the same?

✳

Two weeks after my interrogation, while becoming impatient about my status and still wondering where you were, a letter from my sister arrived. Prisoners were rarely allowed mail; it was felt to offer false comfort, as well as pose potential dangers, even though every missive was read before delivery.

Eduardo, when I saw the return address, I was shot through with relief. I imagined a funny-sad composition that would mix anecdote with assuagement, that would say what she was doing to free me.

I wasn't given the letter immediately; I was told I would receive it in a few hours. My sister became all at once a savior to me; to still my anticipation, I recalled early moments of sibling worship. When we were very young, I would thrill to her arrival at the playground after school. We would hop on our bicycles and ride around Great Falls, fomenting adventure wherever we went. We were particularly good at making up games, and one of our favorites was called "Helen Keller." We would go to one of the town's supermarkets (not one that served our family, of course) and zigzag up and down the aisles while she played a blind girl and I her custodial brother. (We had just seen *The Miracle Worker*, a movie about Helen Keller, on television.) She would grab at items on the shelves, crying "Waah-nt, waah-nt." I would issue a reprimand: "No, Helen, no. You can't have that." We would make a couple of rounds in the store to signal our presence and then head for the register, where the candy was kept. Making sure there was some easy mark of a madam on her way to the check-out, we would slip in line just before her and begin the performance. Sarah's hand would clutch a candy bar and mine would slap her down. "You know we have no money, sister," I would say. "I guess we'll just have to go home hungry," she would reply with a broken heart. Invariably, the missus would take pity, buy us what we wanted, and pat our heads as she disappeared out the door. I must have been around 6at the time and my sister 8.

Finally, I was given the letter. As I opened it, I knew I would find no vestige of that mischievous cheering spirit. "Dear John," it began, "I have no idea where this note will find you (if it finds you) and of course that is part of the problem. I don't know if you are languishing in some horrid stinkhole of a prison or are merely under a sort of house arrest. All that the Cuban authorities have told us is that you are 'in custody.' They won't even tell us the nature of the offense other than that it's 'serious'—this, despite repeated efforts by me and John and the lawyer we have engaged to investigate. His name is Miles Alderman. He used to work for the State Department and is now a partner at Saks, Korine, which I'm sure you know is the leading New York firm dealing with human rights law. (Speaking of law firms, we have told Harrison that you contracted a weird sort of tropical illness and are now convalescing in a hospital down there and will not be back to work for at least another month. When your boss asked why you didn't come back to New York to recuperate, I lied and said some of the best tropical-disease specialists in the world are located in Havana.)

"Miles assures us that he is doing everything he can to get to the bottom of this. Needless to say we are worried sick about you and wish there was more we could do. I have tried and tried to get permission to come down and visit you but so far nothing. Andrea and I commiserate daily on the phone. I'm sure we'll get you out, though the attorney says it could take some time.

"Jackson sits down at the kitchen table every night to write you. I would enclose one of them, except that the woman at the Cuban consulate said that, if a letter is more than one page, it has no chance of being delivered; the odds are low enough as it is. So you will have to content yourself with…" And then there in my nephew's hand was "Uncle John, when are you coming home? You promised to take me to a Knicks game. I love you. Jackson."

I wept.

Rebecca resumed: "That's all for now. Rest assured that we are doing everything that we can for you. Love…"

✳

The first indication that my inner peace was starting to fray took place about a week later. The signs were subtle. I began leaving meals unfinished. I no longer hummed along to cell singing. I stopped composing letters in my head to you. (Perhaps you wish I'd stop now? Not a chance: not quite yet.) Till then, I would begin every morning and evening with silent notes to you, even though I had no paper. Sometimes they were only a few words long: Where are you? What makes your days bearable? Wanna fuck? Sometimes they consumed Leonardo-length notebooks in my head: I would goad you to stay strong, keep heart, think clean thoughts—except about me. Through the ether I would pass along diverting histories of American boxing, Russian bear-hunting, Ethiopian horse-rassling: any activity so pugnacious it would keep you from going soft. I hoped you were using jail time (I assumed you were in jail) for physical training. Wouldn't exiting prison fitter than you were upon entry be a great rebuke to the authorities? Most of all, I encouraged you not to stop loving me. Whatever my doubts, I believed that, without your love, all that was in front of us would be behind us. Perhaps that would have been better; perhaps then I could have rotted away without fear of losing face. After all, when one is afraid of the future, death always seems easier.

I also began to lose interest in the weather. "So what?" you are saying. "What could be more banal than a preoccupation with that?" But you must understand, the glimpse of nature that filtered through my ceiling hole or that I saw on the roof was essential. I began to estimate, based on the glimmer of a passing cloud over the roof, the exact moment when it would rain. Oddly, I looked forward to precipitation: It provided a respite. (Until it started dripping non-stop, as it has been almost all night.) Guards scurried to patch holes, set pans under leaks; it was a high-pitch performance, and all the prisoners relished watching it.

I began to understand why old people grow similarly obsessed with climate: Sitting on front porches of their nursing homes or retirement villages, they have been relegated to the status of plants, and what should concern flora more than an interest in light and water? Prisoners are plants, too, but gnarly vines rather than placid ferns.

I began to study other prisoners, to see how they maintained their sanity. The longest-serving among us (in my first corridor, no one had been there longer than a year) observed a physical regimen—calisthenics, shadow boxing, running in place. And they did not forego sexual needs. If, like me, any of them had loves outside, they surrendered their scruples. Not by forming violent, symbiotic attachments; among the two dozen or so prisoners there were no pairings-off that I could discern. The sexual connections were less tactile, more imaginary. Since my cell had an obstructed view of most of the corridor, I did not often see guys jerking off, but I developed keen antennae for their occurrence. Late at night, I would sense some guy getting off, and it would make me long for you. Several times I suspected that the guards had made prisoners service them. The abuse of authority sickened me. But perhaps the parties all enjoyed themselves. And who am I to sit in judgment, to say that some of these prisoners were not more content than I was? Perhaps happiness is only unhappiness that is better tolerated.

As it was, all I had to cling to were remarks you had made to me apropos of nothing. Seated on the roof under an overhang one day, looking across an asphalt lawn and down a wide grassy passageway toward the sea, with nobody about except a pair of greasy guards posted near the exits, and with a makeshift pen scratching notes on the back of my palm, I jotted down an exchange we had before falling off to slumber the third night at Alma's.

"I don't want to go to sleep," you said, "because I'll be removed from you for hours and hours."

"Don't worry," I replied, "we'll be in the same dream."

"Can you guarantee that, Johnny Boy?"

"Of course."

Those people who might overhear such a conversation and condemn it as jejune blather, mere baby talk, have never been in love or, worse, never listened to themselves talking to the dog.

But feeling for you couldn't carry me through, not always. Shadowing the love was a terrific anger, not at you but at my situation. Although I couldn't deny my guilt in abetting our flight, what had I done to deserve so much time in a Cuban jail? Why wasn't I being extradited? On Benitez's and Frogger's next visit, as Benitez and I sat at a table in the interrogation room, I submitted to their pro forma questions before exploding.

"Why the fuck am I being detained so long? Why can't I find out more about my situation?"

"John—may I call you that?—your case is proceeding."

"Proceeding where? I've been detained for more than a month now without knowing if there's even the possibility of my getting out? Or at least transferred back to the States." The prospect of extradition and the loss of proximity to you only increased my fury. I began to cough, and when I regained my composure, I shouted, "I've been coughing all night for almost a week, and no one seems to believe I'm sick. If I can't see a lawyer, can't I at least see a doctor?"

"I'll see what we can do," Benitez said. Frogger stood at the door, ready to summon reinforcements, if I would have veered seriously out of control.

I leaned over and nearly spat in Benitez's face. "See what you can do today!"

In that sealed room, with chipped white paint on the walls and tropical mildew dotting the furniture, it felt as if no one could hear me, and my questioners, who might justifiably have matched my insults with verbal volume of their own, stayed mute. My cough cleared up eventually, but I never was granted a lawyer.

*

I saw Benitez and Frogger a few more times in the following weeks, but little further was revealed. They kept asking me questions about you, which I mostly refused to answer, and gave me few clues about my status. We settled into a kind of Mexican standoff.

One evening, two months after I arrived at Morales, a guard told me to be ready for "leaving the prison" in the morning. I allowed myself to hope I was being sprung. And I wasn't, of course: I was being taken to your trial. Two guards took me out of jail and put me in a police car for the ride over.

The trial was at the other end of Havana from the prison. As we drove along the seaside corniche through the city, among the crumbling remnants of colonial architecture, past the Soviet-bloc concrete neighborhoods that seemed to house so much of the population, I looked at it all with resentment. Would I ever be released? I saw children playing beneath palm trees and a boy vaguely resembling you as he rode by on a bike, and I yearned to take a walk in the sand unescorted. I longed to breathe unfetid air and move about freely in the sun. But I had been tense for so long that I wondered if I could ever again learn to relax.

The court was in a semi-modern building, one of the many pre-revolutionary constructions intended for one use but refit for another. Before its transfer to the Justice Ministry, the building had been a private school. The architect had lavished care on the entryway, as if to give visiting parents an immediate jolt of grandeur. The classrooms, however, which now contained the tribunals, were small. The courtroom into which I was ushered had only two modest windows. In front of one of these sat the prosecutor. The judge, who was elderly, and the jury, nine men and women, were already seated. The prosecutor was on the right-hand side, and two other lawyers, for the defense, were on the left. I had not been told whether I would be required to testify—a sign of how cruelly I had been kept in the dark.

I had been allowed to wear my own clothing to court—khaki pants and a blue chambray shirt—which should have conferred dignity, but instead, as my police escorts brought me inside, made me feel dowdy. Even the lowliest audience observer looked better-dressed than me. Benitez and Frogger appeared, and we sat in the back of the room.

I hadn't seen the pair for more than a week, and they looked fatter: Powdered sugar was invisibly present on Frogger's chin.

I needn't say that I had trouble understanding why I had been arrested, pushed to testify, and then left with so little follow-up. What kind of system was this? Looking at the judge and jury, I could not even admire the dispatch with which Cuba brings some people to trial—less than three months after our apprehension. I sat for a few more minutes, sunk in profound confusion. Then it hit me: I was being administered an informal polygraph test. Instead of wires affixed to my temples, I had detectives monitoring my eyes. This was a gamble, of course. By not filling me in about your trial I would have to respond to the drama with an unmistakable degree of truthfulness. My reactions could bolster or betray me.

I don't think I gave them much data; the fact that *you* were on trial hit me suddenly; I had been so worried about my situation that morning that selfishly I had barely spared a thought for you. I spent the minutes between my realization and your appearance trying to steel myself against a breakdown. The only way I could do this was to remove myself mentally from the court. I thought of my father and a trout-fishing trip we had made to a stream near the Grand Tetons. I never got the hang of the casting, but I spent hours watching Dad acrobatically arch his line to and fro in water that glistened like diamonds.

Then I heard your name: Eduardo Orestes Ortiz de Montellano Garcia. You walked into the room from a door on the left side. You were wearing prison blues, darker than my usual uniform. Your head was shorn. Your hair is so dark and lush that you'd think I would have regretted the loss. Instead, I found you more striking than ever.

I found myself resenting the indestructible quality of your beauty. What wicked delight I would have taken, had three months of confinement left you unattractive. You would have then been brought down closer to my level. And I still wanted us to be close in any way. We had shared so much. In fact, I had thought that the only difference between any two people was who had suffered and who had not; or better yet, who had suffered and survived, versus who had suffered and thrived. The only chasm I saw between us (at least initially) was the chasm of sorrow. I wanted you to join me on the other side.

From movies we imagine that a defendant entering a courtroom behaves like a star greeting his public. But the humiliation of handcuffs dictates that nothing could be more false. You scurry hurriedly to your seat and the safety of turning your eyes away from those in the gallery. This is what you did. In a flash you had sat down. You did not even scan the room—for me, for your mother. I did it for you and found your mother nowhere. Her absence was the day's most telling omen.

Your name was called; you stood and stepped forward. You stood very tall, your arms hanging quite limply at your sides. The charge was read: murder in the third degree. How did the defendant plead? You looked at the attorney next to you before mumbling, "Not guilty." *Well, well,* I thought. *You are going to fight this thing. And why not: You are a boxer.*

The judge said, "In the matter of the People's Revolutionary Tribunal versus Eduardo Garcia in the death of Pepe Oyon, the court will now commence hearing opening statements by the attorney." I looked around, thinking mention of the deceased would trigger tears from a mamacita somewhere, but no group of gallery visitors behaved in any way that suggested family.

The prosecutor spoke first. Wasn't he annoying, this young man of medium stature? I would have called him handsome, had his hair not sat on his head like some untended garden. He said that you had known the victim, had been seen occasionally talking to him around Coppelia Park, and that you had been heard warning him that, if he did not stop hanging around his friends, you, Eduardo, would "have to take care of it." The judge asked you if you had known the victim, and you replied that you had seen him once or twice around the square. This was consistent with what you had told me.

The prosecutor added little else, except that through "reliable testimony and hard evidence" he would show "without margin for doubt" that you had not only committed the crime but had meant in advance to do so. I looked at the jurors to see how the statement had played, but, to a person, they may as well have been knitting.

Your defense attorney rose next: an ex–drill sergeant of a man (where in the hell did you find him?). He wore a cheap suit of gray-and-white checks and cleared his throat so often, he damaged the effectiveness of his speech. He said that you had acted in self-defense and had done so only after the victim had struck the friend with whom you were hanging out. At the mention of my name, or at least my role in the affair—I was the proverbial but not yet euphemistic "friend"—I tightened, expecting to be asked to rise. But the attorney moved on. He said that Pepe Oyon had had a knife, that he had brandished it in your face and that you had struck him only after it became clear that, if you did not, the boy would use it. He said you were reluctant to use your fists, given that you were nursing a hand injury that kept you from your true love: boxing for the national junior team. The judge asked you how serious you had been about boxing. You mentioned, seemingly without much emotion, your pride in being named to the national squad, and the judge assumed a look of paternal satisfaction. I did not mistake His Honor's pleasure for favoritism. There was no question in my mind that the judge had been installed at this trial for very specific reasons, and even though I was not yet sure what they were, I was not so foolish as to see in his face anything other than the mannerisms of a martinet.

The judge went impassive a moment later and asked you suddenly if you had ever been in love. A veering from the crime night to lofty sentiments did not surprise me. Emotion might reveal the reason for the "crime."

"Well, there are many kinds of love. Love of family. Love of country. Love of the great, glorious revolution. Love of self. Which of these do you mean?"

"Romantic love," the judge replied.

"When I was 15," you said, "I fell in love with a girl in the class above me. Her name was Yolanda, and we used to take walks together on the beach. I thought that my love was reciprocated, until one morning I received a letter from her saying that she had to go away. I never heard from her again. But I did love her."

There was nothing embarrassing in what you said and I had certainly heard about Yolanda before. But hearing the information in a courtroom struck me differently. A ridiculous remark whispered in private can sound colorful; revealed in public its hue changes horribly. It's a little like having a bank officer look at your credit report: The scattered occasions when you paid your credit-card bills late now look, toted up on paper, like the pathetic patterns of a spendthrift. I was stung to hear Yolanda's name again. Perhaps you had loved her; even a puppy love long extinct unnerved me. I could not get over the fact that you, when asked if you'd ever been in love, had mentioned only a silly schoolboy crush rather than your liaison with me. Of course, I did not expect you to proclaim Our Love boldly, at least not on the opening day. Your giving a hint of us, however, would have helped to hold me together. It might have been as simple as appending to your Yolanda story a statement like "And there have been others." It may strike you as sad that I hoped for so little, but it was only because there was so much to endure.

Given that you had cracked the door to your sentimental history, I assumed that the judge would have pried it open further. Why broach such material if you're not going to go all the way with it? Silly me: The judge had merely established his ability to elicit information, and the power that ability conferred. He pondered your answer for a moment, then, in response to a motion brought quietly to the bench by the prosecutor, declared the court adjourned until the next day.

From lunchtime, when I was returned to my cell, until 5 o'clock that afternoon, when Benitez and Frogger paid me a visit, I turned over the details of the morning session. I was amazed how little time I spent wondering what was happening behind the scenes at the trial: just who was being punished. How unsophisticated I was to the symbolic power of a drama, let alone one so inherently charged as the one that takes place in a courtroom. Now I realize that a drama can only rivet our attention insofar as we, the audience, while watching the event taking place in the present, are collectively aware of a greater event occurring simultaneously, of which the drama's participants themselves are unconscious. I realize as well that only one thing can bind a group together tighter than collectively viewing a misfortune: collectively talking about it.

(Speaking of offstage drama, rats are now scratching industriously at the walls of my cell as I read this section. Having often seen rodents here, you'd think I'd have grown used to their sound; and I have, I suppose. It is only tonight, when I am trying to hear the precise placement of my thoughts, that the noise has become annoying.)

As the afternoon of the trial's first day ticked by with aching slowness, and despair crept into my cell and my heart, I thought about something Spiderman had said to me shortly before he was taken away: We think in eternity but move slowly through time. But I couldn't meditate on that idea for long. I had not been fed anything since early morning, and hunger gnawed at me.

By the time the detectives arrived, I had calmed down somewhat. The three of us walked out into one of the prison's few exposed areas, a small courtyard with a forlorn-looking jacaranda tree. Seagulls cawed petulantly overhead, and I could hear the distant sounds of a radio merengue. I also heard the faint slap of waves against a shore. We sat around a small table. Though the detectives were armed, I was kept in handcuffs, as if to remind me of the desperate dynamic of my situation.

"We are still interested to know whether you will testify in the case," Benitez said.

"But why am I so crucial? There is no question as to who caused the death, or why. Eduardo Garcia acted in self-defense. This is the truth and the only scenario I am willing to corroborate."

I had thought I had said nothing of import, but Frogger's eyes brightened and his brown face glowed nearly pink with pleasure. "So you do agree to testify?" he said.

"What's my choice?"

I was aware of having decided only just then to cooperate, and before I weakened further, I thought it best to change the subject. "Since you're getting a little of what you came for, I would like to know a few things in return."

"Go ahead."

"Who exactly was the victim?"

"Pepe Oyon? No one of any importance. His father was a farmer who had come to Havana to work as a janitor in one of the municipal buildings. His mother is dead. And he'd been in trouble with the authorities a few times."

"What about the boy with Pepe?"

"I'm afraid there's nothing we can tell you there," Benitez said. "Only that he'll be testifying soon."

"Then perhaps you can at least tell me something about why Eduardo's mother was not in court today."

"Victoria Garcia has been very ill lately. She is currently convalescing outside Havana."

All kinds of images flashed before me: a soft-white hospital along the shore where gentle nurses applied cool compresses to your mother's forehead while a strolling minstrel sang love songs in the courtyard; a plain concrete building the slate-gray of cinnabar in a nondescript suburb where no-nonsense attendants dispensed Thorazine while patients on the ward moaned for their mothers; a harsh-brown prison in the furthest Oriente province where sadistic guards lashed out verbally at mewling political detainees.

"Do you expect that she will appear in court at all?" I asked.

"It is doubtful," Frogger said. "It is thought that the proceedings will go more efficiently if she is absent."

Of course it is more efficient, I thought: If you deny an accused person the solace of seeing his mother he will have one more reason to be cooperative, even if that cooperation entails lying.

I asked where you were being held during the trial. Benitez smiled, and said, "Don't worry. He's being allowed to live at home."

I felt relieved and grateful at this news. No doubt Castro, seeing your mother as one more ex-(girl)friend to be gotten rid of, took pity on her son and acceded to a last request: "Let him live at home." Spare you, her boy, the violence and predations of prison. I also felt a stab of jealous anger that you were in your room, surrounded by heaps of Garcia Marquez and Stephen King while I, whose crime was so minor, was languishing in jail.

"Didn't you think it strange," said Benitez, "that the judge asked your friend this morning if he had ever been in love?"

"Nothing in this trial would surprise me. Why would that?"

"Of course, the fact that you and Eduardo Garcia were lovers— that you are a homosexual—will certainly come up in court."

I'm not sure what offended me more: Benitez's use of the past tense to describe my relationship with you or his description of me as a homosexual. My relationship with you still existed, as far as I knew; and as for the word "homosexual," it should have been a non-issue. Yet he had pronounced the word with such distaste that I was amazed. Much as I was terrified to profess my love for you publicly in Cuba, I was thrilled by the way it might mark us out as different from others. Whether I wanted one or not, my love for you was giving me an identity. And I was realizing that, despite my loathing of being labeled, to possess an identity may be inevitable: In refusing one, you acquire another.

I began angrily to pursue the subject, but a guard appeared, and the interrogation session ended.

As I contemplated what I would say about our relationship in court, it was inevitable that I thought about whether I was setting myself up to play the victim. Even though no portrait of Saint Sebastian is a fixed part of my mental gallery (in all the old paintings he looks to me like a pin cushion), the role of martyr tugged at me tidally. It is such a tempting part to play. As victim, you always have an answer for the unanswerable "Why?" "Because they did it to me." No matter that the only place you can go next is to be fitted for your halo or become boringly bitter, embracing victimhood still appeals. It simplifies.

But thoughts of victimhood would take me nowhere; in truth, I had agreed to testify partly to see your face—head-on, rather than in profile, as it had appeared fleetingly in the courtroom when you had turned to converse with your attorney. Even though I could conjure up at will your big dark eyes, slightly asymmetrical lips, beach-bronzed coloring, their brightness was dimming a bit. I needed fresh impressions.

I also needed contact with your youthfulness. Why I required it just then was a little mysterious to me. I guess I was beginning to grasp just what function age was playing in your hold over me. I told myself, however, that what attracted me to you was your aura, a word that, despite its overtones of overpaid charlatans nattering on about the blue or red light bathing one's body, continued to have meaning for me. In whatever shade surrounded you was where I wished to be.

How strange it felt to have to confront the youth question yet again. It was reminding me of my own adolescence. Is it the memory of our own youth that so seduces us in the presence of others' adolescence? Not that my teenage self held much interest. What a callow lad he was, racing about, feigning interest in others, but always worried only about his grades, his status, his ability to enroll at a top college. How slowly everything then moved for me!

I suppose that my hunger for your youth also connected me to Josh. Those last weeks with him had provided enough sorry smells, sights, and sounds to last a lifetime. The nighttime coughing, the daytime incontinence, the hollowed-out look in his eyes at all hours: Why would I *not* want to replace these with a steady unembittered voice; a youthful, firm body; and face eager for everything? I began to understand why children and the elderly are so far apart in age yet can seem so indissoluble in spirit. What could be more connected than the ancient lady sitting quiet as a cat by her window and the child racing down the street outside, shouting, shouting?

Mentioning Josh again makes me sorry that I offered you his description so sketchily. Let me here insert a few more details. Anatomical ones—why not? He had a great ass (ah, those few inches of ivory on which I nightly wielded my brush!) and a rather small dick (which painted my portrait pretty regularly, too). That first night of the trial, I turned millions of such impressions over in my mind; I had to masturbate myself to sleep, alternating between memories of Josh and memories of you.

✳

Benitez and Frogger said I would not be testifying for a few days, so I was not sure that they would come back to fetch me the next morning. But they arrived even earlier than their counterparts had the day before. They laughed and joked in the car on the way to court, as if they'd just cracked the crime of the century and needed to celebrate. I kept expecting them to prepare me further for my eventual appearance, but we barely exchanged a word.

Though we reached the courtroom just a little after 9, everyone had already assumed their places. In fact, both attorneys were huddled in conference at the judge's bench. I asked Benitez to ask one of the other spectators what was going on. We were told that the defense attorney had made a motion to dismiss the case. Rather than respond openly to the request, the judge had called the lawyers up for a parley. A minute later, the judge dispatched the lawyers back to their tables, announcing, "The motion has been denied."

I assumed that the procession of witnesses could commence that morning. Instead the judge asked that you stand. You were dressed in a blue serge-like jacket and khaki pants.

The judge asked you if you understood the gravity of the charge against you—that conviction for it would mean a very long prison term, possibly for good; and did you want that when you had in front of you a life which, if no longer brimming with promise, at least with a proper confession and ensuing reduced charge would not be irreparably diminished?

You answered calmly that you had acted in self-defense and were confident that the court would find in your favor. You understood the charge very well and thanked the judge for reminding you of its seriousness.

The judge removed his glasses, a habit I immediately recognized as a sign that he had not received the answer he sought and how disappointed it had made him. Although he said nothing to indicate that he had more than a legal dossier's worth of knowledge about your life, the way he turned over the spectacles in his left palm, the mock-concern of it, made me realize again that this whole trial had probably been mapped out in advance. And while that possibility promised to reduce the suspense to quite dispiriting levels, I did not feel as crestfallen as the reader of a whodunit who has divined the killer prematurely and must now decide whether to plod on till the end. I felt more like the late-night viewer who, 10 minutes into an old movie, realizes with a start that he has seen this picture before, but looks forward to the next 80 minutes anyway, to the glimmering possibility that the story will end not quite as he remembered it.

Still turning over his glasses, the judge glared at you, asking, "I assume you have been asked many times already to write out a confession?"

"Yes," you replied.

I could not believe how perfunctory the judge's question was. It was very well-known that almost the sole goal of every investigator is to extract such a document. I had been so far spared severe pressure to do so because I had not been formally charged. But I had heard about the rudiments of the drill from my ward's Maria Callas. He told me that in revolutionary Cuba each presumed offender was assigned to a state security officer whose sole objective was to obtain a confession. The process of investigation, accusation, and interrogation had to produce the desired result. G-2 (the security branch) had no concern for ethics—or for punishment. Its goal was an admission of guilt.

While the judge asked a few more questions as to just what you had admitted to, my eyes barely left you, you whose body language—head erect, except when the judge's voice dropped to low levels, and you had to shift your shoulders to attempt to hear him—was my sole indication of the true state of your feelings.

You began a dry recitation of the "crime."

Isn't it extraordinary how the details of a sudden death can mutate so quickly from momentous to mundane? The bloody blow that brutally ends a life becomes a mere collection of bent knuckles that collide with the dull planes of a recessed forehead.

"Sir," you said hesitantly to the prosecutor, "it was a very busy night at Coppelia. John Webster and I had gone there to have a good time. Not to meet anyone specific.

"Did you see anyone you knew there?"

"Yes, sir, a few people. We chatted with a lot of them but with no one for very long."

"But you saw the victim there?"

"Yes."

"Did you talk to him?"

"Briefly."

"About what?"

"I don't remember. Probably just said hello."

"Did you notice him following you out of the park later?"

"Not at first, sir. John and I must have been walking for a minute or two before we noticed him."

"Then what happened?"

"Well, John was scared. I was, too, a little. But no way was I going to run away. Even though he—I'm talking about Pepe—was holding a big stick."

"So you confronted him?"

"Absolutely. He told John he wanted his sneakers. No way was I going to let that happen."

"Did you tell him that?"

"Yes, sir. I insisted that he and his friend get out of there. But then he came at John with the stick. That set me off."

"You couldn't have thought it would be a fair fight?"

"I didn't really have time to think about it, sir. My fist hit his face"—at the mention of violence the courtroom moved forward as one—"and I heard a kind of smack. I must have got him pretty good on the jaw. But he came back at me. That's when I lost it a little, I guess. Started to feel a little blood on my hand."

"Why didn't you stop?"

"I don't mean to be respectful, sir, but have you ever boxed?"

"No."

"Well, if you did, you might realize that once you get into the rhythm of the punches, some of the force takes over. You feel driven; you don't hear what anyone is shouting at you. But I think it's important to point out that I didn't seek out the fight. Pepe tried to rob my friend. And he struck me. I'm a man; I struck back."

Though you ended your story on a proclamation of honor, a moment later you sobbed, just once.

What a brilliantly underplayed gesture that was! I had an overwhelming urge to rush forward, put an arm around your shoulders, and announce myself as the "friend" who was being mentioned. Without your mother or any loved ones about, who else could console you? What would it cost me to make myself known? It would be no surprise to the judge or attorneys, who certainly had been made aware of my presence. Something, however, held me back: My cowardice? My desire not to upset the proceedings? My guilt?

The judge was not satisfied with your concision and so began the laborious process of asking you to repeat certain narrative details, as if repetition would dislodge something essential. This took up most of the rest of the morning. The defense attorney would occasionally jump up to voice an objection, remembering, perhaps, why he was there, and the prosecutor once stood to demand a clarification, but otherwise nothing prevented the session from settling into a kind of tropical torpor from which I doubted we would ever emerge.

Shortly before noon, the judge put back on the glasses that had lain to his left for hours, signaling an adjournment for the day. You were whisked out the door, lost to me for another 21 hours.

As I exited the courtroom, I heard one of the spectators mutter, "I thought this was going to be a case about murder. But it's just one more love story. Does everything have to come down to that?"

I considered this view for a second: Do all stories have to return to attraction, exploration, abandonment? The car took me back to jail through a tropical rain, and as I watched children splashing gleefully in puddles, an archetypal image of joy, of freedom, I answered at least a qualified yes. For what form other than the love story so compellingly subsumes both the heart of religion (worship) and the core of human science (selection)? Yes: Science, you say. From our talks I know that you do not like to think of love, or life itself, as mere chemical phenomena, the result of combining nucleic or amino acids. You consider such terms to be, as Keats put it—a poet I was heartened in New York to hear you like—the "unweaving of the rainbow." I do not agree. Deeper understanding of observed phenomena is to me much more thrilling than one more unprovable theological assertion about the stars. But since your preferred mode is the spiritual-poetic, let me address that. How I cringe at the greeting-card sentimentalists who say love is an eternity, as well as at those who claim that love should be lived only at the moment of its occurrence. The time of love is neither great nor small; it is the perception of all times, of all lives, in a single instant.

Given this statement, why do I believe that, despite its persistence, the love story has been so seriously wounded in our age? I could reply that after Auschwitz, Hiroshima, and *The Population Bomb* there was no way it could do more than slouch into the new millennium. Or that the proliferation of pornography—the mistaking of the sex scene for the erotic encounter—has drained love of its "soul." But others have already offered such obvious commentaries. In fact, I think that the most wounding blow to the love story was struck by the cinema, the very medium, ironically, through which it was carried into our age. For the heart of the love story is the contemplation of the icon, and the hurtling velocity of the moving image makes such a painstaking process difficult. In the words of an alarmist: Speed kills. The force of the flickering format distracts the mind from the imagination and thought necessary for the deepest affections. Other fast forms (the telephone, the computer) have also had their deleterious effects. Ah, for a return to the epistolary era, the days and weeks spent waiting for a reply to one's missive, colored by the recollection of what one has mailed and the anticipation of what it might elicit. How instantaneous response has curbed all that. Don't be cross with me for this kvetching. If, like some jerk of a cultural contrarian, I rue modern media, I also know that there are times in an attraction when speed has its place. Especially at first. But I think that this is true of late-night pickups rather than romantic encounters. When you want someone to fuck you, you're hoping he'll hurry up; when you want someone to love you, you're hoping he'll slow down.

※

I began to be convinced that, if only I could testify and corroborate your story, everything could be put right. I would look at you and draw strength from your expression and eloquently dispel any doubts about your intention. But since I had not been contacted by your attorney, I had no idea when I would have my chance.

That night after supper, I began preparing what I would say. My testimony would be ridiculously simple and essentially the same as yours: You had acted in self-defense. I struggled to make of my speech an Aristotelian piece of rhetoric, but as the hours passed and sleep didn't come, I realized that any attempt at oratory would be ambushed by the prosecutor. I listened closely to my fellow prisoners' medley of coughs, mutterings, and muffled shouts, and superimposed on them, as unobtrusively as the ticking of a clock in an otherwise quiet room, a speech of such mythological proportions that even if it did not earn you your freedom, it would earn us both a place in paradise.

I would stare at your face for encouragement, your fierce eyes like two panthers straining against the net of your lashes. Ladies and gentlemen, I would say, like some cockeyed emcee. I would stand before countless eyes, congeries of hands folded upon knees, poorly shod feet placed on stone, tightly closed mouths set all too prematurely in judgment. I would stand before this statue-still assembly and say, "This boy you charge with murder took a life not just in self-defense, but in token of his love for me."

My feeling for Eduardo Garcia must be blown up in full view today, even though it took me 33 years to attain such a state. I was waiting for this young man before he even had a name, a face, when he was still only my distant joy and happiness. I searched and searched among the crowd of the living for this creator of my future delights: I looked at men as if I was staring at people passing by in an airport terminal: to be sure they are not what one is looking for.

What a fool I was to be wrapped up in the composition of this florid peroration. This fantasy was nothing but a distraction, a displacement of my anger—that I was not free to profess my love for you openly, resolutely, whether in a cold courtroom or on a sweltering street corner. As this anger took hold of me in my cell, I pounded my fist on my bed frame, so loudly that a guard appeared, demanding that I stop. When I regained a measure of calm, I made a brief analysis of what your case would eventually mean for me. Although you had already given me clues that all might not be right between us, I was still desperate to see your face—not just from across the room but up close. I wanted to stare into your face, which contains, as one of my prison books puts it, "undertow eyes." Yes: undertow. Your eyes dragged one in, "like the undertow of a wave retreating from the shore on stormy days."

Do you remember how, on one of our first nights at chez Alma, I sneaked up behind you in that primitive bathroom? You must have heard my footsteps or caught a glance of me in a wall mirror, for you said, "Is anything wrong, Johnny Baby?"

And I said, "No, nothing. I came to dive into the waves of your gaze."

And you said, "Man, you're worse than some of those poets they gave us to read in school, not because they were artistically inspired, but because they sang the praises of the revolution."

"Yeah? I'll try not to embarrass you again with the sappy stuff." But I did; I have.

✳

It must be as painful for you to be reading about the trial as it is for me to be writing about it, so I will try to be brief in narrating its remaining scenes.

When the other boy took the stand the next morning to testify, I did not recognize him. On an unlit street, he had looked short and scruffy. On the stand, raised a few steps above everyone except the judge, he acquired stature, and his impeccable haircut and dress-to-impress clothing imbued him with an air of respectability.

The judge asked the other boy to state his name.

"Orlando Merced Callende," he replied confidently.

"And where do you reside?"

"Here in Havana. I live with my mother and work in my uncle's grocery store. My father is dead."

"How do you know the defendant?"

"We were in the same school. Different classes. I was in the same class as Pepe."

"How old are you?"

"I'm 19. I graduated last year."

The judge smiled, an avuncular smile that rekindled my paranoia about the proceedings, since nothing the boy had said logically warranted such approval. The judge asked the boy to describe the crime night.

Orlando said that in the park you and he'd had a discussion, a rather tense one, before the "murder."

"And what did you talk about?" asked the prosecutor, taking over from the judge.

"About something shameful in his personal life."

"And what was that?"

I braced myself for something that would force me to reorder my view of you; instead, Orlando said something that sent a ripple through everyone else in the audience.

"That Eduardo Garcia is a faggot."

I looked over at you to monitor your body language. There was no movement: Your shoulders, head, and back remained erect against your chair.

"And what did you think of that?"

"I thought what everyone normal thinks: how low, disgusting, and decadent it is. I hoped he would never make a pass at me."

I felt a stab of indignation, but also a little gratitude, that the trial's subtext—hatred—was now out in the open. The hatred that you find in so many respectable people. The hatred they feel for the imperialist, the African, the atheist, the Catholic, the Jew, the nomad, the solitary, the poet, the homosexual. At the heart of the hatred: fear! The day my indignation dissolves, I shall fall in a heap, a marionette with snipped strings.

"Did Eduardo ever make a pass at your friend?" the prosecutor asked.

"Not as far as I know."

"Did anyone ever call Eduardo a faggot to his face?"

"Are you crazy? He's a champion boxer. Except Pepe. He wasn't afraid."

"Afraid of what?"

"To tell Eduardo that being a faggot is an insult to the revolution."

"When did he tell him this?"

"A few days before the incident. They ran into each other at the gym where Eduardo trains. Eduardo didn't want to hear about it."

"But Eduardo had been injured and was training irregularly. Are you sure he was there?"

"Yes," Orlando said with impressive composure. "I went to pick Pepe up so we could go to the movies, and he told me all this."

"Hearsay," the defense attorney cried, but the judge merely glowered at him.

"Why do you think Eduardo was upset by all this?" the prosecutor continued.

"Because he was afraid that Pepe would say something to his trainer, and that he would not be allowed back on the boxing team."

"He said this to Pepe?"

"Yes."

"What exactly did he say?"

"That if Pepe mentioned anything to the trainer, Eduardo would track Pepe down and kill him."

After a few more questions, the witness was turned over to your attorney. He made attempts to destroy Orlando's credibility. He reminded him that the quarrel that night had not been over Pepe's blackmail threat but over sneakers. Orlando replied that that had been a smokescreen. Pepe was merely taunting you, reminding you who had the upper hand. He wanted to embarrass you in front of your American friend. He said you had threatened Pepe again that night in the park, but that Pepe was not afraid.

Your attorney poured scorn on Orlando's story, but it was no use.

Of course, if it could be shown that Pepe's accusation was untrue—that you were not, in fact, a faggot—then perhaps the defense attorney could reverse the trial's momentum. But that would require me to lie: to say that you were not a faggot, that you and I were friends, nothing more.

That night in my cell, the way to save you became clearer.

To paint you and me as the story of two friends, rather than two lovers would be easily accomplished: No one had seen us making love, and no one in Cuba had heard us talk about our sexual relations. Not even Alma.

*

The next morning's session started late. The handful of approved spectators milled about; the attorneys kept checking their watches. I had hoped you might be brought out to join the waiting and that, in the course of our collective time-wasting you would look back and see me, thereby making things less charged when I took the stand. But you remained offstage.

At 10 A.M., an hour after our regular start time, the judge emerged from his chambers. He immediately removed his glasses and started fidgeting with them. The change in his demeanor made him look human rather than omniscient, and the vulnerability was heightened by the fact that, as was Cuban practice, he wore no robes. He looked like he would rather be anywhere than there. He called the session to order, and you were brought out.

I was called to the stand.

I walked slowly past the lawyers' tables, not looking at you. I had spent the week staring at your back from the rear of the room and now you, as I mounted the witness stand, would have for a moment to do the same with me. When I turned around, neither the fear I had anticipated nor the smile I had hoped for was on your face. Instead, there was calm. Our eyes met; there was acknowledgment and a quick nod. That was all.

I stated my name, and the prosecutor asked me why I had come to Cuba.

I replied that I had come with an American brigade to join the harvest.

"How long were you scheduled to be in the fields?"

"Six weeks."

"And did you stay the whole time?"

"No."

"And why was that?"

"I was tired of the work."

"So what did you do?"

I said I had long wanted to see more of the "great and revolutionary" country of Cuba, so I left the fields and came to Havana. I was prepared to talk about my leave-taking all morning if necessary, but Benitez and Frogger said the prosecution would not be interested in that—that I had done nothing illegal by leaving early—and they were right.

"How soon after you arrived in Havana did you meet up with the defendant?" the prosecutor asked.

"The second day."

"Where had you met?"

"New York."

Annoyed at my curt answers, the prosecutor asked me to describe the circumstances of our meeting, taking as much time as I needed.

I told the story with generous detail, didn't you think? It seemed so long ago that I was already compressing details then.

"Señor Webster, what exactly happened the night of Pepe's murder?"

"I think one can hardly call it a murder."

"What, then, would you call it?"

"An accidental, highly regrettable death."

"But how can you call it accidental? You have heard Orlando explain how Eduardo threatened Pepe?"

"Yes. But that was not the subject of discussion the night in question. Shoes were."

"Your shoes?"

"Yes."

"But isn't it possible the shoes were merely a pretext? That Pepe had been threatened for a second time by Eduardo at Coppelia Park that night and that he felt it necessary to let Eduardo know that he was not going to be intimidated?"

"I don't know. I know nothing of the threat that you mention, and I was with Eduardo in the park the whole time. Isn't it more probable that Pepe and Orlando were merely young hooligans who saw a pair of sneakers and decided that they wanted them?"

I could hear you chuckle as I said this, though I didn't dare look at you. Everyone else in the courtroom was quiet. Though you had asked the prosecutor if he had ever boxed, it is not the custom at trials for witnesses to question the prosecutor. But now the question had been asked, and everyone was waiting for an answer. Instead, the prosecutor brushed the question aside with an arrogant counter-question.

"Isn't it possible that Pepe chose to confront Eduardo when you were present precisely because you had something to do with the nature of the threat?"

"I do not understand what you mean."

"I think you do. If Pepe was going to remind Eduardo of the threat, what better time to do it than in the presence of Eduardo's current…lover?"

If the prosecutor thought the ominous drop of the word "lover" into the glass was going to shake me—or the rest of the court, where the emotional temperature seemed to remain unchanged—he was mistaken.

"But are you and Eduardo lovers?"

"No." I didn't dare look at you.

"Really?"

My denial had been terse, matter-of-fact, but in order to prevent it from upsetting my composure, I went on the offensive.

"I find it interesting," I said, "that a prosecutor concerned to pin premeditation on my friend would ignore the import of his own words. You keep referring to Pepe's activity as a 'threat.' Doesn't that word suggest to you that it was not Eduardo but Pepe who instigated the entire aggression?"

Once again I felt that the courtroom itself demanded an answer of the state's attorney. He was not so quick this time to dismiss my question with one of his own.

"Might the judge remind the witness who is on the stand here?"

The prosecutor's reply came across as defeated and pathetic. I could feel the air go out of the courtroom. I had won the exchange and while the lawyer waited for the judge's reprimand, which came dutifully, I looked over at you. You were grinning. Elation coursed quietly through me. Our solidarity remained.

The prosecutor spent the rest of the morning going over details of the night of Pepe's death. Were you surprised that I did not challenge him a second time and in fact submitted quite compliantly to his questioning? He did not succeed in tripping me up. But it was clear that I would have to undergo another day on the stand.

That night in my cell, I waited for gloom to descend. Benitez and Frogger told me I had been horribly insolent: If I kept up this tone, I would certainly be found insubordinate, a charge more serious than the American "in contempt." I could be sentenced to prison for decades. (At that point, no one was yet talking about the death penalty.) Why, then, was I so happy that evening, as happy as I had been since I had first seen you on the street and imagined for us a shiny future?

From this distance, I'm not sure I can describe so intense and therefore so fleeting a joy, but in looking back at that session, I have the feeling that, curiously, I hadn't noted then the very thing I had indeed noted most of all. Staring at your eyes that morning, I had seen someone with whom I was not only in love, but whom I loved. However, I still wanted to make love with you; in the courtroom, if not on the witness stand, fantasies of sex flickered constantly through my brain. But I no longer worried that my complex nexus of feeling for you was only an illusion that my mind had manufactured to gratify my ego, or that my heart had dreamed up as proof that Josh's death had not robbed all my emotions of their edge.

This sense of conclusion did not unruffle my emotions, however. When the prosecutor asked me to describe our relation and I had answered "friends," I had felt dishonest, as if I had just demeaned what we shared. Conversely, when he asked if we were 'lovers' and I had answered 'no,' I had felt absolutely honest in my answer. "Lover" belonged to the realm of the "feminine," and I—and I hoped you—had made our exit from that kingdom. Henceforth, you were in fact my "friend." Given your age, you were my "boy-friend." I was very comfortable with that description. This all seemed natural to me then. It was only later that I realized that this was merely my attempt to begin pulling apart from you.

✳

The pace of the trial picked up. It was only much later that I found out from Demosthenes why. The proceeding had begun to make the news back in the U.S.: Demo had learned this from a foreign visitor who had told his sister; there was no report of it in the state-controlled Cuban media, nor any commotion outside the court building to suggest anything newsworthy was going on. But to prevent any flare-up of international interest, the trial would have to conclude soon.

In court the next day, as you may remember, that high official from the Justice Ministry showed up. I could hear a silent "har-rumph" from the official as people were evicted from the front row to make room for him and two soldiers. Everyone was now on best behavior, and the official, an old, ferret-faced man, was obviously a Castro spy, but I didn't care. I did nothing. Except: notice the weather (hot, humid) for the first time in days and how it was stifling the courtroom. Except: cast a quick glance your way to enjoy your reaction, which consisted of your eyes nearly popping out of your head. Except: to continue speaking.

"Reebok is an English-American brand of sneakers," I said. "They have been around for about a decade but have become fashionable only in the last few years."

The prosecutor continued with an antimaterialist fervor that was nothing more than a grandstanding play for the official's attention: "Do you really think that Pepe Oyon cared about the brand of your footwear?"

"If he did not, he gave quite a performance of pretending he did. After all, he was wearing sneakers already. Apparently, he liked my Reeboks better."

"Aren't you exaggerating? Who in Cuba would commit violence just for shoes?"

The brazen stupidity of the question amused me. If the prosecutor was going to impress our visitor, then I could, too.

"Perhaps you are right. It is only in a country like America, poisoned by centuries of capitalist greed, that a youth on the street would care so criminally about something as inconsequential as having his feet covered comfortably."

As I said this, I realized the danger of making a mockery of the proceedings. Clearly, the official had not come to court on a hot summer day to hear about shoes.

What had he come for? I suspected that you knew better than I. I relished the fact that it was for me—not Orlando, not some later witness, not for the verdict or sentencing—that he had shown up. I felt hopeful: The official's presence indicated that the regime was taking the trial very seriously.

The prosecutor went to his desk to consult some papers, and the judge wiped sweat from his brow, and I was dying (as I was all that week) to know what you were thinking.

The official was not adept at waiting. As the prosecutor kept shuffling papers, he pulled at his Castro-like beard, adjusted the pistol cinched to his belt, and made the lawyer the target of a thousand malicious looks.

You kept your eyes on the floor.

The prosecutor found what he was looking for: a magazine article.

"I have in my hand a copy of a magazine article dated February, 1985. Do you recognize yourself in it?" He showed it to me. Although the paper was yellowing badly around the edges, I had no trouble recognizing the photo as one of Josh and me. A gay glossy had been doing a Valentine's Day feature on couples who had been together for more than five years, and we were Exhibit A.

"Yes."

"And who is that with you in the photograph?"

"My friend Josh."

"According to the article, he was more than a friend. According to the article, he was your lover."

He showed me the photo again, as if that would make his observation incontrovertible. There were Josh and I, laughing at a midtown Manhattan restaurant. We must have had a few cocktails, because I was smoking a cigarette and Josh was sucking on a cigar. It was a happy scene, and I had no wish to disclaim it. Before answering the question, however, I glanced at the official, whose face betrayed surprising curiosity.

"Yes," I said."

"So you do not deny you are a homosexual?"

"I loved Josh. I gladly admit that."

"And you admit that you are were the lover of Eduardo Garcia?"

"I have told you that he is my friend. I feel a tremendous loyalty to him."

"A loyalty?" The innuendo dripped from the prosecutor's mouth.

"Let me put it in a way that you might understand. Eduardo Garcia is like a younger brother to me. He is my comrade: If we were on the field of battle I would gladly take a bullet for him."

At the mention of "battle" a reverent murmur rippled through the room.

"Yes," said the prosecutor. "Your attempt to paint pictures of Homeric valor are very touching. But you have not answered the question: Were you having sex with Eduardo Garcia?" I had not looked at you the day before when a similar question had been asked; I couldn't bear to. That day, though, I was merely confirming my previous testimony.

I looked over at you, asking for permission. Your eyes seemed to give it.

"No, I wasn't having sex with him."

I looked at you again. You nodded almost imperceptibly, and I felt a cleansing sense of relief.

My lie, of course, may have opened the door for your future falsehoods, though in admitting this I must also observe that I was trying to *save* you. "But whether I was or I wasn't," I said, "what could that possibly have to do with the death of Pepe Oyon? For it *is* a death we are concerned with here, isn't it?"

The prosecutor was not to be beaten, though. Do you remember that crude interrogator's trick he resorted to, asking me to go over material a second time, trying to break me down through tedium? I thought of this as I repeated details to the lawyer. I also thought of much gentler circumstances: how lovers grill each other this way; how love itself is a perpetual interrogation; how the interrogation process showed me a method of explaining myself to you. I thought of how I had asked you over and over for the names of boys you'd KO'd and how you in turn had asked me for the lyrics to "Shaft" or "Super Fly." These repetitions were crucial. For what we may have been looking for in each other was, despite our differences in age and culture, the ultimate sense of feeling at home, though the true home of our longing was not the longing but the search itself.

When the prosecutor asked me to describe our meeting for the third time, your attorney objected that I was being "badgered." But the judge, seeing that the official had perked up once the techniques of torture were employed, overruled him emphatically.

As my voice went on autopilot, my brain kept speculating about why, beyond U.S.-Cuba relations, a Castro confidant had shown up. Over the years many family members of Castro's close circle must have fallen into trouble, and surely he had not sent aides to their trials. What was it about your family that was different? I thought back to some of the things you had told me about your mother.

To begin with, you said, it was unusual for a woman to hold such an exalted position in the regime, especially a woman still relatively young and attractive. Your mother was, after all, barely 40, and, as I had observed at the Angolan consulate, she was still quite able to inspire lascivious glances. How had Castro, I wondered, found a way to respect both her shape and her savvy?

You said that your mother's power flowed from her ability to forget. Other officials saw their friends become casualties of the regime, and then could not serve it unwaveringly. Your mother, you insisted, let such things wash over her. A neighbor, a cousin, a husband: Anyone was expendable. Yes, even a husband. Enraged that your father, before his terminal illness, he was seeing another woman, Victoria did not use her influence, even when her husband begged her to do so.

The prosecutor droned on, his questions becoming more pointless and long-winded. I looked at you, and suddenly realized that someone besides me might have strong feelings for you. In other words, I, who was so tempted to judge your mother for her cruelty toward a wayward husband and insensitivity to a gay child, instead felt a stab of sympathy for her. You were all she had. Of course she must feel a murderous, Medea-like rage. How strange it was to notice an emotion so basic that I should have been aware of it all along. I should have noticed it both for myself and for you. It might have changed our story a bit, made it possible yesterday for me to see you.

But then I suddenly remembered something you had said about your mother as we were walking in Havana one evening that week after our reunion. I had mentioned that a boy passing us on the street looked a little like Josh, and you had said, "Funny, isn't it? Josh was taken from you; now you take me from my mother."

"Señor Webster," the prosecutor was saying when I shed the distracting thoughts, "did you at no point during the night in question, while the altercation was taking place, consider that you yourself might had had some influence over the event?"

"How could that be? I had no idea who these hooligans were?"

"No influence?"

"I do not understand what you mean. If you mean, did I try to stop the fight, no, I did not. But it happened so quickly it would have been impossible to intervene. Orlando did not intervene, either."

"I do not mean influence the outcome of the actual fight. I mean influence Eduardo's behavior so that he would have no reason to be under threat for any assumptions about his antirevolutionary behavior. Do you feel no responsibility there?" The prosecutor was setting me up, I hope you realized, as a *brigandista* and self-proclaimed friend of the revolution who had done nothing to ensure your ideological correctness.

"No. I felt no such responsibility." As I answered, the prosecutor smiled, and my heart dropped. At this trial, I had first been a spectator, then a witness. It was dawning on me that I was quickly becoming a codefendant.

As if to confirm my premonition, when I returned to my quarters that afternoon, changes had been made. The message that a Castro advisor had shown up at the trial hummed along the invisible wires that connected jailer to prisoner and cell to cell. Benitez and Frogger ferried me back to jail as if nothing special had occurred, but I guess that that, too, was part of the mood shift. The prison's tactics were much more noticeable. For one thing, no singing was allowed that night in my ward. More important, all my books—a concession on the part of the prison warden—were taken away. The words of others, whether sung or set down on paper, were now going to be denied me.

Three more days passed. Each morning I arose monkishly at dawn (prison is so metaphysical!), prepared myself for court, and just as I had achieved focus, a guard appeared at my door to tell me I would be staying in. On the fourth day I observed the same regimen, but instead of sifting calmly through my thoughts as soon as my ass hit the floor, I was thrown off-kilter. It was the heat. Summer seemed unending. I had been told that heat in Cuba is always humid, sticky, inescapable, but I did not believe it could be worse than the baking I had survived every summer as a child on the Plains, or worse than the physical enervation I had undergone during my first August in New York, when I lived without benefit of air-conditioning. And maybe the weather wouldn't have struck me as so severe if I hadn't been in a prison near the sea. The lack of ventilation conspired all morning to suffocate me. Flies amassed frenziedly in the air, and I could practically hear the lice replicating with shouts of glee.

The next morning a guard shouted my name at the ward door and said that I had to gather my belongings. The announcement set the other prisoners' tongues wagging. Someone shouted that I would be set free; someone else, that I would be taken back to the sugar plantation to toil until my case was settled; and a third voice piped up, predicting that I would be taken to another prison.

I placed my personal items in a soft pouch that one of the guards had given me. My emotions soared and sank within a few minutes.

A guard came to fetch me, and I walked down the corridor, handing out my provisions to men at random—here something for the calypso singer, there an item for the opera queen. I passed out goodbyes like business cards.

I was resolute that upon reaching the ward door I would not turn and survey everyone's face a final time. Even though not one of those hombres had become a trusted intimate, I still felt connected to them. Certainly it would have been more honorable to merely disappear. Just before I reached the door, however, the calypso singer, Manuel, began singing "So Long, Farewell," from "The Sound of Music." My guard tried to shush him, but that only made him sing louder. "So long, farewell, *auf wiedersehen, adieu…*" Soon the Top 40 specialist chimed in, and a few seconds after that, in a piercing descant that soared precariously above the other voices, came Callas herself. I turned and took in everyone's faces for as long as I could, before the guard shuffled me on my way, and reinforcements arrived to put a clamp on the ebullient cacophony. I was so moved that I couldn't cry.

And where was I going? Our ward was separated by labyrinthine corridors and two courtyards from the hulking, ominous prison proper. Every time we passed through the outdoors, I was sure that I would find my sister, or Andrea, or even you on the other side. I imagined how thrilling it would be to sleep in my own bed again and walk the streets of my New York neighborhood. The guard and I negotiated our way, and the air, even summery and sticky, was restorative. The only time I observed normal activity was when we walked past what looked to be a booking station. New inmates were being classified according to everything from crime to age to marital status. Previously, when I had caught sight of new inmates on my way to the courthouse, I felt sympathy toward them and the horror they were about to undergo. I also felt gratitude that at least I wasn't on one of their wards. Now—suddenly and sadly I realized that I was not only being kept at Morales but transferred to the other side—I was.

I was taken to a penalty cell.

"I want to see Benitez!" I shouted at the guard. "What the hell is going on?"

The guard merely shoved me into the cell with a little laugh, as if in silent silken revenge for some long-ago slight suffered at the hands of an American. I learned later that these cells were merely a way station to more permanent quarters, but at the time I was sure I was being tossed in the dungeon and forgotten.

Compared to that cell, a dungeon would have been a day on the strand. The cell had a dirt floor. It was only about five feet high, so I moved around with a stoop, not that I moved around much, since the enclosure was only about three feet wide. There was no mattress, only a tattered blanket and pillow: these were already home to colonies of fleas and ants, and they were not going to relinquish them without a fight. There was only a hole in the ground to relieve myself, and I wanted to do that as little as possible. I imagined myself a small rodent, disappearing down the small hole in the cell wall. (Until this time I had fantasized sporadically about burrowing a prison escape; I was an American and was soon going to be released.) Worst of all were not the crude deprivations but the lack of anyone within earshot. There was, in other words, no one to whom I could complain. And if one cannot complain and be heard, is one human?

I was sure that this point would be my lowest. Possibilities were gone. I would not live to be an old man. I would not sit in bed at 90, the only one of my generation who had reached such an age. I would not be an old man who still dreamed of getting it up, still dreamed of hitting a homer in the ninth inning of Game 7 of the World Series, who still waited for someone to throw him a surprise party or even just serve him breakfast in bed.

If I had been taken to the penalty cell upon my arrival at Morales, I should never have survived. I don't necessarily mean I would have died. I mean that I would have been shattered mentally. I would have been too concerned to maintain my dignity, both bodily and spiritually, and would not have allowed myself to sink into the pure animal state necessary to endure. Yes, I had become an animal. I spent the hours in fierce preying-mantis battles with the lice; I talked to them; shrieked with glee every time I smashed one against the filthy floor. I whistled like a bird, chattered like a monkey, roared like a lion. My behavior was Bedlam in miniature.

A week later a guard arrived, and we retraced the path through the prison back to my old ward, where Benitez awaited me in an office. He said Frogger had been called away on a family matter. He then apologized for the severity of my cell. My case was becoming much too conspicuous since the official's appearance, and it was "thought best" to keep me away from other prisoners so as not to "spread rumors."

"I am glad to know that I am considered important enough for the rumor mill. Is my case still making headlines in the U.S.? Is my sister going to be allowed to visit? How's Eduardo?" My volley of questions indicated my jagged, disoriented state. I was not lucid enough to display calm curiosity.

Benitez smiled wanly, failing to address my queries.

"Of course you realize by now," he went on, "that there has been a change in your situation."

"Huh?" I grunted. I tugged at my dirty, tattered prison uniform.

"There has been an extraordinary reversal of testimony at the trial."

I had been disappointed too often to feel joyful.

"Who has reversed himself?"

"Orlando."

"He has admitted that Eduardo never threatened Pepe in the first place?"

"He has admitted that Eduardo did not kill Pepe at all."

Benitez's statement was so preposterous that I imagined for an instant that he could only mean one thing: Pepe was not dead, and the trial had been nothing but a sham, a sick masquerade designed to humiliate your mother.

"He has testified that the killing was committed by you."

I suppose I could have protested that you yourself had admitted doing the killing, that everyone had agreed on that one fact. I could have pointed out that what little physical evidence there was pointed in the same direction. But that would have been obvious and pointless. I was much too worn out to attempt logic. Instead, as Benitez began to outline what he wanted, I thought of how the one thing I wanted was not beauty or money or even, please forgive me, someone for whom I, without exception, came first. What I wanted was freedom. Without that everything was only a concept.

"Has anyone else bothered to back up Orlando's testimony?" I asked. "Eduardo, for instance?"

"Eduardo says the same," he announced.

I gave myself excuses for you. You had to submit to pressure. You had no choice. You were no more responsible for recanting than those prisoners, so vacant-eyed, whom wartime enemies brainwash and put on television to denounce the cruelties of American imperialism.

"Did you torture Eduardo?"

"No," said Benitez, meandering into an assessment of who belongs to the "torturable class" and why.

"Does Eduardo know that by reversing his story both he and Orlando have committed perjury? I assume perjury is a concept understood even in a revolutionary court of law?"

"Perjury is only possible if the witness is acting freely, without pressure."

"And how am I supposed to have applied pressure to these boys?"

"To Eduardo, through your sick homosexual wiles. To Orlando, by his fear that if he said anything else, you or Eduardo would come after him."

Between him and his partner, I had always taken Benitez for the less dangerous fag-hater. As the word "sick" spilled over me, however, I realized that the more insidious homophobe had always been Benitez. His silence meant merely that the reservoir of vituperation was less frequently drained.

As Benitez mentioned more evidence against me, I wondered, *Was I so expendable?* Was the lobbying of my sister and the attention devoted to my case having no effect?

Benitez said that the Cuban system had no desire to prosecute me, even though what few relatives Pepe had would be upset if I were not convicted and executed. If I would sign a detailed confession explaining that I had been the one who had beaten Pepe to death, then every effort would be made to extradite me to my homeland. I thought "extradite" an odd verb to apply there, given that no witnesses to my alleged crime would be sent back with me to participate in a trial that an extradition in principle implied. It took me a moment, a moment in which the weak sunlight in the room suddenly flared and fizzled, to realize that I was being offered my release.

"What do you see as the likely scenario if I refuse to confess?"

"Is there another scenario?" Benitez asked. He got up, walked over the window and paused. "If you do not do as we say, you will undoubtedly face the death penalty."

I came close to leaping and tackling the man at the colossal injustice of this, even if he did carry a gun. I suppose it might be more satisfying for you to hear that I had tackled him. But if I said I attacked him, I would be lying, and the whole point of this letter is to see whether, after having lied so much (you lied the most dramatically, but certainly I have been false, too), I might not see whether sincerity can restore me.

At that moment, I thought I still wanted to see you again, and if I offended Benitez, that would certainly never occur. So I said, "I'll think about it."

My reply was so terse that I would not have been surprised if I had been taken back to a cell even more cramped than the hole in which I had spent the previous week. But, as if to soften my resolve, I was transferred to a lockup nearby the hole, which was more like my quarters in the political prisoners' ward. The cell even had a barred window. The inmates on this corridor immediately struck me as tougher than the songbirds I was used to; fewer canaries, more bull thrushes. One of them sang frequently, the same prisoner who tonight (it must be 4 in the morning by now) cries out in his sleep.

I spent the rest of the day turning over in my mind the abrupt change of events, seeking clarity but finding only chaos. You will no doubt be unsatisfied if at this point I still express no hate toward you (perhaps you think you deserve it; perhaps you do). But that would have helped nothing. I had such incomplete information that to direct all my energy toward cursing you might have made me feel retroactively foolish. (That's so like me, isn't it? I'm always anticipating my emotions.) Besides, Benitez's news relieved me a little. I cannot say why. Perhaps because a death that wasn't my fault had for so long felt somehow as if it were, and a death that now was my fault felt suddenly as if it weren't.

✳

The calm didn't last. Despite the wretched conditions of my imprisonment, I had managed to stay healthy. But that night I developed a fever. I slept badly. It was as if some tropical flu had finally caught up with me. Near dawn I fell asleep and dreamed of vast palm trees bathed in sunlight, deep rivers flowing alongside the branches, ships that drifted solemnly with the current, me sailing in all of them, waving to myself like someone saying farewell (to you?) or eager for an encounter (who next?)

I woke up, and the day, so slow in coming, arrived suddenly, like a door thrown open, the murmur of the prison merging vaguely with the noises of the city somewhere outside.

I felt my forehead. It was still bathed in sweat. I thought not of my temperature but of the moment at that Old Havana hotel with you, when the excitement of our first week had waned, as we are told is only natural, because nothing fades more rapidly than passion, and I was terrified of what dull routines would arise in passion's place. I did not want our relationship to evolve, I was caught in its grip, just as I was caught in the grip of a flu virus right there in prison, and I did not—most emphatically did not—want the fever to abate but thought only of how, were you there, I would have had an acceptable pretext to ask you for comfort, and how you, traitorous but attuned to my obvious longing to be treated and nursed like a child, would have obliged.

But then not you but Demosthenes arrived. I had expected the usual gruff guard to show up at my door that morning. But instead of a burly, surly sort, the kind that makes me realize once again that the difference between keeper and kept is only who turns the key, there was a tall young man with thick blond hair and few words. Demosthenes. Age 21. He came to bring me breakfast—for a few days then, I was kept apart from the other prisoners—and as he slid the bread and coffee through the bars of my cell he looked at my face and saw how little color must have been there.

"Sick?" he asked.

"Yes. The flu, I think."

He disappeared and a moment later returned with two aspirin and a rag and a cup of cold water.

"Take the pills with the water, and then wet the cloth and apply it to your forehead. That should help stanch the fever."

I wanted at once to know how someone capable of such a simple act of kindness could have ended up working in such a brutal environment.

"Thank you," I said. "Is this your usual ward?"

He nodded.

"Have you worked here long?"

He shook his head. His silence amused me: Once again a classical name was proving a misnomer—unless he had reserves of oratory that would make me yet believe him a proper Demosthenes.

He was wearing the usual dark-blue prison guard uniform, but his shirt had a big rip in the right shoulder.

"What happened to your shirt?" I asked him.

He pointed down the corridor, past a cluster of cells that I could not see clearly and were almost out of earshot.

"One of the other prisoners tore it?"

He paused, as if divulging an act associated with another of his charges would betray a confidence.

"I was unloading boxes this morning," he said, "and caught my shirt on the top of a handcart."

I had never observed guards doing much manual labor; in fact, I assumed they chose their profession precisely to avoid developing the sweaty brow of the cane hand or the furrowed brow of the warehouse worker.

"Do you have someone at home who can mend it?"

He shook his head: No.

Whether that meant he lived alone, which I thought was unlikely, given your country's housing policy, or with someone who was bad at darning was not clear.

"Your mother must know how to mend things."

"My mother is dead."

"Recently?"

"Last year."

I felt relieved by this information. He had experienced a recent adult loss; he had visited the other side. This was another reason to trust him. And when our trust did blossom, enough for me to enlist him in a scheme to smuggle letters out to Sarah, letters which were never answered, a little of my faith in the world was restored. I wanted to tell him the day we met how desperate I was to trust him, but that would have been so far outside the code for proper prisoner-guard behavior that I knew it would make him flee.

He fled anyway, but not before saying "Feel better."

✳

During the week, I received no visits from Benitez, nor any other communication concerning the disposition of my case. My concern about the future waxed and waned: I could wake up in the morning feeling calm and bright, certain that wheels of which I was unaware were turning vigorously, and that I would, despite being "convicted" as a "murderer," be freed before month's end; by nightfall I would be unimaginably anxious. I was sure Benitez was right: I was to be executed.

My new surroundings also contributed to my mood swings. This part of the prison where I have spent so many months now was much less secure than my previous ward. Criminal and political prisoners were mixed, although there was not much collegiality between them—to put it mildly. Sensing this, officials rarely allowed them to congregate at the same time in the small dim room that served as a recreation facility. In this way, volatility was lessened.

Though I was branded with a criminal offense, I was placed with the politicals for recreational purposes. In these times I got to know some of their stories. No doubt a few of them were exaggerated, but I got a general idea of how they were treated in this part of the prison, and how their treatment differed from that of the "criminals."

I have been ashamed to learn from these harshly treated men what I should have realized in the other part of the prison. But in my first ward, this other side felt at a safe remove; one heard of its harshness only second-hand. Now there was no way I could avoid confronting its reality and that reality's meaning—if "meaning" has a place in a world so devoid of basic human regard. The relation of meaning and suffering I thought I had figured out with Josh. There was not one, of course: Meaning derives from reflection, and reflection is the province of the healthy. The truth of this was made clear to me the evening I arrived home from work and found Josh in a physically wretched state. Entering the bedroom, I tried to cheer him up:

"I think you've been spending too much time figuring out just who's going to live on your block in Whore Heaven and it's tuckered you out."

"John, from here on out I'm no longer worrying if I'll make it to Heaven; I'm worrying if I'll make it to the bathroom."

But Josh's case had not taught me everything there is to know about suffering. Not by a mile. The suffering of those denied dignity, to say nothing of freedom of movement, seems to me equally devoid of meaning.

As I got to know the other men better in the weeks after I refused to cooperate and my capital fate started to become clearer, until the warden arrived yesterday and said cryptically, "Prepare yourself," of course I did not forget you. It certainly occurred to me that Benitez's revelation might be merely a tactic to elicit information from me and that your situation might be as precarious as ever. I nonetheless felt relieved at even the suggestion that you might soon escape detention—if you were indeed still locked up.

Even as I felt relief, however, another emotion sometimes traveled in its wake: fury. You might already be back walking along the Malecón with its caressing breezes, obnoxious traffic, and ostentatiously romantic couples; and here I languished in Havana's most notorious prison. I was reaching the point where the putting-myself-first pose had ceased to be interesting. Why do I think of a line from a movie, *Old Acquaintance,* that Andrea forced me to watch after calling and waking me up one night at 3 A.M.? Perhaps because in this scene Bette Davis, playing a beleaguered artistic novelist, says to a younger woman, "It's late, so late, and I'm very tired of youth and love and self-sacrifice."

Before my case deteriorated completely, I was visited again by Benitez. He came to my cell this time, an extraordinary concession given his aversion to the lockup. It was almost as if he himself had once been behind bars, and counted it a badge of his present situation never to have to revisit those painful days.

He entered the cell, glanced around for a place to sit, and, finding none except the bed where I was perched, decided to stand near the semblance of a window.

"Conditions have improved since I was last in one of these," he said.

"Fuck you."

"Do they have you mingling much with the other prisoners?"

I thought his choice of verb overly precious: Jail was hardly a high-school mixer.

"Sometimes during recreation periods we mix. But you know all this."

"I should, I suppose."

There was no coyness in Benitez's voice, and for once it occurred to me that he might not be privy to my entire situation.

"You could find out every movement of my day any time you wish," I said.

"I am told that you spend a lot of time pacing back and forth in your cell."

"How else am I to maintain my sanity now that my books have been removed?" I said. I could have added that, unlike most of my fellow prisoners, who had been given specific sentences and could mark off the days, hours, and minutes of their confinement, I had no imposed endpoint and thus had to make up my own goals daily.

"You could have a few of them back if you would write a confession."

Literary effort begat literary effort, in other words.

"I know. But there is no guarantee that such an act will gain me anything more. You have even threatened me with execution."

"What is it you seek in addition to the possibility of extradition?"

"I wish to see Eduardo again."

Benitez twisted his face into a mask of suffering, as if it were he, not I, who was daily deprived of dignity. I found his contortions funny.

"You know that is highly unlikely."

"No, I don't. Seeing Eduardo again has never been discussed as a condition of any agreement."

"Why do you want to see him again? Why not go back to your own country and leave him alone? He has said that you killed the boy."

"Haven't you ever been in a situation where the solution is clear to you and yet you find yourself unable to choose it?"

Benitez flinched.

"Of course I have. But that is not the point. You have disrupted more than one life by your obstinate conduct on this island. I think you might want to keep that in mind as you contemplate your next move."

"Cut the shit. Let's go back to my confession," I said.

"Your confession, yes. Why are you so hesitant?"

"Have you given me any reason to trust you?"

"The fact that you are still alive, that your relatives know you are alive."

I looked around at the cell—at the seatless brown commode, the little metal shelf over the rim, which held my tin cup and spoon. Through the makeshift window I thought I could see the branches of a palm tree stirring from a soft breeze. It was a mirage. There was no tree; it was hot, and sweat had created large concentric rings under Benitez's armpits.

"What will you provide for me if I promise you, right now, that I will write you a confession?"

"Favors don't pay for promises; they reward deeds."

"I think you should make an exception in this instance."

"Tell me the nature of the favor."

"It requires nothing except that you answer two questions."

"Why not turn me into a genie and ask for three?"

"Two will be sufficient."

Benitez stood at the edge of the cell, sphinx-inscrutable. Whether he would answer me straight or in riddles was not clear. I stood up, planted myself confidently against the wall and fired away.

"Have you received any more letters on my behalf from my sister or anyone else, and if you have, since I assume you read them, what do they say?"

"We have received several letters from your sister through her attorney. She and her—your—family are fine, and of course they are worried about you. But of course you know they have been told many times, the last time only a few days ago, that you are alive."

"What did the letters say?"

"As I've said, they express concern. They mention an American lawyer who has been working on your behalf with the State Department. They mention that your case has gotten press attention."

"Has anyone else written?"

"Is that your second question?"

"Yes."

"Some woman by the name of Andrea. Her letters are full of odd references. Attempts at humor, I imagine. We have had no contact with her. I assume she is in touch with your sister. Is this woman, this Andrea, your girlfriend?"

The question was posed without irony. Benitez was just macho— or naïve—enough to think that I could be fucking you and yet have a legitimate girlfriend back in America.

"Of a kind," I said.

He smirked: Andrea must be my mistress or my whore. I did not have the heart to tell him that she was merely—especially—my friend. In my experience, it is impossible to explain to most men how a friend of either gender can be so much more a part of one's life than a lover or a spouse. It was one more example of the "other side" syndrome. Either you had crossed over and required no explanation, or you had not, and did.

I was pleased by Benitez's cooperation, yet I found it surprising that I did not ask about where you were. I must have hoped that even an indirect inquiry would yield such information. I hesitated, framing the question in my head.

"What is my fate?" I asked him. A bonus question. "You mentioned, very cruelly and cavalierly, that the wheels are in motion for me to be executed. I've been tortured by thoughts of this in my cell for days."

"I must admit that I do not know. Your question certainly must be one that occurred to everyone involved with the case. Much is rumored, but who knows? I think in some ways it is preferable not to know. Then things might change."

I could not agree with Benitez that in this case it was better to have no firm knowledge. Prison had extinguished many things in me, but not my curiosity. The detective's praise of "not knowing," however, I found redemptive. Not to know whether God, love, or justice existed, or even whether one would wake up from any given night's sleep: What serenity there seems in that! In point of fact, all such uncertainties can be excruciating.

He and I talked for a bit longer of what form my confession would take. He was concerned only that it include certain facts: that I had been with you that night; that I had no knowledge of any animus you may have harbored toward Pepe or Orlando; that I became involved in the altercation only when I saw that Pepe had a knife; that my blows had been the final ones. Benitez did not care whether you had struck Pepe initially or not, only that I had finished the job. You had merely meant to scare the boys away, but I, enraged, wanted to kill the chief perpetrator. I had not come forward sooner because you, sure that your mother's connections would serve to get you off, had insisted that you yourself claim responsibility as the sole assailant.

(Forgive me if I do not here express resentment at being the fall guy. It was your giving me up that enrages me, not the result of it. Does that sound strange? The result, after all, may be my execution: Shouldn't my mind be concentrated, have been concentrated throughout this document, on that? Perhaps, but if I am killed this morning (and it is "killed," not "executed," since I did not commit, nor was I properly tried for, a capital offense), I at least will not have to live out my life bearing the scars of your treachery. I'm sure you would object that "treachery" is too strong a word. It isn't to me. I was the one who was to have made the sacrifice, and you took that satisfaction away from me. You robbed me of the only role I know how to play in the face of difficulty: the propitiator. You may have thought your deceit would save me; instead, it may destroy us both, or at least, since I will never talk to you again and do not want to seem presumptuous, destroy me.

Benitez's recital was such a tidy-sounding story that you'd never have guessed how much suffering had been necessary to compress all the facts. It was so horribly neat an explanation that remorse for the boy's life that had been taken welled up in me again, as overwhelmingly as it did when we were on the lam. Once Benitez, having promised to provide me with a supply of note paper, finally left, I walked over to the toilet and threw up. I never felt more remorseful. Not all the vomit made its way into the bowl, and as I sat against the wall of my cell, staring at the pool of human waste and struggling to collect my breath, I thought of how happy all those dogs around Andrea would have been at the sight of this feast, and how grateful I would have been, had any of these creatures appeared just then to keep me, a Lazarus, company.

✳

Of all that I have revealed to you tonight, perhaps for only the following will the gods truly curse me: I am about to break a promise to your mother. Yes, your sad, sweet, tough, elegant, brokenhearted mother paid a visit to my cell a few days ago, and asked me never to tell you she had done so. In breaking that vow I am all too aware of the irony: I berate you for your public infidelity and then turn around and smudge my own honor. This is a moral failing on my part; but, I remind you again, not one that will keep people in prison or possibly cost them their lives.

Her arrival at my cell that afternoon, in the company of two guards, wasn't a complete surprise. Although I hadn't given her much thought in prison, her appearance had a logic to it. After all, haven't you always said that she likes me? So there I was, immersed in one of my few remaining volumes (by a bad Communist poet); I felt a shadow fall into the space separating the leaves of the book; a voice, mellow and low, spoke; I looked up and there she was. I sensed that some of her coloring had gone since I last saw her, but her makeup was effectively applied so any facial dimming may have been a projection of my own undoubted prison pallor. She did not look at me with pity, for which I was grateful.

She was dressed in a simple yet superbly cut cotton suit, in the pale yellow of frozen butter. She had lost a little weight but still made quite an impression: So sharply was her behind cinched in her skirt I was surprised that whistles and hoots had not heralded her arrival for me as she passed through my ward's corridor. Perhaps the guards had cued the inmates to stifle themselves.

I hope it does not shock you to hear me refer to your mother as if she were just a common piece of ass: In fact, her effect on me was somewhat grander than that. It had been so long since I had interacted with a woman up close that I felt a sudden impulse to kiss her hand, even as my curiosity about her motive for coming inspired much baser impulses. As the guards let her into my cell and stood watch just outside, I expressed none of these feelings. I motioned for her to sit on the bed, and she accepted my offer. I stood near the windowless aperture in the wall.

"I suppose you must be wondering why I have come," she said.

"No. I'm wondering what took you so long."

"Well, my absence from the court must have told you something. I haven't been well; I've been away."

I intend no slight if I point out that my own mother, even if she had been breathing her last, would have crawled to court every day, oxygen tank in tow, if her son had been on trial. I suspected that this may have been your mother's nature, too; I wanted to understand her situation almost as much as I wanted to blame her for my predicament.

"What has been ailing you?" I asked, anxious to let her know I was not going to let remarks pass without elaboration.

"Asthma my whole life. It got so bad earlier this year that I had to leave Havana."

"I'm sorry."

Your mother crossed and uncrossed her legs nervously. The provocative gesture activated something primitive in me, reminded me of my sexual connection to you. For a moment, I wanted to strike her, to avenge all the pain I thought she had caused the both of us. When the impulse abated, I felt I could at least try to listen to what she had to say.

"I'm sure you must wonder if I've been responsible for everything. What has happened has had something to do with me, but any serious damage has not been of my choice. In fact, I've been working on your behalf."

She paused, like a clairvoyant waiting for a word or gesture that will allow the psychic reading to continue. I didn't move. Her story would have to unravel unaided.

"It is true that when I began to discover the nature of your relation with my son I was not pleased. He's all that I have. I didn't find out because of anything he has told me; while you were cutting sugarcane and he was away watching a boxing match one night, I found one of the letters you had sent to him from New York. I could hardly speak. I didn't confront Eduardo, though. When I calmed down I mentioned my concern to a colleague of mine in the Justice Ministry; he was the man you eventually saw in court. I never thought you'd leave the cane fields prematurely. I only hoped that when you finished your term you would be so apprehensive that you wouldn't want to linger long in Havana. When you came back to the capital, it didn't take me long to figure out you'd returned. Eduardo was so happy all of a sudden. Ever since his injury he'd been so glum, and then all at once the sun came out."

To hear your mother admit that I had given you joy: How happy that made me!

"My first impression of you was good, but I didn't want him to see you. But I thought, if I forbade it, he'd only run away. And then he ran away anyway because of that boy's death. I was so upset that Eduardo had vanished. I couldn't think clearly at first. For days I had no idea where you two might have gone. When I finally thought of Alma, I assumed the police would go down there, apprehend you, and bring you back to Havana to clear things up. Because the death seemed like an accident, Eduardo would be exonerated and you'd be shipped home. Then things got very complicated."

"Wait a minute. Did you think of Alma on your own? I thought Eduardo tipped you off that day when he called you."

"Eduardo didn't call me until after the arrest."

"That's impossible. He told me he called you."

"I'm telling you, John: He didn't call me."

I felt angry: Once again you deceived me. Blood rushed to my face. Who the hell had you phoned?

To my surprise, your mother had stopped talking. Her story had been proceeding at such a steady pace, however, that I saw no reason why her loquaciousness wouldn't resume.

Still, I reassured her. "Please, go on. Nothing you tell me at this point can affect you or me more adversely than what has already happened."

She took a deep breath. Her hesitancy was born of fear, but it was beautiful.

"Well, I guess you could say that I lost control. A higher power—and I'm not religious, so I think you can divine my meaning—intervened. I was obviously going to be punished for some past transgression. I still don't know what it was. The revenge would involve my son."

I sat there thinking: If this is true, there goes my conspiracy theory. I refer not to your leaving me vulnerable, but to my most paranoid prison scenario. In it, you never loved me at all but were your mother's agent to see if I were CIA.

"The first sign of my compromised position was the operation unleashed to capture you two. A helicopter—could you believe it? Somebody wanted no slip-ups."

"And then you weren't allowed at the trial. That must have been painful."

"Awful. I was kept under surveillance as I tried to calm my asthma. I expected the worst. I was so surprised when the trial turned away from Eduardo and toward you. I had nothing to do with that, but I hope you won't think me cruel toward you if I say I'm glad my son is being spared. I'm still not sure why you are being threatened with execution, but every time I've tried to do something for you, I have been told to shut up, or attention will revert to my son."

It was fascinating to hear all this, but I had to keep in mind that your mother is not the *dea ex machina* of this tale: She couldn't explain why I have been assigned a terminal fate.

"I've been more than threatened, Victoria. My execution has been hinted at for sometime next week."

Her face went ashen; she muttered, "I'm sorry." She must have sensed that her sympathy would do nothing to help me and that my good feeling toward her was in danger of dwindling. She veered away from my external situation and back to you.

"I hope my story has put a few things in perspective. But that's not the primary purpose of my visit."

"What is?"

"It may sound crazy, even a little obscene to you at the moment, but I've really come to speak to you about the future."

"You have a real sense of gallows humor, don't you, Victoria?"

"What do you mean?"

"I mean that if I'm released rather than 'executed,' I'm going to be escorted immediately to the airport by men with guns. I don't think you need to worry that your son and I will run off together. And since it's unlikely he'll be let off the island anytime soon, I don't think you need worry that he and I will set up housekeeping in New York."

"Eduardo's behavior lately has shown me that he is capable of anything."

"So what are you asking of me?"

She was quiet for a moment. In this interval I thought for some reason of my own mother, who had a similar habit of taking long pauses before crucial statements. I thought of my own mother in a pink surgical gown, wasting away on a hospital bed, and I felt suddenly solicitous of you on the day that your mother dies. Prematurely,

I express my condolences. How many of them we have in our hearts, the dead! Each of us carries his own cemetery-full.

"I'm asking you to give up your connection to him. To sacrifice those feelings."

"You're asking me to give him up forever?"

"Yes."

"Do you have any idea how hard that would be? Do you have any idea how much I love him?"

"I know that it would be hard, but you're handsome and young enough to find someone else in New York."

"Please don't say that. It's Eduardo I love."

"You know that he's a man, and like most men his eye tends to wander."

"But why should I give him up?"

"Because a mother is asking you to."

I've spent years and years trying to reach a place where I no longer do things primarily to please my mother, or her voice speaking to me in memory, yet there I was, inexorably succumbing to the notion that I must do something to please yours.

"How can I forget him? Even if I told him I didn't love him, he wouldn't believe me."

"Then refuse to see him. Benitez has arranged, as part of extracting your confession, for Eduardo to come visit you. Promise me you won't see him. It will be easier on you."

"Please leave."

"What?"

"Leave. I'll think about what you've asked."

"Thank you."

She called to the guards, and got up to go. (If you're thinking that I refused to see you yesterday in deference to your mother, you're wrong. My reasons will very shortly come clear.) There were so many things I probably should have asked her as she left—if she could phone my sister and say I was OK, if she could work on the cause of my clemency. But I said nothing further. Until now. Then,

I merely touched her hand and watched as she disappeared down the corridor.

✳

"John, wake up."

It was afternoon; another day had passed; I had dozed off after hours of wondering about my fate. I had drifted gratefully into sleep. Once again, in prison sleep provided my only real comfort. Each time I surrendered to it, I had the sensation of surrendering to a companion. It was particularly welcome when dreamless (one could say that every day sleep awakens us from life). And even when it leaves us, it takes several seconds to remember all our sufferings.

That afternoon, the remembering took a little longer, because the voice rousing me belonged to Demosthenes. His presence had become more and more welcome. This annoyed me somewhat; I had spent so much time staring straight ahead at you that, without quite realizing it, I had boarded myself up against anyone else entering my inner sanctuary.

What saved Demo for me was my lack of sexual attraction to him. Don't misunderstand me: If he had offered, I would have accepted. After all, deprivation demanded contact. But I would not have accepted out of passion, direct or sublimated. I would have done so out of an altogether odder obligation: friendship. I do not remember when I first realized that this is what Demo and I now shared. We cannot tell the precise moment when friendship is formed any more than we can pinpoint the millisecond at which we fall asleep. As in filling a vessel drop by drop, there is at last a drop that makes it run over; so in a series of kindnesses, there is at last one that makes the heart overflow.

My relations with Demo were marked by a feeling of having been coaxed back to health only after months of strict attentiveness. Demo did not ask "How are you?" every morning out of habit. He paused before the first and second words of a greeting, a caesura that conveyed genuine concern. Long after I had recovered, he slipped me all manner of things—vitamins, extra food, water—to ensure my well-being. Every one of these gifts comes back to me now like a vanished thought; a shy, slightly troubling confidence, like soft music you have to listen to in order to hear it. To convey them all, I would have to write in whispers. But, then, isn't that what I have been doing here all along?

So I developed a profound attachment to the jailer. What could be less resistible than someone who nurses you? I remember when I was in the hospital in New York for a week once with pneumonia (as you know, I am HIV-negative, but upon hearing my diagnosis people assumed the worst), and how the frequency with which people showed up to visit permanently altered my attraction to them. Josh, dear Josh, took time off from work, so his place in my affections remained secure. Andrea came next: I thought she would be kept away by her extreme self-involvement and aversion to bedpans, but no: She arrived every morning with flowers. There were other people—good friends, I had thought—who found multiple reasons for not showing up. Many of these were understandable, but try as I might to understand them, I could not. We try not to gauge affection by anything so grossly quantifiable as the number of hospital visits. But we do gauge. We do.

Be assured that Demo did not replace you in my deepest, most complex affections. He did, however, do something else. He showed me that perhaps you might not have mortally wounded me after all: If I survived, there would be others who would have an interest in me and whose interest might blossom, if not into emotional fidelity then at least into genuine, honest regard. After Josh, I had wondered the same thing: Would others still find me attractive? I thought you had been the healer.

Demo at first did nothing more than bring me news of the outside world. In a country with controlled media, you might think: What could he possibly know of truths beyond the island? But of course such an attitude is only the arrogance of those who come from countries where media is controlled in other ways. Demo's news was not the sort that fills time slots on CNN, although if I pressed him, I was able to learn where wars, famines, hurricanes had happened lately. His news was of a more natural, less fear-inducing order. Had it been a good season for tomatoes and corn, was the Havana baseball league loaded with talent this year, or did this week's games give grounds for worry? His news displayed a deep connection to the rhythms of daily life, rhythms that, unlike those of prison, were natural and relaxed rather than enforced and unnerving.

About a week after he first brought me aspirin, Demo brought me something else that without authorization would have been considered contraband: a few of my belongings. Nothing conspicuous; nothing that could not easily be hidden in my mattress. A few photos from my wallet; a leather belt Josh had given me; a newspaper clipping announcing, with a photo of you, your latest triumph in the ring: That was all. I asked him why he had brought the items, and he shrugged his shoulders. The next morning, however, he confessed that, when his mother died, the only things that had eased her out of this world into the cold earth were photographs of her family and a few figurines. He thought I should enjoy the same courtesy.

I was startled to hear this. It was the grand compassion associated with someone in intensive care or on death row, not someone who was about to compose the confession that would ensure his liberation. I told myself I had mistaken his intentions. Surely my situation was no longer precarious, and his gestures were signs of generosity, not pity. But when a day, then two passed without Benitez coming to see me, and without anyone providing me the pen and pencil with which I was to write my confession, I began to wonder whether I had been condemned and Demo had been sent along as my death angel.

Such a person (I say angel in the most figurative sense) always appears. The person is almost never a member of the family, rarely even a longtime friend. Whether nurse or neighbor, chaplain or shaman, the angel shows up and commits acts of compassion that, unconnected to personal history, have simple, powerful effects on the ill one. A spiritual hypodermic, these acts usher in immediate results. With Josh, the angel had been someone from his office, a young woman who brought over some documents one night and was a daily visitor until the end. My father's angel had been a cleaning lady; she was sent to replace the woman who had worked for our family for years but who could not confront the evidence (blood, bowels, boils) of her longtime employer's decline.

Like all angels I have known, Demo's gestures had a slightly ghoulish tinge to them. Why, for example, should he have brought me my belt? Prisoners' garb requires no fastening; we were denied even slim ties or shoelaces, for obvious reasons. Was the provision of a belt Demo's version of the cyanide tablets slipped to soldiers about to drop down behind enemy lines, to ensure that if they were captured they would have a sure exit before divulging state secrets?

Strange to say, but until the arrival of that belt I had given no thought to suicide. Though I had always believed it to be a potentially rational choice, some vestige of Protestant training told me it was a sign of sickness. I looked on life with the indifferent eye of the sick person. I thought, *Why spoil the suspense by choosing the last moment myself?* I forgave myself my faults, just as I hoped my family and friends would forgive me after my death. I no longer reproached myself for being excessively moved by human beauty, for having risked everything to have another look at your face.

Demo divined this mood in me. He never pushed our conversation to the point of asking too much personal information. It was as if he could treat me with sympathy only if he knew nothing intimate about me. I speak of my history, of course; in prison, he knew everything. He knew when I had to shit before I did.

One morning a few months ago, Demo said that Benitez had arrived at the prison that morning but, before coming to see me, had been suddenly called back to his headquarters.

"Did he give a reason?"

"Why should he give a reason?" Demo said. "Benitez is an investigator. He does what he wants."

There was such contempt in Demo's voice that I thought he must have done time or at least been subjected to serious investigation. Nothing in his narrative, though, corroborated my hunch. Though he was in authority, he himself seemed to despise it.

Demo finished work each day around 5 in the afternoon. He only came to see me in the morning, though, so when he arrived at the cell the day after Benitez's aborted visit, just after his shift finished, I was surprised. He was excited; he had something in his hands.

"Sugar cake from my sister. I thought you'd like some."

We both knew that guards were forbidden to give provisions of any kind to prisoners; we both also knew that the regulation was flouted all the time. Money, though, was usually involved, and Demo made no mention of a kickback.

He passed the piece of cake to me. It was covered in a white cloth. I insisted that he share it with me. He protested, but finally took half.

We stood less than a foot away from each other, separated by bars, munching the sweet crumbly confection. I suppose the bars should have made me feel sad, spoiled the moment, but they did not.

"It's delicious," I said. "Is your sister a good cook in general?"

"Yeah. Ever since my mother died she's done all the cooking in the family."

"Do you cook?"

Demo looked at me as if I'd asked whether the moon were purple.

"So your sister lives with you?"

He paused. "Yes."

I suppose I should have felt grateful that someone so softhearted—for though I knew Demo's job required him to be potentially brutal, I needed to think him kind—had a culinary sister to look after him. Instead, I thought only of what such an arrangement might require him to sacrifice: his privacy. Never would he have an evening when he could entertain a lady friend. I hoped his sister, like that of the crazy cop with whom I had first crashed in Havana, made outings to country relatives.

As if to retaliate for my prying, Demo posed an equally invasive question. "What about you? Do you have sisters?"

"One. She lives in Connecticut."

"What about the boy here in Havana, your friend, the one who everyone says was your accomplice in the crime?"

I was disappointed that Demo described the fatal night as a "crime"—should I have disabused him of that notion, or did I command more respect if I was thought somehow criminal?—but heartened that he had chosen to ask me about you instead of only my blood relatives.

"Well, he's a boxer. A champion boxer." I was still so proud of you then.

"Where has he competed?"

I enumerated your career, such as I remembered it. In fact, I know it very sketchily. Only two bouts can I describe in any detail.

It was at this realization, of just how little I knew you, that I hatched my plan. How little I knew you: That's a partial untruth. I know the smell of your breath, dry and slightly sour in the morning, sweet at noon, acrid at night; I know the lines in both your palms, intricate as your footwork in the ring; I know the sound of your feet, soft and determined when shod, cavalier and clumsy when not. I know your skeleton. But of the skeletal history of your achievements, I remain in the dark. Though you shared them with me often, I have let them pass through my mind's sieve. But that is why I devised the plan. I would write two confessions: one in which I would halfheartedly relate to Benitez and the security system what they wanted to hear, and one in which I would explain myself to you. Should the system betray me and decide to do me in, I did not want the guilt of not having unburdened myself fully to follow me to the gallows. And, as I've implied throughout this document, I could never have made this outpouring in person.

But to whom could I entrust such a document, should the worst occur? Such a letter was not likely to be brief and easily squashed into the bottom of a shoe. Who could lug such a tome forth from these walls? Demo.

But how would I ask him?

"Demo?" I felt as nervous as a schoolboy at his first dance.

"Yes, John?"

I looked at him for a moment, trying to telegraph my request silently, to spare myself the embarrassment of having to say it aloud. I thought of all the phenomena forever out of our sight—bacteria, viruses, pheromones, radio waves, the ozone—and wondered if not just the intent but the details of a request could be transmitted wordlessly.

Then Demo said, "You have something you want me to do, don't you?" and I became a believer. (Dawn may now be gathering, but there is still no need to call a priest.)

I paused. The only problem with having him as the potential courier of my mini-memoir was that he would inevitably be a character in it, and I wasn't sure if I wanted him to read it out of curiosity and stumble over some semi-sexual reference to the brush of his hand across my thighs. I remember how mortified I had been to come across the contents of a college roommate's journal and find small sharp remarks about me piercing the notebook's soft vellum cover. "Webster insufferable! Webster a complete asshole! Webster once again insensitive beyond words!" What if Demo took similar umbrage? What a fight there might be! I could just imagine: Me climbing the scaffolding and his hot sweaty hand reaching up from below the stairs to exact revenge.

"Yes, Demo," I said, "There is something I wonder if you'd do for me."

He listened.

*

The night after I made my deal with Demo, I slept peacefully, interrupted only by a dream in which you and I made love in a pastoral setting: a calm at odds with my confused, resentful feelings toward you otherwise. Around 10, Benitez showed up to visit. One trip to my cell, however, had apparently been enough. We met in a common room up front.

The detective paced around at first, starting and stopping conversation. For a minute, we sat for a while in silence. To lessen my anxiety, I smoothed my hair out with my hand; this was easy to do, since prison rules allowed me to wash it only once a week, leaving it full of grease.

He handed me a sheaf of loose-leaf papers and some pencils.

"I hope you understand the importance of making a complete confession," he said. "Otherwise nothing will proceed as I've outlined."

I said I understood. (I will spare you having to read the actual text I submitted a few days later; compared to this letter, wouldn't that confession be beside the point?)

"Do you really understand? Do you know that if you don't do what we've agreed, who knows what will happen to you? You will disappear, and everyone would simply think you had vanished for good into the nether regions of the prison."

I said that everyone knew what prison I was in and that if I disappeared, I could be said to be have been stabbed by some deranged inmate, and true enough, no one could do anything about it. No matter how many news stories had bannered my name back in the U.S.

"It is my duty to tell you," Benitez said, "that, despite what I've been promising will happen if you confess fully, something may go wrong; the worst can happen: You may be kept in prison or even—I must say it, though I don't want to—be executed."

Though the thought of execution had made me nearly sleepless for more than a week, I was still unwilling to show Benitez that I felt fear.

I absorbed his announcement and said, "What is the second thing?"

"That I have a communication for you—from Eduardo. Here."

I took the letter back to my cell but did not read it right away. Just as on that first morning in your apartment, when you and I had held rather than ravaged each other, I delayed the gratification. I knew that this would increase my anxiety about the letter's contents, but I had so staked my life around the doctrine of not knowing that I decided, *What the hell—after so many months, why not adhere to my principles a while longer?*

Besides, while in jail I had grown so accustomed to a certain view of our relation that I did not want to discover that it had been spoiled by a few strokes of the pen. It wasn't the notion of us as a serenely loving couple that your communiqué threatened; that had been jettisoned long before. It was, rather, the reverse: me as a romantic soul who had been abandoned. Strange: I never liked myself more than in those moments of reverie when I imagined myself cast aside.

After supper that evening of Benitez's last visit, I took advantage of the half-hour allotted to me in the hellhole of a rec room. I had tried to keep my nose clean so as not to cause trouble with the other inmates, but the fact of having a cell to myself had produced bad feeling anyway.

I lasted only a few minutes in the rec area. I could wait no longer to read your letter. I went back to my cell, sat against the wall, and to the soundtrack of shouts coming from the rec room and a belching contest from the unit next door, consumed it. Forgive me if I insert it here. You don't have to reread it, of course. But you may want to, before you look over what follows. I'm also placing it here because I have no desire to take its pages with me, should my life be spared. I want no concrete reminder of our time together. Though I no longer want to see you, I remain a believer in at least the symbolic value of our time together, and like any believer, I want no material evidence to color my conclusions.

Dear Johnny Baby,

I've been sitting in my bedroom these many weeks. First, I was in an empty apartment, unable to exit. I stare out my bedroom window at the café across the street, the café where, well, you know. I try not to sit too long. I don't want to get fat, man. So I get up often, to do pushups, work with my dumbbells, jump rope. The downstairs neighbors hate the noise. In a prison about all you can do is exercise. But why am I telling you about prison? You've been in a real one all this time. Is Morales as bad as they say? Alma's oldest son (Alma's fine, by the way) was in that prison for a few years. But he never talked about it.

Oh, Johnny. It was so strange to see you in court those days. I was more scared for you than for me. You should at least have had your family there, for moral support. I didn't have my mom in person, but at least I was getting letters from her every day. I kept waiting for it all to be over so we didn't have to face each other like that anymore. Then I thought we would have a chance to hang out.

Now I guess I should cut to the chase. What happened that night was a tragedy—for Orlando, for his loved ones. But also for us. I see now that we should have come clean about it from the beginning. Running away like that made us feel that we shared a big secret. And maybe even that for a while we had a shared destiny. But what we did was wrong. Our actions resulted in the death of someone, and won't it be more difficult for our love to continue because of that?

My mother returned home not long ago. She looks a lot better. I thought she would have been worn out from worry, but instead she seems refreshed. She says that it was good for her to be removed from the noise of Havana for a while. Now that she is back, she once again wants to turn her full attention toward fulfilling the goals of the revolution. "The goals of the revolution": I know you'll laugh a little when you read that. You're suspicious of all revolutions, of the crimes that are committed in their name. But you do not disbelieve in them. No, you're too ardent a personality for that. You are a man of great passions, Johnny Baby. That is why people are drawn to you, and also what gets you into trouble! Even my mom says so.

I know you won't like the easy tone of this letter. Does it reflect what you like to call my "boyish indifference"? Why does everyone find fault with the good things about me, even my maturity? Why does everyone underestimate me just because I am a teenager? Even you do. Don't you know? I love you in my own way. Perhaps less than you do me. But I do love you, Webster. You are the first man I ever hit the road with. Before you, no man had ever stared at me with such a true, tender intention. Our times en route were the best days I've known. Ever.

There's something else I need to say. I've been afraid to all along. But I have to now. That day at the post office, when I said I called my mother? Well, I didn't call her. I called my friend Maria, the mulatto girl we saw in the park that horrible night. We barely spoke to her then. I didn't want you to get upset. I mean, she's more than my friend; she's now my girlfriend. She wasn't really my girlfriend while we were together. I'm not that cruel! But since I've been confined to the apartment, Maria's been allowed to visit, and we've been talking. About many things, the way you and I do. I feel close to her, and, yes, we've done it. Had sex, I mean. I enjoyed it. I was surprised I did, since I thought I could only really enjoy it with a guy. But with her, well, something happens. Her skin is smooth, her fragrance wonderful. I want those sensations to continue. She has thick, jet-black hair and brown eyes. You'd like her. I'd like you to meet her.

They tell me our court case is going to be wrapped up soon, and then you'll be going home to New York to see your sister and Jackson and Andrea. When the case is settled, all I want to do is go to Coppelia Park, listen to the car radios, and have some ice cream. I'll begin plotting my next visit to New York, all the things we can do together, if you still want to see me. Mostly, though, I want to study and to box. Did you hear that since my hand healed I've won all my fights?

I guess that's all for now.

See you soon,

Your friend Eduardo

Many things flew through my head after I read your letter. They are the same things that fly through my head now, proving, I suppose, that reaction and reflection can sometimes be the same.

I was not disturbed that you have so matter-of-factly accepted the need to reassign responsibility for Pepe's death. You know that your blows were the lethal, the only ones. Why, however, are you so accepting of the falsehoods that have been pressed on you by the authorities? For so long you appeared to be considerate, kind, dependable: a trinity of qualities that, so blinded was I by the their presence in an 18-year-old (by their presence in anyone!), I mistook as signs of moral clarity. To find that you are, after all, transparent in your application of ethics is dispiriting. In saying this I do not reveal some outmoded bourgeois standards; for you, I thought, as for me, loyalty was the revolutionary virtue par excellence, and how can you be loyal to a person if you could so blithely betray the truth? Of course, it occurs to me that in glossing over this matter you may merely be adhering to some higher principle. Namely, that saving my skin is more important than telling the truth. This thought, oddly, provides no comfort.

It was in mulling over your unstated motives that I was forced to consider whether I should believe anything in the letter at all. Perhaps I should treat it as the work of an unreliable narrator: You were under duress and nothing you say can be taken at face value. This possibility unnerved me briefly. But then I realized that whoever vetted your letter would have seen through so elementary a tactic. Besides, it is more tantalizing to accept you at your word: Assuming you are sincere gives me more grounds to suffer. More retrospective meaning! You wronged me, and you cannot even talk about it. How weak.

If your half-cheering, half-discouraging tone had been the brainstorm of some investigator determined to drive me to confession, the move was brilliant. If the letter had been only lovey-dovey and too much when-will-I-see-you, I might have considered confession unnecessary and settled back into complacency, awaiting the day when you would show up at my cell to turn the key. If the letter had been terse and chilly, it would have had a similarly dampening effect. To deny me any satisfaction would have increased my resolve to provide no satisfaction to the authorities. But by interspersing your letter with tokens of affection, you ensure that I'll want to see you again.

I'll cooperate with you, as I have with the authorities. I'll gain my freedom, perhaps even see you again. Little did I know that, tonight, awaiting my sentence, I would not want to. That I would instead still be seething.

I resented how little compassion you evinced for my imprisonment. True, you did not wallow in pity about your own confinement. But you were kept at home; I had endured deprivations of the damned. I also resented you for not envying me my situation. What? you ask. Why would you possibly do that? Because at some sea-deep level I have learned things—about you and me both—during my jail time. I won't say, however, that it has given my life suspense, even though the fact that, as I write this sentence, I still await the outcome of another kind of sentence indicates otherwise. I certainly don't believe that at some subconscious level I wanted to be locked up. In any narrative of confinement, cruel-hearted readers will always look for the moment when a minority character shows self-pity so they can cry "Ha! Once again, the minority story is about prisoners and victims." It doesn't occur to them that an identification with any powerful person or idea is a strategy for not giving in to victimhood. Certainly, I had fallen into this class. During my first weeks in prison, I was sure that to desire anyone would desecrate my spirit and to consort with the jailers would compromise my sense of dignity. Where had this strategy gotten me? I was horny all the time, and until Demo appeared I was unable to allow anyone to help me. But of course how could you understand any of this? You've been too busy pining for Maria.

You mention her in your letter quite matter-of-factly, cruelly insensitive to how her existence might affect me. With that bit of news you have wounded me. I've wept. Did you think I would stop thinking about you if a woman entered the picture? This would merely be an example of what I might call the affectional fallacy, with which our age has been so obsessed that future generations will think we went mad. The fallacy—that one's identity depends crucially on the gender of what one fancies—is ingrained in us now as irreversibly as the scent of Winstons in wool, and will be even harder to get out. (Of course, I am talking about the heart here; the politics of preference, designed to combat oppression, are another matter.) One's patterns of loving have always seemed to me less a matter of identity than of freedom of expression. It does not take a historian, even one as expert as you, to realize that throughout time sexual acts and tendencies have varied very little. What changes is the layer of lies surrounding them. If you went off with a Maria, you might fool others, but you would not fool me. Just because she's pregnant and you brought her along to the prison yesterday to underscore that fact, doesn't mean your hard-wiring has changed.

You can't imagine how crushed I feel, and how dubious about your prospects. I know that if you end up marrying her (that your future may not be entwined with mine: I can hardly believe I've finally said that), it will be to become an official parent. Why do I shudder for this child? (Why wouldn't I, like the Shakespeare of the sonnets, want my beloved to transmit his beauty to another before he dies?) Perhaps because I fear that the child is, despite what you say, the product not of love but of convenience. True, once the child is born your marriage might blossom a little. Your relation with Maria will once again become sweet and no longer require any passion. Your passion will once again focus outward. You'll cruise Coppelia, looking not for Maria but for Mario. I see you returning from one of these wayward outings and being led into the nursery to say good night to the peaceful child. Why do I feel sad at the prospect of this infant's image? Aren't infants supposed to bring us joy?

If your choice of gender did not undo me, your desire to be faithless did. I feel a twinge of sympathy now for a friend of mine, whose husband left her for a man, and who said that it was not the homosexuality that bothered her; it was the treachery. I know that we had sworn no eternal pacts, yet each day we had spent together harmoniously had seemed to me the implicit building of a bond, of which the fidelity played a part, and of which uttered oaths would have been spoiling. In fact, the power of what I feel, have felt, flows from our silence on the subject. Our fidelity was based on a silence that grew and grew. I realize now how mistakenly one can interpret a silence. In my first prison ward, men kept equally silent about just how spiritually stifling our conditions were. But at least we could express this silence, render up all the sadness it contained, because we had music. Music expressed our heavy hearts, without us having ever to explain why.

I can, I think, overcome my fury at your faithlessness, though not at your bringing Maria with you to prison yesterday. (Talk of "Prince and his girl," I guess, was not merely code.) This gesture was why I refused to see you: I cannot lend my support to it. In my sadness I try to be understanding. I try to accept what your youth dictated: that I would not be the only one. Certainly, I flattered myself that in me you had found your one and only; Josh had met me when he was barely older than you, and hadn't he remained constant, more or less, till the end? Part of me acknowledged, however, that there would be others after me or, perhaps, during me. You were not even out of your teens and were driven by that lust that your age confers. How could I satisfy you? Why would I want to? The truth is, I didn't want to. To be your only stud was a responsibility I pursued only temporarily. I wanted to be your main partner—sexually, emotionally, even domestically, or so I fantasized, despite the cultural and geographical odds against that—but not necessarily the sole provider of stimulus. By being silent on that subject, I thought we had an understanding there, too. I didn't mind the idea that our lust would evolve into compassion; I remember my great-uncle George once saying of sleeping with my great-aunt Marie: "I do not feel anything when I brush up against my wife's legs, but mine ache if hers do." I imagined our relationship would become rather like what one has with a simpatico feline: In the evening, the cat ventures forth to the yard, the attic, the other room, to do what he must do, but he always returns at bedtime to be stroked, to nestle next to you, or at dawn to awaken you, just like a man, whiskers rubbing against your chin. If I can already imagine that love receding, like the view from the back of a tunnel-traversing train, and can begin to contemplate a day when my fascination for you will seem rather puzzling, I will not pretend that, whatever our apparent incompatibilities, you were never really my type. You will be my type as long as beauty and sex and a sense of history, to say nothing of good manners and high spirits, continue to have a hold over me.

How pathetically long I have gone on about your brief letter! I am not even sure you have been allowed to express yourself freely in it, and still I respond, as if every word were a bloodstain smeared across a cave wall, and true. Even if your words are not authentic, and all my words are just Talmudic tugging on a suspect text, one thing you wrote I absolutely know is accurate: your saying you don't know me. During this entire letter, I have felt a duty to respond to that. How could you know me? So much of our time together was spent worrying about who might lurk in the next bend in the road, and when we were not thus fretting, we were, contrastingly, enjoying sensual (if misleading) silences together. But I can enjoy such silences no longer, which you might by now have guessed is another reason why I could not have stood to see you yesterday: There would have been too many of them. (Unlike now, when the silence of a prison dawn has been broken by voices in the corridor, one of them a woman's. Andrea? Sarah? Has American diplomacy triumphed?) The fact that we conducted our affair mostly in your country meant that you were always explaining Cuba rather than Eduardo, and in New York I was so busy extolling the scenery that I never got around to me. (It sounds like my sister. And an official of some sort.) All these things, it appears, conspired to deny you my narrative. (It *is* my sister, and she's addressing the man with her as "Congressman.") No more. By the time you read this, I will, it appears, be free. If it wasn't presumptuous, I would say that you have my forgiveness; but it is not you who have made a confession. That act has been mine. I have confessed; I have told my story.

I must place these pages underneath my pillow. They're here.

✳

I know that you will never read what I am about to write, but I am going to address it to you anyway. Maybe David, who is sleeping in the other room, will come across this journal-like entry and find it a sign that I am finally putting Cuba behind me. Or maybe I will tear up these jottings as soon as I have set them to paper.

This month, December, there have been parties every evening after work, and I find myself attending every one of them. Tonight, I stumbled out of the office into the cold outdoors, speedy and self-aware with drink, just as theatergoers were crowding out of restaurants onto the sidewalk for the collective push toward some ultimate 8 o'clock curtain. I'm not sure why I have been so hungry for good cheer this season; perhaps because I have found a new job, at last one I like, and am trying to display my feelings publicly; perhaps because after avoiding Christmas for so many years, first because of my Jewish boyfriend, then because of latent Scroogism, I am attempting to compensate; or perhaps because after so much effort spent trying not to turn into my holiday-loving father, I have unconsciously jelled into a reasonable facsimile of him anyway, at least at Yuletide.

The job I have taken for a giant media company in midtown Manhattan seems a suitable compromise between the warring factions of my spirit: the restless, occasionally loony piece vies constantly with the side that longs to be kept off the streets at 3 o'clock (A.M. or P.M.). My satisfaction at work also has to do with the agreeable camaraderie I find there. A collection of mellowing rebels, my division, which is devoted to public relations for high-tech products, on most days reminds me that I am not alone in my metaphysical dissatisfaction, nor in my desire to discipline it by means of a regular paycheck.

After work tonight, I made my way over to a little bistro in the West 40s. I took my time, marveling at the way rushing individuals surrender their individual gaits in deference to those of the mass. I cleaved to the section of the sidewalk nearest the buildings. The night air, so wetly cold that it stung the sinuses like a rapidly gobbled Italian ice, took the edge off any slight egg-noggy inebriation.

David—olive-skinned, short, slightly overweight—was already seated at the restaurant. As the maître d' led me across the room, I caught my boyfriend's eye and laughed heartily, as if I'd just heard a joke I couldn't wait to share with him. This joviality wasn't the effect of alcohol only. Slowly, nonalcoholic spirits have been seeping into me since escaping your country two years ago. Just after my return, I felt as if some inner sentinel had been standing guard, strictly prohibiting any joy, but now that it has relaxed its watch, I find I am again able to savor the daily absurdities that continually parade past me.

The bistro wasn't exactly my favorite. We settled on it as a compromise: David wanted to go somewhere fresh, bustling, and French; I desired hamburgers and quiet. So we ended up at Raoul's: nominally Lyonnaise and nearly new. The pre-theater diners had left, and the restaurant's emptiness moved me. I have always been stirred by places the crowd has left behind.

David stood and hugged me, and my warm glow increased. Like so much else about him, his greeting was direct. A kiss on the mouth would have struck me—and you, too, I'm sure—as too pointed a display of affection, and a handshake would have constituted a kind of lie. An embrace expressed a confident relation between us, while leaving open the possibility of a more private intimacy. There is, I must tell you, something warmly restful about this man, whom I met through a friend. After the jolting berths and rickety transfers of you and the two or three guys who came afterward, I think I am finally breaking the post-Josh pattern of fear, need, and humiliation. Most mornings now as I shave, I think, *How lucky I am to have David,* not least because there is something sweet and soothing and above all necessary about reliving the dramas of my past with someone as generous and funny and not quite handsome as he is. If he had had no real interest in my history, I could never have fallen for him; with someone unmindful hanging about, the days when memories of you and Josh overwhelmed me would have been too painful.

Why? Because if I had thought that writing our story (and let's be frank: though I hate to call it therapeutic, my prison confession was more for me than for you) would have freed me from it, I was mistaken. Ironically, if the Cuban events had remained with me in the fast fashion with which they had unfolded, I might have been able to make my peace with them sooner. But they coalesced more slowly around the purer, more powerful conclusion that was much more difficult to discard. However your action was intended, I could no longer even think of rationalizing it. It was simply an act of betrayal.

I sat down at the restaurant table and took an immediate swig from the vodka martini that David had taken the liberty of ordering for me. Such small considerate gestures are typical of him. At first I'd resented what they symbolized, thinking that accepting them would consign me to a premature domesticity (how long before we take up bridge? plant a garden? acquire cats?). But I am learning to view his behavior more gratefully. With him, perhaps acceptance is not, as I used to fear, just a kind cover-word for resignation. My sister is encouraging my efforts here. "Don't take David for granted," she counseled me on the phone a few nights ago when I confided my feelings to her. I told her that I am afraid that being with David is just a little too safe: a predictable retrenchment. It suggests all too natural a pattern. In one of my prison books I read that societies also have these vital rhythms: periods of the cult of youth are followed by periods marked by the veneration of old age; the exaltation of motherhood and the home are followed by free love; war and the hunt are trailed by the contemplative life. But my personal oscillations suggest a less pendular pattern. Just as with you I combined introspection with intensity, so perhaps with David I can meld meditation with mirth. Sarah certainly thinks so, and since the day when she won my release from prison, through a magnanimous, persistent enterprise mind-boggling in its maneuverings, I have tried to be better at heeding her advice.

Even as I have gotten progressively worse at listening to Andrea, especially her thoughts about my love life. She claims to like David, but is, I can tell, more emotionally isolated, now that I again have less time to devote to her. She finds consolation in the recurring part she has on a television soap opera, a historical rompfest called *Ladycrackers*. And she still calls me at night to ask if I'm watching the late movie.

But enough of the supporting cast. Why have I been thinking about you tonight? Maybe it was the bistro's recorded music, which was very Paisley Park. During one blaring number I fantasized that you walked into the restaurant, and that a *Way We Were* ending—in which the lovers are reunited and tearfully realize the rightness of their long-ago separation, even as they remain more in thrall than ever—ensued. But I have heard nothing of you since the day Sarah and I and Congressman Jerry Williams, a Long Island Democrat acquainted with Castro, boarded a charter plane in Havana.

And what about me? How should I characterize my prospects? Shouldn't I indicate whether I am happy or sad? Or announce that the question of happy or sad is really beside the point since my story is true? Or insist that my Cuban adventure in the end mattered not at all, swathing our story in some kind of higher meaninglessness? Or even curse you one last time?

I'd rather tell you about David and me and our plans. We are going to Barbados for New Year's. We plan to snorkel, ride horses, play golf (another sign of creeping senescence!). When we return I will go to work, to the gym, and to hospital where I volunteer on Saturday afternoons. I will think of you and sometimes still feel hurt, guilty, used. I will not resist these emotions. I will allow them to rise and fall in me like footsteps. I will not even mind if every time I hear a Prince song on the radio or in a restaurant, I ask myself, *What is Eduardo doing right now?* The way I did the morning after I had made it out of the sugar fields and sat across from your window, sipping a café.

Acknowledgments

The Serbian writer Danilo Kis allayed forever my anxiety about being influenced by stating in an interview I once did with him that "originality involves knowing the great literary works of the past and adding the drop of one's own authenticity." While such indirect inspirations are too many to list, I would be remiss if I did not cite a couple of works that influenced the depiction of Cuba in this novel: *Trading With the Enemy* by Tom Miller and *Before Night Falls* by Reinaldo Arenas. I hasten to add that I have never set foot on that Caribbean island. If there are details in *Last Night* that do not ring unerringly true to Cuba experts, I can only reply that this is a work of fiction with no aspiration to documentary-exact fact.

Several people provided helpful criticisms of this novel in its various stages, including Lindsley Cameron, Ethan Silverman, and Cynthia O'Neal. Erica Silverman, who agented the project, provided both emotional support and professional prodding. Michael Lowenthal and Tom Steele contributed microscopic readings of the manuscript, and Greg Constante, Scott Brassart, and Matthew Van

Atta of Alyson were also of great assistance. The person most vital to the novel's publication was Judy Wieder, who additionally has been enormously encouraging to me in my job as editor in chief of *Out* magazine. I would also like to acknowledge the daily help of the *Out* staff, especially Bruce Shenitz, Jeffrey Epstein, and Bryan Buss, and my assistants Jon Cipriaso and Paul Davis. For advice on the book's baseball matters, I tip my cap to A Player to Be Named Later.

As Danilo Kis reminded me, a book is the product not of its author's reading life; it is also a distillation of his interactions with family and friends. Thus in addition to those mentioned above I must also note my indebtedness to my mother, Ann Lemon, for imparting to me a love of music and reading; to the late Fred Souza, for having been a once-in-a-lifetime soulmate; and to Bill Schneider, without whose love the author would, quite literally, never have made it to his "Last Night."